ONE MORE BODY

A Moses McGuire Novel

By Josh Stallings

Copyright © 2013 Josh Stallings

All rights reserved under International and Pan-American Copyright Conventions.

Published in the United States by Heist Publishing

ISBN: 978-0-9910544-0-4

WWW.JOSHSTALLINGS.NET

DEDICATION

For Jared James Stallings, my son and one of the bravest men I know.

ACKNOWLEDGMENTS

A huge thank you goes to my editor, the ever amazing Elizabeth A. White, her thoughts and comments were always insightful and drove me to write a better book. To Erika my harshest critic and strongest supporter. To my earlier readers, Holly West, Thomas Pluck, Neliza Drew, Aldo Calcagno and Fingers Murphy, for stumbling along with me in the early drafts and always adding to the later ones. To my siblings Larkin Stallings, Lisa Stallings and Shaun Anzaldua for their kind words and undying support. To Sabrina E. Ogden, McDroll and all my other online friends who keep cheering Moses on, my deepest appreciation.

CHAPTER 1

Ensenada, Mexico - November 10th.

Sitting on the beach with a dead woman might drive some men mad. I found it reassuring.

Mo, this can't last. Your life? It is fucked up even by your nonexistent standards.

Mikayla sat in the sand between my legs, back against my beer gut. Sweat ran down her shirt, the wet fabric clinging to the scar from her self-amputated breast. She'd done it to keep the ex-KGB from kidnapping her and selling her into prostitution. She was an assassin. A dead one. Her personal body count topped twenty or so pimps. She lost count in a whorehouse she torched in Tel Aviv.

"Sitting on a beach with a ghost is fucked up?" I asked her. "Men paying to rape a kid? Much more fucked up. Men getting rich selling boys and girls? Much more fucked up. Eating Vicodin and chasing it with therapeutic levels of cold Mexican beer to stop the spike nailed into my temple? That shit is minor on the scale of fucked up."

Is it working? Drugs? Whiskey?

"Keeps the barrel out of my mouth."

Thing is Mo, ultimately it wont, can't. Only death brings peace.

"I'm done, out, no more. You, the sun, Angel. This is my life."

Oh, Mo, no. This is R & R. Her callused hand rested on my knee, her razor out of sight for the moment. She'd been at war as long as I'd known her. We'd gone into a house full of trafficked girls, left their captors bloody smears.

I have to go, Mo.

"Another fifteen minutes, give me that."

Fifteen.

I could feel every vertebra as she pressed against me, her muscles taut. She was never fully relaxed, even in sleep.

"Given enough time, could you...me?"

Old man, you are crazy. She blessed me with one of her rare smiles. It showed her gray, steel teeth. *Mo, if I ever chose a man, you would top the list.* This was the most I had ever heard her speak, her voice rasping from disuse.

"Maybe we could have made it, you and me."

No. You are a Viking. When you go it will be alone and soaked in your enemies' gore.

"I don't want to, not anymore. You know what I did to that girl."

Never forget her. Never. Rapist. Victim. Collaborator. Hero. There is no middle ground for us, Moses, none. Rapist. Victim. Collaborator. Hero. You and me, we have no choice.

Although she didn't move, I could feel her body lighten.

"No, you said fifteen minutes."

It has been that and more, I'm tired. Her body was no more pressure than a silk scarf. And then she was gone. I looked out over the Pacific, Angel, my Bullmastiff bitch, at my feet. I felt hollow with Mikayla gone. Eating painkillers like Chiclets could only quiet the dragon, but never slay it. Mikayla,

I didn't have to explain. She knew already. If talking to a dead assassin brought me peace, so fucking be it.

I lay back, letting the hot sand warm my back, work its magic on my tore up muscles.

"Do as I say, or spend the rest of your life back in the pen." The stranger let her hand rest on the butt of her Glock. She was short and lean, maybe 5'5", built like an athletic boy. Flat chest and ass. No meat on the bone. Her face was moon shaped and the only soft part about her. She had full lips, no lipstick. Her hair was in a tight, short afro. She vibed cop.

"Better keep the pistol hidden." I took a Pacífico from the galvanized bucket full of ice at my feet. They were six-ounce cuartitos, so you were never drinking warm beer. Perfect. I cracked a Vicodin between my molars. If she minded, she didn't say so. She didn't move. Hand on Glock. Ready.

"A narco bandit makes you for a cop, your head will wind up on a pike. They actually do that shit down here. Medieval country." I could see myself reflected back in her Ray-Bans. She was wearing slacks, shirt and blazer. It was 80 degrees in the shade of the palapa. I offered her a beer. She shook her head. I tilted the bottle up. It was cold and fresh and I finished it in one steady gulp. I dropped the bottle and grabbed a new soldier. She was playing stare down, real *he who talks first loses* bullshit. So I made an obvious show of checking her out.

"Enjoying the view?" Cold.

"Not my type. I like my women with a few more curves and a lot less pistol."

"Strippers, right?" She was right. I had been with my share of strippers. Women: they twisted me every way possible. Some used me. Some cared for me. Some died. Some were broken just for being near to me. Now the only woman I was interested in was dead.

"Did you come down here to ask if I might be willing to toss you a tumble?" I asked. Her jaw started to grind. "I'm kinda in a celibate monkish phase. Sure you don't want a beer?" I rolled the bottle over my forehead, let the ice water cool my face. I looked out over the Pacific. Never get tired of the view. Angel lay in the sand at my feet chewing on a pork bone. On the table was an old ghetto blaster. I turned The Pogues up. Nothing like *Rum, Sodomy & the Lash* to lift my mood. "And the Band Played Waltzing Matilda" was playing.

"Can you turn that down?"

"No, this is the good part." I sung along: "Those who were living did their best to survive in that mad world of death, blood and fire."

The music died. She held the plug. "Not a fan of The Pogues? Lady, do you have any saving graces?"

"Mr. McGuire, I didn't drive all the way down here to be ignored, eye fucked, watch you drink beer and listen to crap Irish music. Do I get the cuffs out, or do we talk?"

"Crap? The Pogues?" I stepped into her face. Ok, my chest into her face. At six foot four I towered over her. I invaded her space. "Don't like The Pogues? Get the fuck off my beach."

"That's not how this works." She gripped her piece.

Angel looked up at her. Feeling the threat, she let out a low growl, like one of the hounds of hell had been pissed off. "Lady, you have extradition papers?" She hard eyed, but didn't answer. "Didn't think so. Park the attitude before my dog does something wrongheaded, and you get a permanent limp."

"That bitch moves and I will put her down." She eased her hand into the trigger guard. Angel tensed her haunch muscles, ready to spring.

"Angel's fast. Money's on her."

"Lowrie said you'd be a dick."

"He send you down here?" Detective Lowrie, LAPD. I wouldn't call him my friend, but he was an honest, no bullshit cop. Rare in LA.

"Yes. He said if I needed to find someone lost in the sex trade you were the man to see."

"I don't do that anymore."

"He said you'd say that, too."

I didn't tell her that the last time I went blazing Mikayla had died at the hands of Xlmen, a Mexican hunter. Gregor, a soldier who trusted me, lost an arm and almost bled out in a San Burdo whorehouse. We painted the walls with Russian pimps. We saved the girls. Some made it out, some were hooking again before we left town. On me. All that was on me. I led them into it. I didn't tell the lady cop about the teenaged girl I raped. I didn't tell her of the dreams that never left me. Instead, I sat down and offered her another beer. "Come on, I'll rustle us up some fish tacos. Enjoy what's left of the day before you head back to Los Angeles."

"You want the hard way? Fine." She moved behind me, dropping a hand on my shoulder like I was a recalcitrant schoolboy. "You're a felon reported to have been using a firearm. Oh yeah, I read about you in the *LA Times*. Big hero. Strike three, you are out." I heard a soft whistle, felt air move toward my head. Something heavy hit the base of my skull and I went limp. And then I fell into a deep pool of black.

I hurt.
I hurt fucking bad.
Bile backed up into my mouth.
My head was pounding out a slow painful cadence.
Wake up, Mo. Sleep when you're dead.
I heard Mikayla's voice, but her body was gone. When I opened my eyes, I saw that someone had turned the ocean on its

side. The surf sparkled silver in the moonlight. I looked around as far as I could without moving my head. A Glock lay in the sand, a pair of Ray-Bans not far from it. My beach chair was lying by me, bucket of beer toppled, ice a drying puddle in the sand. Somewhere off in another land I heard Angel growling, something in her mouth muffling the sound. It took all my strength to sit up. Fireworks exploded behind my eyes.

"Help, please." Her voice was a soft whisper. I turned my head, searching for her in the dark. I saw eyes first, her dark skin fading into the shadows. I struggled to make sense of the scene. Reaching up, I found the cord and pulled. Light flickered on. She was on the ground against the back wall of my beach shack, Angel attached to her right arm. Rivers of drool spilled down. Angel kept her eyes pinned on her prey.

"Best advice, don't move if you want to keep that arm."

"Do I look like I'm moving?" she whispered. I plucked the Glock off the sand and held it casually aimed at her. I searched around and found what I was looking for, a small leather bag filled with lead shot.

"A blackjack? Really? How old are you?"

"Thirty-eight."

"Blackjack is some old school bullshit. Where'd you find one?"

"It was my father's." She looked down at her arm vised in Angel's mouth, then back at me.

"Angel." I snapped once and Angel released her grip and came to my side. The stranger was tough, I'd give her that. She stood up, stretched out her shoulders and cracked her neck, but didn't bitch.

"You going to shoot a cop? How stupid are you?"

"Pretty stupid. Ask anyone." My head was still pounding. "This ain't LA. I toss your body in the sea and the local policía will give it a couple of hours then move on to something that pays better."

"I don't beg." She was cool. She closed her eyes. Ready.

"And I don't kill people. I'm done." I popped the shells from the gun's mag one after another into the sand. I cleared the chamber and handed her the empty Glock. I kept the blackjack, figured I had earned it.

She slipped the automatic back into its holster. "I have more ammunition in the car."

"I'm sure you do." I uprighted my chair and set two beers on the small table. She sat down, looking at me. I patted the pockets of my Hawaiian shirt, didn't find what I was looking for. Scanned the sand where I had fallen, found it. I picked up the pill bottle with my Vicodin. I crunched a painkiller and chased it down with a deep swallow of beer.

I don't know how long Angel had her pinned, but it must have been hours. She was rubbing her forearm. I held up the Vicodin. She shook her head. I put a bottle of mescal on the table. She didn't refuse that.

"She's thirteen." She was looking out to sea.

"Ok, who the fuck are you?"

"Detective Rollens, LAPD." She dropped her badge on the table. It looked real enough. "My niece. Thirteen. Vanished. Left home, never made it to school. Gone."

"I'm sorry. But—"

"I know. You don't do this anymore."

"Can't."

"A guy from vice thinks he saw her on the stroll. Saw the BOLO too late, hasn't seen her on the street since."

"He have any idea who she was working for?"

"Ten different pimps work the stroll."

"Ask all ten."

"Think I didn't?"

"You do it in an interrogation room?"

"Of course."

"Didn't ask hard enough. Not by an LA mile. Motherfuckers lawyered out before you finished the papers, right?"

Rollens slid a picture across the table to me. It was a young girl in a cheerleader uniform. She had cornrows with little bows at the tips. I poured myself a healthy shot.

"She's a heartbreaker." I forced myself to really look at the snapshot. Take it in. "You want me to come up and go after these pimps hard? That's the reason you're here."

"I want you to help me find her."

"It is never that easy." I held the picture of the baby in a cheerleader uniform and took a long pull off the mescal.

When I first moved to Ensenada I went to an AA meeting. I was willing to try anything to remove the spike from my head. "Whatever you have done, son," said the sixty-year-old, sunbaked dude wearing a Margaretville t-shirt and a peaceful smile, "anything, you write it out. Then you tell God and another human. Then, if you want peace, you become willing to make amends for all you have done." And that is where he lost me. What exactly was the amends for all the killing? What was the amends for raping a teenager? The wreckage of lives I had shattered? He said I shouldn't worry, he had heard it all. I'm sure he was wrong. Besides, no one needed to carry my water for me. I had developed a program of my own, a careful balance of booze and painkillers. Get it right, this mixture will keep the ghosts at bay. Get it wrong, you tip the scale into oblivion. Stay away from stimulants. Try not to think about shit. Talk to dead friends. On really rough days, I toss a line out past the breakers. Fish while Angel chases the gulls.

It wasn't a bad life. I owned a house and a shack on the beach. I'd made a truce with the local Don, Señor Sanchez; I agreed not to kill his man Xlmen, he agreed to leave me and my friend, Adolfo, in peace. Adolfo's wife was learning not to fear me. Their kids would come down and play with Angel. I didn't have much. I didn't need much. I stayed away from women. It was simpler that way. The last woman I had been with had been a teenager, a child really. A sick fucker had dosed me with Viagra and stuck a gun to my head. '"She wants you to have her precious cherry, to save her whore sister. How fucking sweet, no?" He would have killed the girl, slow and ugly.

So I raped her.

Maybe I chose right. Maybe I didn't.

Either way, I had no need to revisit those feelings.

After almost a year I finally stopped waking in a panic, sweat slick sheets wrapped around me. It wasn't peaceful, but it was as close as I deserved.

I set the photo of Rollens's niece on the table. I took the mescal and walked away, down toward the surf. She followed me with her eyes. I was sitting in the sand, my head on Angel, necking the bottle when I heard her car roll away. I crunched a Vicodin between my teeth. Fuck it. I popped a second, chasing them down with mescal. I was going to need all the help I could get to keep the dream away tonight.

There is a moment, one perfect moment, when the world goes cotton ball soft and there is a layer of gauze between me and all that went before. Somewhere off in the fog I had done some fucked up shit. But here it was all warm and well.

I was at peace.

CHAPTER 2

Compton, California - October 31st.

Freedom was walking to school, running late, again.
Third time since entering the eighth grade in September. It
wasn't her fault there was a line to get in the bathroom this
morning. They didn't understand she needed to keep her
grades up. She had plans.

She had just crossed West Rosecrans Boulevard when
the fresh looking car pulled up beside her. She could see herself
in the smoked windows. Something was wrong, alarm bells
clanged in her head. She wanted to run, but it was like in a
dream and she was stuck in slow motion.

The back door opened behind her.

"Andre, grab the bitch."

She turned to run.

Arms caught her shoulder and spun her around. A man
with dreads and a scruffy beard held her. She noticed he had
dark stains in the pits of his Rocawear.

He wrapped his arms around her and dragged her
toward the back boor. She snapped out of her dream. She
screamed. She kicked. It made no difference. In seconds she
was tossed into the back seat and the waiting arms of a thin,

ashy man. He put a hand over her mouth and whispered, "You bite me and I will break your ugly neck." He made a crunching sound like chicken bones being broken.

And they were gone. Speeding away from the curb. Moving into traffic.

When they passed her middle school, she could see all the kids lined up, most in costumes. Her so-called mother said Jesus Christ didn't like Halloween; it was a devil's holiday. Her friend Julia was bringing her a sexy nurse costume Julia'd worn last year. Freedom couldn't hear the playground over the thumping bass of J Cole's "Can't Get Enough." *I love it when you give me head, I hate it when you give me headaches. ... I'll beat the pussy up, that's the hook right thurr. That's the hook, right there...*" Freedom and Julia had danced to that song, lip-syncing into a straightening iron for a microphone.

Then the school was gone.
They slid through traffic.
No one knew she was in the ride.
No one.

Freedom watched the streets turn unfamiliar. The men sat on either side of her. They laughed and passed a joint around. They spoke as if she wasn't there. Called her their little money pot. They laughed about the fun they would have with her.

"You like fun, right?" He was in the front seat, looking directly back at Freedom.

"What?"

"Don't play stupid, bitch."

"Sorry, what did you say?" His hand was moving so fast it struck her face before she knew it was coming. It stung. The world was moving like a video where they removed a piece and put in stills. Jagged, no fluidity.

"Stupid bitch gets beat."

"You tell her, Zero," the driver said. He was watching Freedom in the rearview mirror. Eyeing her with brick-red, hungry eyes.

Freedom tried to pay attention, but panic drove her to hide in her mind. More unanswered questions. More slaps. She thought of *Alice in Wonderland*. She liked books better than movies. In a book, she could see Alice as looking like her. In a movie, there was no escaping she wasn't a little blonde white girl.

They were on the freeway.

They were over a bridge.

They were down the rabbit hole.

CHAPTER 3

The sun was burning off the fog when I woke. Hangover is too gentle a word for what I felt. Ragnarök. I felt like the Valkyries had ripped the flesh off my face and put it back on inside out. A goose egg graced the base of my skull. My mouth tasted like I had been chewing ass all night. Standing, I found all my muscles worked in a broken puppet, disconnected sort of way.

Rollens was sitting at my table, fresh and rested. She was sipping a large Starbucks coffee. A man was sitting with his back to me. When I rounded the table, he looked up. Xlmen. The son of a bitch who'd killed Mikayla. This fucking psychopath fancied himself a hunter. Bullshit. Killed her from a hundred feet out. Coward. A chrome .357 rested on the table under his hand.

"This that day?" I asked.

"Day you try and kill me, cabrón?"

"That day."

"I don't know, cabrón, is it?" I was close enough to reach his throat, maybe choke him out before he shot me. Worth a try.

Rollens set a digital camera down on the table. "Might want to see these."

I sat across from Xlmen, picked up the camera. On the screen was a picture of Adolfo standing with his youngest boy. They didn't seem to notice the picture was being taken. The next picture was Adolfo's wife down at the lavandería laughing with some other women. Again, the subjects were unaware of the person taking the shots. These people had taken me in, treated me like family.

She motioned to Xlmen. "The hunter, he took these."

My guts went ice. My head cleared instantly. "You sick fuck." I stared into his eyes long enough to make most men turn away. He didn't even blink. "I will put you in the ground. Piss on your grave."

"I don't think so, cabrón. But you will try."

"Adolfo and his family get harmed..." I hadn't taken my eyes off him.

"I know, cabrón, you will kill me. Painfully, yes? Bullshit." He let out a low, mirthless laugh. Standing, he reached for the .357. I rose fast, tossing the table, flipping the revolver into the air. It landed in the sand next to Angel.

Xlmen moved for the gun, then froze when Angel showed her teeth.

Stepping past him, I bent and picked up the .357. The ivory grip was warm from the sun. Calmly, I pushed the revolver's barrel up against the small man's head and pulled the trigger. The .357 roared. Blood, bone and gray matter plumed. Blowback speckled my face. The assassin fell sideways, blood soaking the sand beneath his head. A group of seagulls screamed and took for the sky. Rollens had her Glock out, aiming it at me. She stood in a classic shooter's stance. Her eyes flicked from me to the dead man, back to me. It was as if she was trying to solve some puzzle. I dropped the revolver into the sand. Slowly she holstered her pistol.

"I thought you were done killing?"

"I guess not. Get his feet." I could easily pick the man up, but I need her complicity. I slipped easily into covering my tracks. Killing him was too easy. Maybe I wasn't a better man than him. Maybe I was just quicker.

Xlmen had left the keys in his Land Cruiser, and why not? Everyone in Ensenada knew his rig, and no one was stupid enough to steal it.

"Follow me," I told Rollens. She was still trying to regain a firm footing, but she did as told.

We drove south, putting some distance between us and town. Angel was sitting in the passenger seat, hanging her sloppy face out the window letting the wind fill the folds of loose skin around her mouth. If she minded the corpse in the back she wasn't letting on.

After twenty minutes, I pulled off the highway onto a dirt road. A few miles up the arroyo I parked behind a granite outcropping. I searched the car. I searched the dead man. I found an envelope with three grand American. I found a Rolex, a good hunting knife, a Remington scoped rifle. I took the watch and cash and left the rest. Travel light and scavenge what you need as you go. It was guerrilla warfare, and I had no base camp for resupply.

I took the five-gallon tank of gas off the back rack and dumped it over the car. Fire is a great destroyer of DNA, not that they would need any to know it was me who killed him. Xlmen was an assassin for Señor Sanchez, a local mobbed-up pimp. Sanchez left me alone as long as I let his boys be. The only caveat was that he had to keep his hunter away from me. For executing Mikayla, I made it clear that if I saw Xlmen I would kill him. A man's word is his bond.

Black smoke rose up in the rearview mirror as Rollens drove her Honda Accord back toward the highway. "How did you contact him? Girl, don't even think about lying to me.

"Girl?" She let it drop. "A DEA agent knew a solid cop down here. Said if any man could put the fear of God in you it was Xlmen."

"You hired him?"

"Yes. I wouldn't have let him hurt your friends. I took those pictures, not him."

"Who the hell are you?"

"An aunt who's run out of options." I had no snappy come back. If it were my niece I would do worse. Hell, I had done worse.

We parked in front of my house. "You certainly have fucked my shit up down here. So I'm in, but I want some things from you. This is over, I want a guarantee that my prior record gets expunged. No more holding this third-strike bullshit over my head. Never again."

"I don't know. Give me a minute." While I went in the house, she walked away trying to get cell service.

I traded my flip-flops and shorts for a pair of jeans and cherry red Docs. I packed a duffle with all I owned; there was room left over. I'd arrived in Ensenada in a stolen Mercedes, not that the dead men I took it from were bitching much. The car was stripped and on its way back to El Norte in days. From a ceiling panel, I took what cash I had left. It and the money I'd scavenged from the hunter gave me a knot of five grand plus change. From the back of my closet I took my 1911 Colt .45 and a cut-down Mossberg. That was it. I was ready to roll. Hefting the duffle, it was light. It was all I had to show for 45 years on planet Earth. That and a head full of trip lines and barbed wire.

I snapped and Angel jumped in the back seat. "How did your call go?"

"Looks good. Not solid, but it looks good. Armed robbery, no one hurt, auto theft, no one hurt. With my and

Lowrie's recommendations, the ADA thinks we can make it go away." I doubted every word, but she was the only bus leaving town so I climbed in.

Adolfo was working the front door at one of Ensenada's legal brothels. He was a good man, knocking out the bills to cover his family. Who was I to judge how he did it? I passed him the door keys and told him the house was his. It was already in his name since Americans can't own property on the coast. Angel stood beside me while we talked.

"Mi hermano, no, I'll hold it until your return."

"I may not make it back."

"You just tired. Rest up, I get Jerry's boat, we go fishing. Or get laid. You feel much better."

"Not this time, amigo. Keep the house. I'm leaving Angel with you, have the boy take care of her. Just save me a room in case of miracles." The house had cost all I had, but the idea of Adolfo and his family moving from their apartment to the beach made it less painful for me to leave. He pulled me into a hug. He didn't say it, but I knew I'd always be welcome. He pressed a small silver medallion on a chain into my palm.

"Saint Jude, patron to lost causes."

"Ain't Catholic."

"If you don't tell, I won't." He gripped my hand. "Vaya con Dios."

I finally broke the hold. I put the medal on over my head. Way I was running, I could use any edge I could get. With a finger snap Angel sat beside Adolfo. She hung her head. I leaned down and let her lick my face. "You don't want to go on this run. Kick back, you earned it. Now stay." She stubbornly obeyed. I moved away and across the avenue. I didn't look back. She was my last attachment to my old life.

In the farmacia, I picked up an industrial-sized jar of Vicodin. The girl behind the counter didn't even blink when I crunched two of them before leaving the shop. Through the window, past the sign promising the best Viagra in town, I could see the street. Rollens's Honda was blocked in by a military jeep. A pimply kid was aiming down with a fifty cal. If he burped wrong the street would be gone. He was aiming at Rollens. She spoke to an older officer. I backed away from the window. Watching. Feeling the Vicodin take hold. Rollens poked her finger at the officer, got up in his face. She had some cojones. Behind them sat a shiny new Lincoln Town Car.

From a pile of souvenirs I took a sarape and a sombrero with Ensenada emblazoned across it. I tossed the shop girl a couple of twenties. Pulling the hat down over my face, I moved down the street, stumbling like a dunk. Under the sarape I held my 1911, cocked and locked. Rollens was yelling about calling the local general in, said she had heat and this captain was going to get fried. On either side of the Town Car stood two serious men. They had black camos and MP5s, those ugly little death-spitters. I stumbled past the man on the left. He laughed, then noticed something wrong. Too late. The .45 was out and pressed into his cheek.

"Put it on the roof," I told the man on the other side. "Do it or I shoot him, then you, then the man in the car." I had the MP5 in one hand and my Colt in the other. Reflected in the windshield, I saw a soldier stepping slowly closer, his AK47 aimed at me. I was fucked. Might as well pull the trigger and see how it would take me.

A blur of strawberry blonde flew into my vision—120 pounds of Bullmastiff in flight. Angel nailed the young soldier in his trigger arm. He fired a few wild shots before she had him pinned on the ground.

Across the Town Car, the serious man let blaze. I spun his counterpart in front of me. He must have vested up, because no bullets came ripping out his back into me. The gunner stumbled back and went down when I emptied the MP5 into his chest. I hoped he was vested, sort of. He took a job that ended with pointing a machine pistol at me. After that it was on him. I had enough legitimate ghosts of my own.

The military boys were standing around, not knowing what to do. I leaned down, pulled off a magazine Velcroed to the serious man's belt. Dropping the empty, I slammed the full one home. I tossed the MP5 to Rollens. "They touch my dog, kill 'em."

I was in the back seat before anyone could clip me. Señor Sanchez was cool and sophisticated in his windowpane-checked, slate-colored suit. "Moses, you are a difficult man to like."

"True. Ask anyone." Soldiers surrounded Rollens. The .50 cal was aimed at the Town Car. I let the barrel of the 1911 rest on Sanchez's thigh. He hit a button and the window opened, flooding us with harsh light.

"Reyes." He called the young officer over. The kid was in his early twenties and sweating, eyes darting between us. "Dile a tus hombres que se retiren."

Captain Reyes looked relieved and snapped a smart salute. The bulletproof window slid back up, silencing the outside world.

"We, you and I, had a deal. I would leave you alone, and you, you would leave my men alone. I only made this deal because I was feeling generous."

"You haven't tried to kill me because you were afraid of the collateral damage I would inflict on you. I took the Russians off the count, you wondered if I could get to you. Right?" I looked at him, then around the car. "I just did." The Vicodin had traded reflexes for bravado. Shit trade if you want to stay alive.

"You shoot me, you and the woman are dead."

"Dumb fucking greaser, you think I give a shit who you shoot?" I started to laugh at a joke he wasn't getting.

"But here you are negotiating for your life, true?"

"Your man—"

"Xlmen, my hunter."

"That psycho midget, he killed a woman I counted a friend."

"And you promised to let it rest if he stayed away and we didn't cause your friend the doorman any trouble."

"Your man fucked up. He threatened Adolfo and his family."

"I didn't sanction that. He was freelancing for Detective Rollens."

No one freelanced on Sanchez. I let the lie slide. "Here is how it is gonna work. I'm leaving Mexico. The only thing that will bring me back is if anything happens to Adolfo Anzaldua."

"Ha. Good man. Loyalty. Xlmen was a good man too, but he liked to wander off script." From a skull shaped bottle he poured us each a tumbler of tequila. "What shall we drink to?"

"Not having to mess up this lovely car?"

"No, a long life. To die with white hair on top and a hot puta under." We slammed back the shots. It went down smooth. Things had gone soft and comfortable.

Señor Sanchez opened the door, leaned out, and moved his index finger in a quick circle. The officer commanded his men to load up, then climbed into the jeep. I walked away from the Town Car, waiting for a bullet to take me down. The Town Car slid away down the road. I snapped and Angel let the wide-eyed boy up. She moved to my side. The soldiers mounted up and were gone, leaving the street empty.

I called Angel. She jumped into the back seat of Rollens's Honda.

"Thought you were leaving that bitch here."

"Changed my mind." Less I left behind, less leverage Sanchez had on me. That's what I told myself. Truth is I needed something real with me. I had shot two men since morning. Angel kept me human. Least I thought she did.

"Are you high?"

"Not yet." I took a long pull on a Pacífico and let my head sink into the headrest. I had not a clue where we were headed, but I sure as hell couldn't stay where I was.

CHAPTER 4

Sunlight playing on a rusted swing set.

Mrs. James pouring pale, watered down blue Kool-Aid.

iPod playing Jay-Z, the earbuds split so each of the best friends got one.

Laughter.

Charles Drew Middle School, one year until high school—King Drew Magnet High School of Medicine and Science.

She was climbing up and out.

Dreamed to be a doctor.

That was forever ago.

That was two weeks ago.

Freedom looked past Zero's sweat-slicked shoulder. He was pounding down. Grunting. Naked, bruised and bloody, she was tied to a dirty mattress. When the first man raped her, she screamed. They stuffed a balled up sock in her mouth. She was choking. Pain filled with fear, or was it fear filled with pain? Word games helped her leave her body. But only for a second. She was a straight-A student. She would prove Mrs. Mayer, her social worker, was right and that bitch at the home was wrong. After King Drew Magnet, she was going to Stanford. She was going to be a doctor—or a rap star or a model, anything but this moment.

The second man was done in seconds. He grunted and climbed off. Stared at her. Angry. "What you looking at, bitch?" He hit her. Her lip bled down over her teeth. It tasted of iron. Her arms strained at the ropes. She wanted to punch this bastard. Make him bleed.

The third man was skinny, with cornrows. He spit on her and laughed when he was pounding on her. His spit on her cheek felt like acid. She closed her eyes. Saw the frog she had dissected in biology, saw the skinny man's guts spilling out.

Sex. It wasn't like in the songs. All that bluster and bitch that, bitch this, suck my dick, strippers busting my nut, making it rain, popping rubber bands, broke bitches disgust me, nappy-headed hoes. Nicki Minaj talked about fucking hard.

What they were doing to her wasn't a song.

What they were doing was full of hate and degradation.

They hated her.

Simple.

In her mind, Freedom smelled chalk. She loved school, was good at it. She had moved in and out of different homes, but school was constant. She loved math and science; they were true. No room for bullshit lies. English? You could say you loved a child and walk away at the same time. Math was truth. Biology was even better. Facts. Attach a battery to a heart and it would beat. Cut the current it would stop.

"Look at me, bitch. I own your ass." The fourth man had bulging muscles and a sleeveless sweatshirt. He punched her in the left eye. He let out a deep sigh when he finished.

The fifth was a boy. Not much older than Freedom. He looked sad, embarrassed, but that didn't stop him. One of the older men stood over them while he did it to her. He laughed when the boy was done and toasted him with a 40. He took a gulp then poured some on her belly, for the dead homies.

They left her tied to the bed. Spread. Ready for them.

But she wasn't there. She stood on West Rosecrans, saw the car roll up. She stayed in that moment. Her last normal moment.

The men left the house. They returned eating Burger King. They smoked pot and laughed. After the sun went down they were drunk. She could hear them laughing. They fought over who was going to fuck her first this time. A deep voice she knew as Zero said he didn't do no sloppy seconds. They threw dice for it.

And she was on West Rosecrans.

And this moment would last forever.

CHAPTER 5

We crossed at TJ without incident. My passport might not stand up to heavy scrutiny, but I was white and riding with a cop. They barely glanced at her ID then let us slide into the land of the free, home of the weak, the broken and the bought off.

The Pacific Ocean blurred by, the beer and painkillers doing their job. I leaned my seat back into a full recline. Angel leaned up and gave me a sloppy kiss. I fell asleep.

In the dream I am killing kittens again. Tiny deformed kittens too genetically broken to survive. They cover the attic. I grab a tabby and snap its neck. I pick another and kill it. They mew and stumble blindly. They will never survive. They must be killed. It is the only kind thing to do. I pick up a ginger. Her eyes are open. She looks at me. She is strong. She won't die. I choke her but she just keeps fighting, scratching.

"You ok? You were shouting in your sleep."

My face was slick with sweat. "I'm solid." I have stopped wondering what the dream means. I know. "Where are we?" The sky was dark with pregnant rain clouds.

"Just passing Dana Point. Be in LA in an hour, plus traffic."

I popped the top on a Pacífico and took a long, deep swallow.

25

"That's illegal this side of the border."

"Rolling with a cop should have some bennies." I crunched a Vicodin, upended the beer and lay back down.

"You ever sober?"

"Not if I can help it."

"McGuire, this isn't a joke. These pukes will kill us both if you fuck up."

"Who? Who, Detective Rollens? Do you know who we are going after?"

"No. But whoever has Freedom is bad fucking news. They will take us out if you don't sober up."

"You say that like I give a rat's ass. You want to ride along then put a vest on and keep your mouth shut. We clear?"

Rollens slammed on the brakes. We went from sixty to zero in a roar of burning tires. I was tossed forward, slamming my head on the dash. Pain stabbed where the beer bottle chipped my front tooth. Angel was wedged against the driver's seat. She was growling, as if she was going to attack centrifugal force. Rollens released the brakes and stabbed the gas pedal down. I was slammed back down into my seat. I could feel blood coming down from my scalp. When we hit sixty-five she backed off.

"McGuire, you really should wear your safety belt. Click it or ticket."

Blood ran down my chin. "I could learn to like you...that or kill you." I laughed. She didn't. "Just so you know, hurt my dog again we'll find out sooner rather than later."

It was raining by the time we hit downtown LA. From the 5, I could see the skyscrapers disappearing into low clouds. Gold and silver towers looming over the industrial train tracks and the Mexican streets of East LA. The homeless collect in downtown. Billion dollar high-rises look down on a legless beggars. My hometown. She held only sad memories. Innocence stolen for five bucks a shot in low-rent strip joints. Booze-addled fantasies of love turned wrong. Dead friends and betrayal. Welcome home, son, grab a glass.

I directed Rollens to the Shamrock Motel in Hollywood. Sunset Boulevard. The dirty section, near Hollywood High School. Three spectral crackheads stumbled down the sidewalk, blocking the driveway.

"What are we doing here?" Rollens didn't look worried, just curious.

"Get us a room."

The crackheads moved out of our way. The place was more of a dump than I remembered. Peeling paint, the stench of puke and piss. A perfect place to get lost.

"Why not my apartment? Cheaper and no bedbugs."

"There are people who might not be too happy to hear I'm back in town. People you don't want standing on your stoop." That's what I told her. Truth was, if she was going to take me down I wanted home court advantage.

The room lived up to the exterior. The floor was covered in threadbare olive-colored carpet with dark stains that spoke of bloody deeds. Rollens stood, not wanting to sit on any surface. Didn't blame her.

"Nice place. Take many dates here?"

Angel jumped onto the bed and curled up. "She'll be getting hungry. Likes carne asada or carnitas. Just have them lay off the beans or buy a gas mask." I headed out.

"Where the hell are you going?"

"Out."

"I ride with you."

"Not if you want to see your niece again."

"How do I know you won't powder on me?"

"I'm down to one good trait: I do what I say I'll do. I'm in until your niece is home in her momma's arms or I'm dead. Besides, I'm leaving Angel with you, so you know I'll be back." I'm sure if I stuck around she would have had more to say, but I didn't.

LA is a car town. Has been since Standard Oil shut down the Red Car lines and sold the world on suburbia. Now they were hustling to play catch up, digging subway tunnels like cash-glutted moles.

I caught a cab over to the Valley, where one of the best motormen I've ever known had his shop. He started building cars to supplement his career as an actor. Acting fizzled, but illegal car builds sky rocketed. If you want to pack ten pounds of dope in a Prius and make sure it could outrun the cops, he'd tell you to fuck off. But if you wanted him to do it to a '67 Chevelle, 20k later and, bam, you'd be rolling down the road in a nondescript rust bucket that could slap a Ferrari.

"Mo, don't even open your fucking mouth. The answer is no," he said when I walked into his office.

"Jay, come on. One for old—"

"No!"

"Don't I always pay for what I break? You know I do."

"You owe me 40 large for the beauty you trashed in Mexico. That and, oh yeah, the Crown Vic you left as collateral. You blew that shit up, too." With movie star flair, he swept his hair back with his left hand. A snub-nosed .38 materialized in his right hand.

"Oh, Jay... fuck. Really? All our years of doing business and it ends with a gun? So be it. But, before you blaze away, listen. Remember Peter? That guy from the *LA Times*? He told me he had paid you in full."

"Bullshit."

"Do I lie?"

"People change."

"Not as much as you'd think. I'll prove it to you. Even with all this drama, you are still going to get me a ride. That's who you are."

"I have a gun. It is pointed at your face."

"Got it. Ok, I need a ride that says dated class, like for a player who has been away for a few years."

He thought about it. I could see I had him. "Fuck you, Mo, fuck you."

"I'll get you your money."

"No, you won't."

"I'll try."

"Yes, you will." He put the .38 down. "So this character we're building, he's just raised? Six, maybe seven years in the joint and takes his short out of mothballs. What was he down for?"

"Pimping. Interstate movement of minors with intent."

"Luxury. Faded but still clean. Not a caddy. He ain't Huggy Bear, and this ain't Starsky & Hutch. Something big enough to roll with his bitches." He chewed his lower lip, looking out a dirty window at the cars parked behind his garage. "Bingo. I got it. An '86 E300. You'll love it. Hell, squint and it almost looks like your old Crown Victoria. You don't have any cash do you?"

"Jay, I'm looking for a thirteen-year-old girl. She's being pimped out. She ain't got a lot of chances left. "

"Stop. Shut the fuck up. You keep talking and I'll be giving you money."

The Mercedes was a large, boxy four door. The silver paint wasn't fresh, but it looked good. Jay opened the hood, a childlike gleam in his eye. "Four-forty-four, Chevy rat, good for five hundred at the rear wheels. Brembos on all four corners.

Suspension's all AMG. This motherfucker can take most sports cars up Mulholland."

"What's the catch?"

"Catch?"

"Yeah, gorgeous, you look like there's a but coming."

"Body armor?"

"Yes?"

"It doesn't have any. Haven't had time to Kevlar it yet. In the plus column, it's light."

"I'll take it."

"A 9mm can punch though that door."

"I'll try not to get shot there then." I tossed my duffle in the trunk, asked him if it had a CD player. He called me a dinosaur, just like the ride. He said I needed an iPod. I told him to fuck off and shook his hand.

"Moses?"

"Yeah?"

"Dude, not my place, but you look like shit. Smell of pills and booze. None of my business, but you get pulled in, I lose the car."

"I'm fine. Peachy, in fact. Give me the keys."

The Benz did in fact have a CD player. *Rum, Sodomy & the Lash* was playing as I rolled down Lankershim Blvd.

I spun my mental Rolodex.

Gregor. An Armenian ex-street thug and true friend. I got his arm blown off trying to rescue the sister of a woman I loved, and he ended up with. He had always covered my ass. Heard he had a baby on the way, or maybe here by now. Heard he'd gone straight. Good for him.

Manny. Persian owner of the titty bar where I bounced for most of my adult life, he had left town. I'd threatened to kill him if he didn't, so that was understandable.

Piper. A last resort. She said she was done with me. Said I brought too much pain with me. But we had been through a lot together. I could have been her man, if I had been smart enough. Maybe she would still help me with information. Maybe not. I was short on options.

Frogtown sits at the base of the Silver Lake Hills. It's a thin strip of real estate pinned between the 5 and the LA River. *Live Nude Nude Nude Girls* blinked over Xtasy, or Pink Pearl as it was now called. It had changed hands and names but still needed a coat of paint. It was just after sundown and the rain was softening the streetlights, though not enough to hide how sad the building was.

"Twenty bucks, ace." He wasn't a big man, but he was black, and that alone scared most frat boys and squares.

"Worked here, back in the day. Just need to see a dancer."

"Doesn't every one. Twenty bucks." I could have dropped him. I gave him a twenty. Maybe I was growing up. Maybe I was just tired.

The room was dark enough to hide the stained carpet and torn booths. A topless kid with fake tits was sitting on the stage. Bored. I was the only customer. I ordered a shot of Jack and a beer back. The girl slid up beside me.

"Hi, handsome." She ran a hand up my arm, squeezing my bicep. "Big man. I like 'em that way. You big all over?" She stared to run her hand down onto my lap.

"Don't do that." I caught her wrist. "I'm looking for a friend." She dropped her shoulders. Stopped pushing her ass and tits out, and relaxed. The boredom returned to her face. She was jaded. Eighteen and getting older every day. Strippers age two years to every straight's one. I watched enough of them come in. Fresh-faced day one, seven months in they looked old and angry. Unless you had money, then they were sweet college students just off the bus. It was always their first night. And you were always special. They'd do things with you in the back room they never did with other customers.

"Buy me a drink." She didn't wait for me to answer, motioning for the bartender. "Vodka and Diet Coke, Billy. Don't water it."

"That's disgusting."

"Said the lone man in a strip club. You smell like a week-old hangover." She took a healthy gulp of her drink. "Don't look at my titties, unless you want to pay."

"Listen, Amber or Ashley or whatever."

"Cherry Red." Her hair was black and cut into a Betty Page. "Used to be a redhead."

"Might want to change the name."

"Too much work. You sure you don't want a lap dance?"

"Sure. I'm looking for a dancer named Piper."

"Why you want her? You don't like what you see?" Give her credit for trying, but the thought of this sad, bored kid on my lap made my stomach sour. I pulled out my Vicodin and crunched two, chasing them with beer. The bartender started to say something, saw my eyes and went back to drying glasses.

"You gonna share?" She eyed the pill bottle hungrily.

"You want to know what they are?"

"Not really." I passed a Vicodin. She swallowed it without a second thought. "Billy, pass me lost and found." The bartender shrugged and passed her a box from under the bar. Rooting around she found a pair of cheap, dark, black plastic glasses. "Put these on."

"What?"

"Your crazy bloodshot eyes are making me feel icky." I put them on. Big, wraparound bug-eyed Bono things. "Not good. But an improvement." Billy the tender looked at me and busted out laughing.

After a few more drinks, I asked about Piper again. They hadn't heard of her. The number I had for her was dead. I'd swung past her apartment before trying the strip joint. A hipster couple lived there now. If Piper never wanted to see me again, she was going to get her wish.

The Vicodin and Jack took hold, smoothing the edges. Cherry Red put on a robe. It was sheer, hiding nothing, but it made her more comfortable. We shot some pool. I needed to map the landscape. A year was a long time to be away from the trade. Cherry Red stopped flirting. She took her pool serious, sunk three balls on the break. She told me Craigslist had stopped taking sex ads and that *LA Weekly* was dead. Most of the girls used websites. "Not me, I don't turn tricks. Draw the line at lap dancing."

I knew the line would shift. But what good would telling her do? Maybe I'd be wrong. Maybe she'd game the system and get out with her head intact. Probably not. My ex-wife had once accused me of oversimplifying the life cycle of strippers. Said I saw them as two-dimensional caricatures. She was a rich little princess who thought her money could fix me. I was young enough to sign on. Fact is, though every dancer I ever knew was a different soiled snowflake, their end run was always the same. Well, almost always.

The music was someone's random playlist. Someone had weird taste, because the hip hop was interrupted by a calliope-playing circus.

"What the fuck is that noise?" Cherry Red asked.

"Soundtrack to life." I laughed.

"Sucks. Cobain, that's the soundtrack for my life."

"Kurt Cobain? Little young, aren't you."

"He's timeless."

"He was a pussy. Took the easy way out. Man should've sacked up and raised his kid."

"Fuck you." She dropped three more balls. I hadn't even touched my cue and was down thirty bucks. When I did get a turn, I dropped two and scratched. "That all you got, old man? Weak."

It cost me fifty to find out about a sex dance club in downtown. "Mexican joint, El Rancho something. Santa Fe, near 6th. They don't even serve booze with the cooze. Ha, I like that. You wanna break this time?"

"I think I spent enough watching you hustle me."

"Then buy me another drink." I did and she kept talking, told me girls hooked out of El Rancho. The only streetwalkers she knew about worked a stroll down in East LA. "Skank city. You catch AIDS just looking at them. Sure you won't let me?"

"Baby girl, love to. But this is work." She was a child. I left before the Jack and Vicodin told me different.

"You ok to drive, old man?" She called as I hit the door.

"Don't I look ok?"

"Nope. You look anything but ok."

CHAPTER 6

When they cut the ropes off her hands Freedom felt a million needles pounding in with the blood. Every muscle hurt. Her vulva was swollen and bloody.

Zero sat in a chair. He had dazzling white Timberlands, jeans and a Rocawear polo. Dark glasses. "Hungry, bitch?" He held a Burger King bag. Shook it so she could hear the food inside. Her stomach flopped. She couldn't remember the last meal. Breakfast. Days ago. What was it, Eggos?

"Dizzy bitch. You hungry, crawl your ass over here. Keep me waiting I'll toss this shit." Zero didn't even care enough to sound angry.

Freedom used the wall to stand. The room was swaying like it was in a storm.

"Lion!" Zero snapped and the big man with prison muscles and an Ice-T braid slapped Freedom.

"I say walk, or crawl?" Lion kneeled down, lifting Freedom's face so she was looking at Zero. He arched an eyebrow awaiting an answer.

"Crawl," she whispered.

"That's right. Well done, little diamond." Zero tossed the bag to the skinny man with cornrows and pockmarks. "SK, feed our little princess, our diamond in the rough." He and Lion left. Soon the PlayStation could be heard blasting.

35

SK had dirty, stained hands. He left black fingerprints on the bun of the burger when he gave it to Freedom. She barely noticed. She wolfed the burger down. Mistake. Her guts clenched. She puked.

"Bitch, no you don't. I paid good green for that." SK pushed her face into the carpet. He wouldn't let her up until she had eaten her own vomit. Freedom slowly mentally dissected SK, cracking his chest open. Squeezing his heart. Feeling it beat. Then slow. Then stop.

"Get that dreamy bitch up," Zero called from the doorway. Freedom kept her eyes closed, operating on them all.

Hands carried her to a filthy bathtub, dropped her in it and turned the shower on.

"Clean your nasty shit up, bitch. You disgusting."

The water was painfully cold. Freedom didn't care. She had lost her way mentally. That bed, this tub, this pain was all there was or would be. LeJohn, the youngest of them, looked down at her. She was curled in a ball. He was smoking a Newport. He pushed the door closed. He listened for the others, but they had gone. He knelt, took up a bar of Irish Spring. "LeJohn. That's me, LeJohn." He tried to be gentle when he washed her. The washcloth was rough and stiff. "I live over on Olive. You know, by the 7-Eleven?"

His voice was so far away. Was he even alive? Was she? Was she a ghost?

My name is Freedom. My name is Freedom. My name is Freedom.

"I'm going to own my own record label someday. H.B.T. Hard Baller Tunes. Gangster stuff. You ever go to Culver Ice Rink over on Sepulveda? Used to love that joint." LeJohn scrubbed her hair. Washed her tiny titties. Her belly, with its pooch of baby fat. Her bruised face. Between her legs.

She trembled when the pain hit, but she shoved it down. She was this moment.

And then this moment.

And then this moment.

And then this moment.

The water going down the drain was rusty with blood and stank of vomit and cum, sweat and piss, her own shit.

When LeJohn helped Freedom stand, she didn't try to cover herself or run or move. "Bring that bitch out here," Zero yelled.

LeJohn put an arm under hers and helped her walk. He sat her on the sofa next to Zero. SK was cooking a spoon of smack. Freedom had seen her father shoot dope, before he died. Swore she'd never.

"Lil' Diamond, you done good." Zero stroked her face. "You took it hard. It don't never need be like that again." Freedom felt a soft prick when Zero plunged the needle into her vein. The room melted. She slid from the sofa onto the floor. The carpet pressing against her naked skin was stiff with grime. She didn't care. Life was soft and pain was distant. She closed her eyes and was gone. No her, no school, no home, no nothing. Let go and she would be gone.

So she did.

CHAPTER 7

In the industrial section of downtown, by day they stitch clothing and stuff toys in crammed, sad rooms filled with wetbacks. At night, there are six or more strip joints selling girls to paw. Above Santa Fe Avenue is a billboard advertising American Apparel. Sweatshop-free clothing it boasts. Has a girl who looks underage, on her hands and knees, ass in the air, smoky look in her dead eyes.

El Rancho was at the head of a dead-end street. Across from it was a shady pool hall bar. I pulled in to park in front of the bar. A Latino cat with prison muscles and tattoos stepped from the bar, pool cue in his hand. He looked at me and shook his head. With the cue he pointed to the Rancho parking lot. No free parking on this street.

For twenty bucks a skinny shaved-headed kid had me park the Benz in a VIP spot near the front door. I guess my thirty-year-old Benz was a luxury car next to the beaters and pickup trucks. The doorman, security guard and cashier were all Latino. I was the only gringo in the place. They charged thirty bucks, and a two-drink minimum for another twenty. They gave me two drink tickets. Red Bull was extra, the casher with a big grin and gold teeth told me.

The main room was dark, with small two-tops and wrought iron chairs. Lap booths lined the walls. Guys sat while girls rubbed their naked bodies over them. Law said the guy had to keep his hands to himself. Long as he wasn't touching her with his hands when he came, it wasn't sex. Down here, those rules weren't even guidelines. A fat man in a wifebeater had his finger up inside the teenager who was dancing for him. She was moaning. He was moaning too. She stroked him through his chinos. He caught me staring and gave me a conspiratorial wink. My nostrils flared. I inhaled long and slow. He needed his head stomped into pulp. He needed his balls kicked up into his chest cavity.

"Que pasa, handsome?" She was young and plump, spilling out of her string bikini. "You wanna buy me a drink, handsome?" She purred with fake lust. Her accent was thick, in an East LA way. LA is the second largest Latin city in the Americas. Mexico City is number one...just. They could forget that in Beverly Hills, but down here it was clear.

I bought her a ten-dollar Fanta. She crawled onto my lap before I could stop her. "You wanna dance, baby? I make you come hard."

"No, I'm looking for a girl, black."

"Fuck her," she whispered in my ear. "I do whatever you want. Wanna go out? I'll suck you off, whole thing, whatever you like. You wanna come on my face? Ok. Tits? Ok. I really like you, baby."

A storm was rushing through my head. I stood fast and she had to scramble to keep from hitting the floor. She was cursing me in Spanish. All I could hear was blood pumping in my ears. I had to get out. Day laborers sat in booths while little girls ground it out on them. Babies. Fuck.

I hit the parking lot fast, door banging against the stucco wall. The security goon started to puff up and move on me. He saw my face and decided to study his shoes. Smart fucking move. From the bar across the street, the tough man with the pool cue watched me smoke the tires leaving. He didn't smile.

Maybe he hoped I'd come to his joint. Maybe he needed to release as bad as I did. Maybe he just wanted to see me go so he could get back to his cerveza before it went flat.

Pogues and a pint of Jack slowed my pulse. I sat behind a liquor store drinking and breathing. Hipsters came and went, laughing and having a good night. Half the factories were expensive condos now. They got their tough on, living like artists while little girls sold their bodies cheap three blocks over. I'm sure these new residents thought it gave them edge, told their friends they lived in the hood. This town would rip open their pale underbellies and eat them dry if they weren't white, upper middle class kids. No one wanted the kind of heat hurting them would bring.

Two more Vicodin, but who was counting, and the world was all soft and swirly. I dropped off the 5 onto Cesar Chavez Ave. The hooker's track was next to a graveyard. Seemed fitting, almost funny. But not. The girls working here were more diverse: some black, some olive, one ivory. Easy freeway access must have brought in a more open-minded group of whoremongers.

A small group of sad looking girls stood eyeing the traffic, scanning for cops and johns. The smiles turned on when I slid the Benz to the curb.

"Shit, a fine cowboy like you? Giddy the fuck up." She was leaning deep into the passenger window and I could smell cheap chemical perfume struggling to override sweat and sex. "For an extra couple of roses, I let you ride bareback."

"Here." I passed a picture of Freedom with a hundred folded around it. She took the bill and slipped it into her bra.

"Wanna suck on my titties? No charge."

"Other than the C-note?"

"Shhhhit, honey, that was a sweet gift." She dropped the picture. I picked it up off the seat. Held it up for her to see again.

"Missing. Comes from a good home. No way she chose the life."

"Just like all of us, honey. Some homes are better than others, but not one of us played Hooker Barbie as kids." She started to laugh and a fleck of blood hit the inside of the windshield. "You best either have me suck your dick, " she wiped blood off her lips, "or move on."

"Last question, then I'm off like a prom dress."

"That's a tired line, but funny. What's the question?"

"BMW parked at the Shell, he yours?"

"You gonna hurt him?" I nodded "Gonna tell him I tol' you?"

"No."

"His name is Paulie, from Van Nuys. Thinks he's straight outta Compton."

I parked at the gas station and walked over to a tricked out BMW 720. It was a couple years old, but packing expensive rims, lots of extra chrome, leather seats.

"Paulie?"

"You a cop, yo?" He was a skinny white boy with gold in his ear, around his neck, rocking a Rolex. Flashing twenty grand in jewelry while his ladies were sucking cock for forty bucks a pop.

"Not a cop. Want me to rip you out of that car to prove it?"

"How the hell would that prove anything, yo? Cops are some brutal motherfuckers."

Kneeling down, I took the buck knife from my boot. I flipped it open as I stood. One motion and it sunk a half-inch into the top of his bicep. He sputtered, too shocked to form words. Looked like it hurt. I didn't give a shit. A turban-wearing gas monkey looked over then shook his head and went back to sweeping kitty litter off an oil spill. I pushed the razor-honed blade in a little deeper. The pimp's right hand was searching the seat. In a flash of steel the blade was against his throat. "Go for that gun. No really, do it. I want you bleeding out. Are we clear on that point?"

He sucked up his pain and let his eyes go dead. "A'ite motherfucker, what you want? You jackin? I paid Zacarías Araya, full boat. His boys will fuck you up for hunting on their land."

"Stop talking." I held up the snapshot of Freedom. "I'm looking for her."

"Never seen her."

"Without even looking you know that."

"Never seen her." He made a play for his pistol.

I ripped the door open and yanked him out, kicked the 9mm out of his hand. I dragged him to the Benz. Pointing his own gun at him, I told him to get in. He was too stunned to complain. I drove us over the 8th Street Bridge and parked in the industrial area, down by the tracks. The homeless men hiding from the drizzle under the bridge pulled themselves deeper into the shadows as we passed. Gun to head I moved him across the metro rails and onto the bank of the graffiti-splashed cement river.

"This is where you die." I pushed him onto his knees. "Tell me about her."

"I don't—" I fired a shot into his shoulder. He fell forward, started to scream. I pulled him back up onto his knees.

"You hear the sirens? No? Yeah, neither do I."

"Fuck you."

"Ok. I have a full clip and all night. Want to talk straight or do I start taking toes?" I pushed the 9mm into his neck.

"Don't. Please. Don't." He was starting to cry, sounding much more San Fernando than Compton. I pulled the trigger, aiming near his leg. Cement chips flew up. He screamed.

"No. No. Please, I want to talk."

"Then start speaking. Truth. I am fighting hard not to kill you."

"I didn't do it. But I seen her. Young-looking black girl. It was her, I'm sure of it. They had her."

"They?"

"Yeah, the dudes in the car. Car she was in. They, yeah, they um..."

"Who?" I pressed the gun harder into his neck to get him to focus.

"I don't know. Yeah, never seen them, the car, none of it."

"Focus. Was she working?"

"Hell yes, putting in time, right?"

"Wrong. Not this girl. She's clean cut. Truth or die."

"Yes, she was. Mean, she never worked the track. No, not that girl. She...right? Never."

"Fuck it." I started to pull the trigger.

"No. Ok. They had her. Beat up. Nice girl like her, gorilla pimped? Made me sick. I don't play that fucking shit. No, not me."

"Gorilla what?"

"I didn't, ok. Never. Not the young girl. Hell, no."

"What set were they from?" Downtown was a patchwork of gang turf, or it had been when I was last down here.

"No set. It's all MS-13 round here. These dudes, ones that have your girl, not gangsters. From out of town, never seen them."

"Truth?"

"Truth." I fired a quick shot taking off his left earlobe. "Fuck. Fuck. I'm fucking deaf." Blood was running down his face.

"Only in one ear. Now truth."

"Yeah, OK, yeah. Fucking hurts, OK? It was a nigger named Titan, drives a custom Escalade. It was him. That is all I know. Shoot me. Won't change it." I slammed the automatic to the side of his head, driving him to the cement. I kicked him twice. He curled up into a whimpering blood-streaked ball. Fuck him. I broke down his 9mm and pitched it out into the river, left him bleeding on the ground. Truth is, I hoped he would die there.

It was after three AM when I got back to the Shamrock. A tired-looking hooker with bad acne scars and a cheap nylon Beyoncé wig came out of the lobby.

"You want to party?" she asked with no enthusiasm.

"No, baby, I'm spent."

"Heard that. My pussy is wore the fuck out." She put a Parliament in her mouth. I popped my Zippo and lit her. "Thanks."

"Not a thing." I leaned back against the Benz for balance.

"You gots blood on your pants, baby."

"Yeah, I guess I do. You ever hear of a guy named Titan?"

"Drives an Escalade? Preppy?"

"That's the guy."

"Never heard of him." She let out a phlegm-choked laugh. "No, baby, you wanna steer way the fuck clear of the negro. He a stone killer. Heard he beat one of his girls into a coma with a Gideons Bible. Or maybe that was Johnny Rey Rey in Tallahassee. Some pimp did that, sure enough."

"Titan sounds like a real bastard.   Where do I meet him?" I pulled a fifty out and passed it to her.

"He lives somewhere in the Valley."

"His girls?"

"Try Sepulveda track.   You know his girls cause those stuck up hoes make a strawberry look good.   Goddess this, Goddess that bullshit." She slipped the fifty into a plastic Hello Kitty purse and moved out onto Sunset Blvd.

CHAPTER 8

Grand Theft Auto was blaring when Freedom drifted back down. In the background of the game Dr. Dre was doing "Nuthin' but a 'G' Thang."

"Damn, look at me, man. I'm a hard motherfucker." LeJohn was pointing at a built, animated character flexing on the TV.

"Meat it up bitch, I'm hunting you." Andre had a soft Southern accent, light skin and his nose was dusted with freckles. He had a ratty beard and unkempt dreads. She knew he was the second to rape her. The heroin took her focus, but not her anger. He would die second. They should die in the order they took her. That seemed fair. She grinned.

Her body hurt. She was curled up on a stained bedspread in a motel room. Outside was a mystery. Any noise from beyond the walls was drowned out by the video game. She felt like she had a bad flu. Her mouth was dry, tongue stuck to the roof of her mouth. The flesh between her legs was raw and burning. Her thighs felt torn open. The two men playing PlayStation had their backs to her. The door was ten feet away, chain off. She could make it. If she was quiet, she could make it. Without moving, she flexed her legs, pressing blood into them. Coiling, she closed her eyes. Ready.

"Motherfuckers!" Light flooded her eyelids when the door opened. "You rather play a video cat getting rich than get out and earn."

"Yo, Zero, you told us keep to her," LeJohn said.

"So I did." Freedom heard him slap the kid. "And here you are. She awake?"

"Not a goddamn twitch," Andre said. Freedom kept her eyes still so they wouldn't see them move.

"You hear about Paulie? That ding-dong works the graveyard? Hell, you ain't left that box, how would you know shit."

"The wannabe ghost?" asked LeJohn.

"Who else, bitch?"

"I don't know."

"You sure as fuck don't."

"You gonna spill or leave us hanging?" Andre smoothed.

"Ding-dong got his ass fucked, rough. Son of a bitch blew a hole in his leg, his body, blew both his ears clean off. Motherfucker's stone deaf."

"Tres? He forget to pay rent?"

"Na, he didn't kick Tres their trib, his head would be on a pole." Zero laughed. "They say it was some Iron Giant white motherfucker."

"Pale giant poaching on a Tres preserve? He gonna get dead hard."

"Fuck Tres. Fuck them. I'll pimp slap those punks."

"Kid," Zero's voice went ice, "don't even whisper that crap. They are no fucking joke. You wanna live? Pay the toll and roll."

"I'm just, well...this Paul Bunyan motherfucker making a play for the track?"

"Dirty Sheila, she say he was flashing a pix of a black girl"

"Man wants a black piece, just have to hit Fig."

"Or close his eyes. All hoes is black in the dark," Andre said, sparking a fat spliff.

"One less ding-dong on the track, nothin' but a thang." Zero ended the conversation.

Freedom's leg spasmed. Traitor. Andre turned a slow pivot, staring at her. "Good morning, beautiful." A gold tooth flashed in his smile.

Zero dropped onto the bed beside her. He rose on an elbow and looked her over. "Looking fine, Lil' Diamond. How you feeling?"

Freedom tried to speak. A rasping croak came out.

"Kid, get our princess some water." He snapped his finger. "No, not tap, fucking dog. Fiji, and in a glass."

The water spread cool down her throat and into her body.

Zero watched, his eyes soft, almost kind.

The other two went back to the PlayStation. The sound slammed in.

"Shut that noise, dumb Negros." From a knot of bills in his pocket he tossed a fifty at Andre. "Take the kid, buy him some lunch." He tossed another fifty. "And get your funky ass a cut."

After they left, he leaned back, rubbing his eyes. "Sorry about those punks. I try to raise 'em up correct, but it almost impossible to make a BMW from a pile of pig shit. Maybe I should aim for a Prius." Refilling her glass, he let his fingers slip across hers. She couldn't remember the last gentle touch. "You probably hate me. Hell, my own momma hate me. But everything I done was to help you bust the cocoon, turn you into a butterfly." He let his fingers drift over her cheek. He lay back. She could feel his heat beside her. She felt a wave of relaxation. She held the water glass to the light, watching white flecks dance in the water.

"Jus' some feel-soft powder. Last thing I need is a needle marked-up Lil' Diamond."

She drank it down. She didn't care.

About...anything.

CHAPTER 9

In the room, I found Angel curled up with Rollens, both fast asleep, both snoring. I lay down on the other bed, crunched my Vicodin and chased them with a Mickey's Big Mouth. Trash beer, but the best I deserved. I didn't fall asleep, I passed out.

Mikayla is leaning against a dented old Ford truck. Dust swirls around her. The blood from the bullet hole in her heart has dried to rusty brown.

"No mercy asked, none given," she says.

"I'm sorry I got you killed."

"You are the only partner I ever had." She smiles, looking off to the horizon. A river of blood flows between us. Blood laps at her feet. She is sinking down into it. It reaches her knees. I can't reach her.

"Moses?"

"Yeah?"

"We are her only hope."

"Whose? Whose only hope?"

"All of them. Every last one. Every...last..."

Blood crests over her mouth drowning out her words, and then she is gone. I look down and my feet are sinking into the blood river. I struggle but the bloody quicksand has me. The blood is warm. It is sucking me under. I can't breathe. I scream but my mouth fills with blood. I am dying. I want to live. I choke and cough.

I am gasping when my eyes open. The sweat-soaked sheet is wrapped around my throat. I free myself and sit up. Rollens and Angel are staring at me.

"Rough night?" Her eyebrow is cocked.

"Ummm." I take three Vicodin with the warm, flat beer. I step into the shower and blood rolls down from my hands and arms. I remember the pimp I tortured. The night is a bit blurry, but I clearly remember his scream as the bullet took off a chunk of his ear. I knew I should care. Also knew I didn't give a fuck. I was rolling hard on the murder mile. Once I found Freedom I would sit back, maybe cry over what I'd done...maybe not. Anger and fear was all that might keep that little girl alive. I didn't have room in my head for one more lost kid. No more room.

The towel was old and took off some skin. No Downy softness in the Shamrock. Dried and dressed, I took Angel for a walk down Highland. I bought a couple of tall boys from an unlicensed taco shack. In De Longpre Park we joined the other burnouts on the benches. The combination of my red, hard eyes and Angel's size kept them from saying shit to us. Angel ate carne asada while I gulped the Olde English. I was on the second beer before my head stopped roaring.

Angel rested her head on my lap. The wrinkles around her eyes gave her a sad, soulful look. "I know, I promised you a life on the beach. You'll get there, this is just a detour." I knew I might be lying, but that didn't mean I didn't mean it.

"Titan? A black, Valley pimp?" Rollens and I were sitting in Kitchen 24, a hipster version of a coffee shop. The pierced and tatted waitress gave me a wide berth as she set down

51

a pile of eggs, hash browns and bacon. I guess even in my bug-man shades she could still vibe my crazy eyes. After she moved out of earshot, Rollens spoke, low.

"Does he have her?"

"She's not going to be the girl you last saw."

"Does he have her?"

"Yes. I'm just telling you, your niece, the girl you knew, she is gone."

"And? So we what? Say it, McGuire...say we're supposed to leave her out there."

"Fuck that. I'm going after her. If you come, I'm just warning you."

"What has he done to her?"

"Enough." I told her where we would look. I asked her to call Vice and see if they had a location on Titan. After stepping outside to make a call she told me he was off their radar. She wanted to know the plan.

"Find Titan. Kill him. Get your niece out. Problem with any of that, Detective?"

"Not a damn thing."

It was early. Titan's girls would hit the track at dusk, or later. The Vice boys hadn't ended streetwalking, they'd just sent it into the dark and made it more dangerous for the ladies.

I needed some normalcy, if only for an hour, so I took Angel to the Silver Lake dog park. Our morning stroll had barely taken the edge off her energy. If Angel didn't get some real exercise we were going to owe the Shamrock for a new motel room.

A cold mist was coming down off the hills as I moved Angel through the sally port. Hitting the yard, she burst off, spraying chunks of mud in her wake.

Helen stood alone, her back to me. She was a sturdy woman of my age. Her hair was cropped tight to her head and she wore a men's plaid Pendleton against the cold. She didn't look at me when I walked up to her. She was an old friend, a TV writer, dank too much coffee and the owner of a Rottweiler named Bruiser that Angel adored. She was also one of my only links to the straight world.

"How are you?"

"Screw you, Mo. Screw you."

"Bruiser looks good." Out in the mist, Angel broadsided the Rottweiler knocking him off his feet. He rolled and had her by the throat. They tumbled, all snap and growl. "Amazing they never break the skin."

"You walked away, never calling, not even an email, nothing. I thought you were dead. You can't do that to people, Mo. Not to me."

There was nothing to say to that, no way to explain how much better off she was with me gone. Angel and Bruiser reared up like stallions battling, tumbled over, then picked themselves up and ran chasing each other across the yard. Helen and I watched the dogs play in silence.

Helen looked at me, letting out a long breath. She smiled and shook her head. "You still miss Kelly?"

"Every goddamn day." Kelly had been my true friend. She had died ugly and I had put those responsible in the ground.

"Me too."

"Sorry I worried you."

"I know you are." We let silence hang between us. Comfortable. Angel lit out, charging across the park with Bruiser at her heels. "Angel looks good."

"She liked Mexico. We both did. You?"

"I fell in love. Her name is Jules, she's my age. I know, don't faint." Helen had a history of falling for women too young and often straight. It had never worked out well for her.

"I'm glad. You deserve someone in your life."

"She moved in. I mean, she still has her house but she only goes there to check her mail. I'm happy, Mo, for real. Someone to come home to, to drag me out at night. I feel lucky, finally."

"She's lucky to have you." I looked from the dogs to where the Mercedes was parked. Rollens sat watching us, talking on her cell.

"You got to go." Helen followed my gaze to the car and back. On her tiptoes, she pulled off my bug glasses and looked into my eyes for a long moment. "You're in more shit aren't you, Mo?"

"No, I'm good." I replaced the shades.

"Yes, you are, you just don't know it."

"Yeah, I'll see you around, darlin'." I snapped my fingers and called Angel. She tore herself away from the battle and followed me out of the park. Helen called Bruiser over. She stroked his face, but her eyes stayed on me. She knew I was full of shit. But maybe she didn't care.

CHAPTER 10

Al Capone's is a strip and tug joint on Sepulveda Boulevard, down below Victory. It's a small squat building in the middle of a large parking lot. It looks like it was built in the 1960's then stuck in a time capsule. Despite the Italian name, and the five-foot photos of white dancers on the outer walls, inside the dancers, doorman and bartender were all black. I dropped the twenty cover and pushed through the curtains. The smell: cheap perfume, sweat, desperation, lust, hunger and Windex.

It was 4:00 a.m. and the Vicodin was taking its toll. I left Rollens and Angel sleeping in the Benz. I'd spent most of the night searching for streetwalkers. If there was a track in the San Fernando Valley, it was invisible. So here I was heading into another strip club. I fell onto the deep velvet couch that horseshoed the room. Pulling out my pint bottle of mescal I took a pull.

"Don't let Tia see that." She was twenty-two, tops. Skinny but fit.

"Tia?"

"The manager. No alcohol with your pussy." I took a long pull and offered the bottle. She took it from me, licking the opening, eyes locked on mine, tongue darting in and out. "You gay?"

"How's that?"

"Most men see me working a neck like that break a sweat. You didn't even crack a smile."

"Girl, I'm old enough to be your daddy."

"But you're not my daddy, are you." She traced my hand with her finger. It was calloused, rough. She worked at more that stripping. "You want a dance in the VIP room? $150 for fifteen minutes. Guaranteed to make you bust a nut." She was tired and only half-heartedly selling it. I slid five twenties under her spangled purse. She looked at it, then up at the stage. "Now that is one ugly vagina. That shit is all flapping in the wind." She was speaking low under the thumping rap. On stage a woman was on her back, shaking her hips out of rhythm to the music, not that the men at the rail noticed. They were transfixed by that three inches of pink flesh.

"When I get up there, take a look. See, I have a beautiful pussy. That girl needs to get some work done she wants to make the money." I didn't have the heart to tell this child that men were so surprised to be staring at a woman's privates they barely noticed more than their own lust. "What are you doing here, big man? Paying me not to dance on you?"

"Looking for Titan, you know him?" She looked away, then down.

"Nope. No, no, no. Never heard of that nigger. Neither did you, you want to see another sun up." She stood up and walked away.

In a blurry stream women came and sat beside me. Soon as one would get up another would sit down. Six beauties and a stack of twenties later I walked out, with no more information than when I walked in.

The sky was paling as I stumbled across the parking lot. I tilted up the mescal, draining it. Something hit the side of my face like a sledgehammer. I fell to my knees. Somewhere on another planet the pint bottle exploded on the pavement.

CHAPTER11

"Who the fuck wants to know about Titan?" He wasn't large, but the baseball bat he was prodding my face with was. The Vicodin were shielding me from the pain. On the other side of the soft cotton barricade this punk banger swung down. The blow hit my gut. I was spewing before I even felt it coming up.

"Motherfucker, that shit is disgusting. You mess up my Fendis you dead." He lifted the bat up. Somehow I knew this blow would ruin my face, I just didn't care.

A shotgun was racked and the bat stopped mid-swing. Rollens pressed the gauge against the back of his melon. His eyelids drooped to slits. "Shit, keep it easy. No need to take my head off, I was just talking to this giant motherfucker."

"Bat." Rollens pressed the barrel harder. He dropped it. It hit the pavement with a wooden thunk. I used to play ball in school, before girls and drugs and Beirut. I watched the bat bounce twice, then roll.

"McGuire?" Her voice was out there calling me. "McGuire? Can you stand?" That was a hell of a question. Rolling over, I sat up. My head was dull and sloshed when I moved it. I wiped the puke onto the arm of my leather jacket. Using the bat as a cane I stood. Legs wobbled. I eye-fucked the young thug. He didn't flinch. I drove the bat down onto his foot. Bones broke. He started screaming. The second blow hit a kneecap and dropped him.

"McGuire, enough."

"Not by a long shot, but it'll have to do." Morning was coming fast. It was time to move, or have the sun find us in a strip club parking lot with a shotgun, a bat and a crippled thug. I dragged him across the parking lot and tossed his squealing ass into the trunk of the Benz. Passed Rollens the keys and fell into the passenger seat.

"Sepulveda Dam, you know it?" I mumbled, trying not to puke again.

"Yes. What the fuck was that? I had a gun on him. Are you crazy, fucked up, what?"

"Drive." I sank down in the seat.

"If you have a concussion you need to stay..."

I was out before she finished speaking.

Tires on dirt woke me. We pulled off Burbank and into the Sepulveda Wildlife Refuge. Rollens swung around the locked gate and down a dirt track. Two hundred feet and the city was gone from view. "There." I pointed to a cutout behind a stand of cottonwood trees.

"Looks like that hurts."

"Huh?"

"Your cheek." I felt it. A lump had formed, blood crusted where the bat had split the skin. It should have hurt. Painkillers and booze are wonderful things.

Puffs of white fluff from the cottonwood danced in the morning light. The moaning had stopped coming from the trunk. I moved around the car, keyed the lock. As the trunk popped open a pistol fired. Flame shot out of the shadows. I fell back, below the trunk line.

"You didn't frisk him?" Rollens was kneeling behind the rear fender. Pulling my .45, I pressed it against the metal wall of the trunk and fired. The thug screamed.

In the backseat, Angel was snarling and snapping at the rear glass.

"Toss the gun out or I empty the magazine."

"Fuck you." His hand raised up and fired wild. At three feet I couldn't miss. I aimed at his wrist and squeezed one off. The slug clipped the top of his thumb, taking a bite out of his knuckle. He was squealing again. I popped up and took aim into the trunk. He was holding his hand, the pistol fallen, forgotten.

"We done, kid?" I asked him.

"We done."

"Then climb out, hands where I can see them."

He hobbled out and I spun him and slammed his hands onto the hood. Rollens gave him a rough pat down. She pulled his wallet, reading it. "Jeremy Greene?"

"Name is Atlas."

"Atlas? You couldn't lift shit, Jeremy." I leaned against the car. The world was bright, my head was starting to hurt. "I'm way too tired to play take your body parts until you talk."

"Mother fuck—you ain't even ask me no question."

"Rollens, I need you to walk. Take Angel down to the river, get her a drink." She cocked her head, not moving. "As a police officer, you don't want to see what is about to happen."

"Alright, he's all yours."

"What the fuck? You goin? No, no, no. I'll talk, but the sister stays here."

"Go on, Rollens." She opened the back door and Angel jumped out. Rollens whistled and Angel followed her. Maybe I was wrong about her; Angel was a much better judge of character than me. Jeremy Greene watched her go. His face hardened. He stared at me, cold, ready for whatever was coming. I slipped the .45 into my belt and took out the picture of Freedom. I held it up for him to see.

"You smoke?" I asked.

"Fuck? Smoke?"

"Yeah, you got a cigarette?"

"No, don't smoke. You fuckin' nuts, right? Crazy white man bullshit going on here."

"Haven't smoked in years, but seems a good time to start." I punched him in the kidney with all the force I could muster. He staggered onto his busted-up leg, it failed and he fell to the ground howling. "See that little girl there?" I slammed the picture into his face with enough force to break his nose. "Titan snatched her off the street. You were there."

"Bullshit I was."

"You were. You rape her?" I ground my boot down on his ruined foot. It was already swollen and spilling out of the top of his loafer. When he screamed, blood from his nose mixed with his spittle.

"Never."

"Could spend all day taking you apart, still wouldn't be enough. Where is she?" I took the pressure off his foot and leaned back on the fender of the Benz. Blood pounded in my temples. White puffs danced in the light. The thug was miles away.

"I don't know shit," he said. "I'm bottom street boy. I don't run with Titan, just do what he say."

I closed my eyes, wishing I hadn't left my Vicodin in the car. "You ever killed a man?"

"What?"

"Simple question. You did or you didn't."

"No. You gonna kill me?"

"Sooner or later. You got to pay for what you done to that little girl."

"Didn't do shit, told you that." I kicked him in the head, but not with much gusto. I was too tired for this crap.

"I don't believe you. Where is she?" I raised my boot over his head and prepared to smash his life out.

"All right! Fuck you. Dial down. I'll tell you what you wants to know."

"You are almost dead, boy. Talk."

"He took her. Titan took that girl. Grabbed her off the street. Raped her. I didn't touch her. Swear to god. Never. Titan did it. Titan has her."

"Where." I kept the boot hovering over him.

"I'm telling you. Fuck! Ok. Where? Titan gots a massage parlor over on Victory. She too young to work the clubs. Swear I never touched her. Never."

He was a liar. I stomped his leg, finishing the job I'd started with the bat. I made sure it would hurt the rest of his life. With every step he would remember what he did to that little girl. I dragged his screaming ass off the road and dumped him in a ditch. I took the cell phone I'd found in his pocket and set it ten feet up the ditch. I figured it would take him a good twenty minutes to get to it. He would call Titan, Titan would come running, and if the girl wasn't there Titan would be in for the same hard ride as his boy.

I was sitting in the passenger seat two Vicodin to the good when Rollens showed up. Angel jumped in the back. Leaning her huge wrinkled face over the seat, she licked me with concern. "I'm ok," I lied to my best, or at least most faithful, friend.

"What happened to him?" Rollens nodded over at the moaning body in the ditch.

"Got lucky. He gave up Titan. They have your niece in a tug joint over on Victory."

"He told you that?"

"Drive."

61

"They won't be open. Did he tell you where they're holding her? Did he?"

I pushed open the door, stood, waited for the world to slow down its spinning, then walked over to the ditch. "Where is he keeping her? No fucking around." I was shouting to be heard over the blood rushing in my head. "Where?" I kicked dirt clods down on top of him. Dust turned to red mud on his streaked face.

It took all he had to focus enough to gasp out his words. "Back room. Victory. Back room."

Rollens drove. I looked down, saw blood was splashed on my boot. I tried to care. Couldn't. The massage parlor was a small single building. Must have once been a dentist or doctor's office, acupuncture diagrams taped to the front window. All trying to make it look legit. *The Feel Better Joy Massage Parlor*, a cheap plastic sign read. *Only $35*. In joints like this across America men were getting off on or in little girls. Killing them a little more with every load they shot. Was three minutes of pleasure worth a baby's life? Fuck it was. Mutilated, broken kittens. Fat fucking men slamming money on counters. Unending chain of pain. Fuck them. Fuck.

The back door caved with a kick. I swung in, swept the room with my .45. Far behind me Rollens moved, Glock ready. In the room, an old TV sat on a desk. A cot. A pile of outdated magazines. A bookcase filled with oils, lotion, and an industrial-size box of condoms. Aerosol lubricant. Medicated douches.

Fuck.

I moved out, down a tight hall. Quiet. Listening. No noise. Opened the first door. Empty, save a dingy massage table. Next room the same. Same. Same. Fuck. Front room had a Sparkletts bottle, chair. No one. I grabbed the chair and threw it at the reception desk. Plaster broke, phone burst. Silence.

Rollens started to speak.

"Don't." I snapped. My blood was up, anger overriding the pain pills and mescal.

In the back room, I found a squeeze bottle filled with alcohol and a Bic lighter on a cigarette burned counter. I sprayed the old magazines and the wall. The magazines lit, burned orange, then blue flames rolled up the wall. The room was starting to fill with smoke when I walked out.

"Why the hell did you do that?"

I looked at her. No words came.

"Just going to make it that much harder to find him."

"Fuck it. Fuck 'em all." Pressed the accelerator down and the car jumped forward.

"Is this the plan, McGuire? Piss everyone off and wait until the ones holding Freedom come after you, then kill them first?"

"Works for me."

"What if he kills you? Or Freedom?"

"Won't happen. I'm death. He's dead."

CHAPTER 12

From up the street, we watched the building burn. Titan never showed. All it brought on was fire trucks, and an older Chinese man, screaming for them to put out the fire. The cops rolled up and we cut out. Slow and easy. Two more Vics. I was fighting to find equilibrium. Maybe in hindsight I shouldn't have demanded to drive, maybe I shouldn't have done a lot of things that morning.

"You gonna make it, McGuire?"

"I'll get her back."

"I know you will." She looked at me sadly, then out the window.

We were on the 101 headed back to Hollywood when the deal went sideways.

I heard the rumble of the SUV as it sped toward me.

A black Escalade started to pass. Why was the driver wearing a bandana over his face?

Fuck. Oh, fuck.

The rear passenger window slid down.

A barrel with a suppressor aimed out.

Flame burst from the machine gun.

Glass shattered all around me. Bullets ripped through sheet metal zinging around the interior. I locked the brakes, spun the wheel. A bullet embedded in the dash sparked and smoked. We skidded sideways across three lanes. I released the breaks and jammed the gas. Hitting the curb, we left the ground and sailed out over the steep embankment. The front end dug into the ivy. The dash was on fire. We bounced up and kept going. One hundred feet ahead was a chain link fence and the street beyond. We were close to home free. Over the rattle and roar I heard the signature *whump* of a rocket being launched. You never forget that sound.

Flame and dirt and torn metal slammed the ass end of the Mercedes into the air. The explosion left me deaf except for a screaming, high-pitched sound. Time stopped. We went vertical. Angel flew past me, colliding with the windshield. She let out a pain-filled yelp. Her head was red and wet. We continued to somersault, coming down on our roof. Blood was running down my face, stinging my eyes. Breath came hard. My seatbelt held me hanging upside down. The world blurred in and out of focus. A hand pressed something against my neck, pushed my hand up, showing me to keep pressure. The blood across my face staunched.

Below me Angel tried to stand, let out a yelp, fell.

Black.

Lights flashing white and blue and red came closer and closer.

Black.

I reached down to touch Angel. My fingertips brushed torn metal. I couldn't see her through the blood in my eyes.

Black.

I fought to scream. A gurgled gasp is the best I could manage. The pain from my ribs exploded into white heat.

All went bright.

A paramedic's voice was distant and unimportant.

If this is the end, the long white tunnel, so fucking be it.

I had a few choice words for the man upstairs.

White.

No more pain.

CHAPTER 13

Lil' Diamond was all anyone called the girl anymore.

"Freedom. Freedom. I am Freedom. Mamma was Mary. Father, John. Freedom. I am Freedom," she whispered over chapped lips when no one was listening.

Slowly, Zero scaled back her narcotics. Told her if he wanted a junky ho he would go downtown and grab one. As clarity returned, she felt the pain of what they had done to her. The rapes had stopped, but she still flinched every time she was touched. That got her slapped. So she learned to take the fear inside, shut herself down. While Freedom was safe, robot Lil' Diamond did just as told.

They gave her hits of chronic. Gin and tonic. Hamburgers. But for every gift she had to give up a little something. A hand job. Letting SK bite her nipple and smile when he laughed at her wince. New rules: leave her pussy to heal, no marks on her face.

LeJohn was sitting on the bed talking real quiet. The others were in the living room blasting GTA. They had fed her Chinese. She had slipped a chopstick under the blanket.

"Lil' Diamond, I ain't like them others."

"How's that? You younger, but you the same."

"No, Lil' Diamond, I really care for you. For real." He looked so sincere. What was he, fourteen, fifteen? Maybe even thirteen, like Freedom. If the chopstick was sharper, she could bury it in his pulsing carotid artery.

"Don't let Zero hear you talk that way." She stroked his cheek gently. "I can see you a good man, but if they think you soft, they will rip you up." Truth was, if they thought he was soft they would have him rip *her* up. She kissed a scar on his knuckle and thought about a scalpel and what he would look like with his tendons cut. How his hand would dangle uselessly.

The video game went silent. Someone had pulled the TV's plug. A woman's voice was muffled, but sounded stern. The door opened and Amethyst scanned the room. Freedom had heard the men speak about Amethyst, the bottom girl. They talked tough about taking her down a notch, but their fear showed under the surface. Freedom had imagined her an older brute of a woman, instead Amethyst was young and beautiful, dark-skinned, fine-boned and blonde, with purple eyes.

"LeJohn?"

"Yes, ma'am?"

"You paying for my girl's time?"

"I was—"

"You were, bullshit. Now you and the rest of these useless Negroes get the fuck out of here before I start taking scalps home to Frankie. Clear?" Freedom watched Amethyst move Zero and his boys out. Didn't ask. Told. And they listened, too.

"Stand up and drop that robe, Lil' Diamond." She commanded and Freedom obeyed. All shyness was gone. Naked, she stood, eyes down. If she looked Zero or his boys in the eyes she took a beating.

"Turn around." Freedom followed the command. "Boney ass, no tits." Amethyst lifted Freedom's face so their eyes met. "Lucky for you, some men like a skinny bitch. Mostly they like tight, warm, wet pussy. They gonna love you. You like it when I say that? When I say they gonna love you?"

"Yes." Freedom mumbled.

"What honey?"

"Yes. I said yes."

"Good." Amethyst passed her a Victoria's Secret box. "These are for you. Put them on, it's time to earn your keep."

"What?"

"Don't act stupid, you are not stupid. Put these on." Freedom held up the sheer crotchless panties. "On, now." Freedom did as told. The padded bra almost made it look like she had tits. "On your knees up on the bed, stick out your ass. Come on, bitch, give me your 'I wanna fuck' look." Freedom went deep into herself, ordered the robot Lil' Diamond to act sexy like in a Nicki Minaj video. Nicki took over. Freedom hid in her steel room. Lil' Diamond robot went onto all fours and writhed, licking her lips, eyes at half-mast.

Lightning flashed as Amethyst snapped pix with her cell. Ten minutes and they were uploaded to sexteens dot com and three other escort sites that catered to men who like them young. Said she was barely eighteen. Barely legal and ready to learn. From her steel room, Freedom watched. Learned. Waited.

"Did that Zero teach you how to put on a condom? No? Son of a bitch rode bareback? You get knocked up Frankie will skin him. No, for real he will."

"Frankie?"

"Frankie. He is the man of all men. Once we get you earning you'll get to meet him. A king. The man is a king and we are all his princesses."

Amethyst taught Freedom how to put a condom on a man with her mouth. If done right, he might even come while she was putting it on him. Job done. She gave Freedom a can of aerosol lube, showed how to spray it on with her back to the John. "If he's sober, he wants to think you're wet for him. But don't worry, most of these first johns won't give a damn long as they can stick their junk in your hole."

The older girl gave the baby a couple of white pills and a big gulp of cherry schnapps. She left Lil' Diamond sitting on the bed and waiting. But not for long.

That day Lil' Diamond fucked twelve men. Most in their forties. Most white. Zero and the boys would bring them to the hotel. Amethyst would deal with the cash, tell the men Lil' Diamond was new, fresh and ready to ride.

At four a.m. the men stopped coming. Freedom ate a burger then threw it up. She lay in a bath. Amethyst sat on the edge of the tub sharing a joint. "First is rough. Gets easier, trust me, Lil' Diamond. After that it's...different. It pays, baby, gives us everything we ever wanted. We have the pussy, they pay for the pussy. Just the way God wanted it, otherwise he'd have give Adam a dick and a pussy so he could fuck himself."

Freedom slipped under the water, watching the bubbles trickle toward the surface.

CHAPTER 14

"Do you know where you are?" He had a short gray beard, wore a lab coat.

"Hell?" I tried to move my arms but they were strapped to the bed rails. The room was white, with rust stains on the ceiling. Sweat dripped across my vision, stinging.

"How long have you been here?" He's writing on a clipboard.

"Forever?" My voice sounds gravely and hollow. Head hurts. Mouth dry.

"Twenty-three hours. Does that surprise you?"

"Can I get some water?"

"In a moment." Fucker had me trapped, and knew it.

"Where am I?" Not sure I want to know the answer.

"Valley Memorial, psych ward. Do you know why?"

"I'm guessing that you think I'm nuts?"

"You punched a paramedic who was trying to pull you from your wrecked car. You sent two police officers to the hospital before they could Taser you. Twice. Any of this triggering your memory?"

Splashes of color. The burning dash. Tracer bullets. The Benz tumbling through the air. Angel hitting the windshield. Angel. "My dog."

"Dog?" The guy in the lab coat looked around my room. "Where? Where do you see a dog?"

"Car wreck. You a fucking idiot?" He stepped back, afraid. I fought for calm, or at least the approximation of it. "There was a dog. Big dog."

"I don't know." Kept his eyes on his clipboard. "I'll check for you."

"Thank you." I tried to give him my 'I won't eat you' smile. May have failed, he still looked nervous. "Think I can scratch my nose?" I rattled my restraints.

"When I return. Let's see how you do." He was gone.

Get moving, petookh.

Mikayla was sitting on the end of the bed in her blood-stiffened black coat. I tugged hard at my restraints.

Yes, yes I see, zalupa. You seriously fucked this up.

She was toying with a straight razor.

"You my fucked up version of a Valkyrie? You here to carry me home?"

No. You need a hero's death for that. Getting blown up in a luxury car? Pussy move.

"Did you always give me this much shit?"

Who cares? That little girl has you and no one else.

"I never forget that."

Really? What is your plan?

A slight Mexican nurse came in. He looked around. "Talk to yourself, gets you an extra 48."

"I was just—"

"Shhhh, Frankenstein, don't give a fuck. Just want to tell you how this place works."

He washed the greasy sweat off my face, underarms and chest. "Want me to wash your junk?"

"No."

"Cool." He had LA tattooed in gothic letters on his neck. After giving me a hot towel shave, he showed me my face in a mirror. It was battered and bruised, a line of stitches ran across my forehead.

"Frankenstein, huh?"

"Seen worse. Once...maybe."

"Comedian."

"Laugh or cry brother." He held a paper cup of pills to my lips.

"What is it?"

"What do you care? I saw your tox screen."

"Patient confidentiality?"

"You rather I think you're just one more violent asshole?"

"What are the pills?"

"Clonidine, for kicking your apparent steady diet of Vicodin. This reduces anxiety, agitation, muscle aches, sweating, runny nose and cramping. Least that's what it says it does. The other is Clozapine. A chill pill, low dose."

"Thanks." I opened my mouth, swallowed them down like a good soldier. "Any chance I could get you to loosen my restraints?"

"Not and keep my gig. And I need my gig." He tipped the plastic cup and I drank it in a gulp. Asked for another and drank that one down, too.

"A question," glanced at his name tag, "Rodriguez?"

"Bobby. Shoot, Slick."

"Has anyone come by looking for me?"

"You on the run? Guy your size, I bet you never won at hide and go seek."

"No, not much. So?"

Bobby looked both ways, then spoke quietly. "Two detectives been by, wanted to question you. Dr. Miller sent them packing."

"Feds?"

"LAPD."

"One of them a woman, kinda short, black, walks like a cop?"

"No, but they asked us staff if she'd been around."

"Has she?"

"Nope. One of the security guys told me they searched the tapes. Didn't find her there either. She the one you been talking to?"

"No, one's a ghost and the other is just disappeared."

"Man, Frankenstein, you got a head full of some weird shit."

"I know. Bobby?"

"Moses?"

"I know the woman I'm talking to isn't really there. I'm not crazy."

"You say so, Chief."

"How many days am I down for?"

"Two, 'less you keep arguing with non-ghosts. Do that, then it could be longer."

"Bobby?" My words were starting to slur.

"No more questions, Chief. Get some sleep. You been on a hard run. Think of this as a vacation."

I know there was something I wanted to say, some tough bullshit about Vikings and vacations, but I was under before it made it from my mind to my mouth.

I'm listening to The Pogues, "The Sick Bed Of Cuchuliann." What album? The drugs Rodriguez gave me scattered my thinking. Rum, Sodomy & The Lash, that was the album. Shane's drunken vocals stroked my eardrum. He sang about an angel at the head of a bed and two devils with bottles in their hands. You need one more drop of poison and you'll dream of foreign lands...

The Root, Beirut, dust, sand, flames. Classified papers swirl around me. Every time I think I can read one it goes up in flames. I know this is the embassy bombing. I know it means something. A marine stumbles past. His face is gone. He has no mouth to scream with.

Me and two other sharpshooters are on the roof. We leave our M40s and take full autos. Tight alleys. Narrow streets. We aren't out for precision. We are out for revenge. Pure. Simple. The building across the street harbors insurgents.

Muslim fighters run out into the street. We rise up. Our M16s shred them. There is movement. I snap a fast burst. Blood sprays. Then... then I notice it was a young mother, chasing her panicked child out of the building. She falls, her arm outstretched, reaching for her son.

"Revenge, pure and simple. Run out in a free-fire zone, it's you." Gunny says. Pours me a tall beer then drops in a shot of Jack. I drink it down in one long gulp. Looking out at the world through the bottom of the glass, I see the mother falling again and again. Jittery, like an old film loop. Would have been funny if it was Chaplin.

It is not funny.

Next time I came to, the restraints had been removed. I was in a new room. The door had a window. My legs felt unsteady when I stood up. Head swam. I pushed on the door and it swung open. The hall was wide. A nurses' station behind glass surveyed the entire area. A man, sixty plus in a torn, red silk smoking jacket walked past me, inches away. I smelled his stale sweat; he didn't know I was there. At the end of the hall was a dayroom with tables, couches. High on the wall a mounted TV beamed a game show. Loonies moaned and wailed. These folks were really fucked up. There was a small outdoor court for smoking. A young man leaned against the one tree, puffing away. I joined him, not because I smoke, but I needed a break from the noise. He told me his mother raped him last night. Told me she used a wooden spoon. Told me she had been dead twenty years and she still won't leave him alone. I wished I could help him. Seems like a good enough guy. I was out of words. I went back and lay on my bed.

I woke again when Dr. Miller entered my room. The drugs they gave me kept me calm, slightly buzzed but not high. "I just wanted to let you know, I checked and there wasn't a dog in the wreck."

"What about the cop?"

"They told me you were alone." He studied my face, looking for my reaction. I gave nothing up. Less he knew about what and whom I cared about, less leverage he had. "We can talk about it if you like."

"What's to talk about? Gone is gone. Dead or run off, but gone for sure."

"Alright. Fine." He looked sad. Walked out. Left me alone.

Angel is tucked into my leather jacket, her floppy puppy ears dance in the wind. Her warmth is pressed against my belly. I feel a rare, strange peace. Angel is her full hundred plus pounds. I feel hot sand under bare feet. Angel moves down to the surf. The water is blood red. Just beyond the breakers, Kelly stands in a white rowboat. She is whole. Alive. I would do anything to hold her. Angel leaps into the red water, paddles out and gracefully climbs into the boat. Kelly cries out but her words are lost to the roar of the sea. I run after them, splashing, diving, swimming. With every wave crest I see they are getting farther and farther away, until finally I lose site of them. I stop swimming and let myself sink. Blood red covers my vision. I sputter. I gasp. I let go and drift lower.

"Moses, can I call you that?" We are in Dr. Miller's office. He has my police file on his desk.

"Sure, Doc, why not?" I construct my face into some facsimile of a calm smile. He scans my file, looking from it to me as he reads. I keep my head in neutral. One of the gifts my monster of a drunken mother gave me was the ability to shut my head down, go numb and not let the bastards see you hurt. You let them know what hurts, they just keep doing it.

"You have done quite a lot of what most would call violent acts."

"Yes."

"Do you consider yourself a violent man?"

"Yes."

"How does that make you feel?"

"Feel?"

"Feel, yes. How do you feel about the violence you have been involved in?"

"Does my answer change when I get out?"

"Yes and no. You are under a 72 hour evaluation. I need to assess if you are a danger to yourself or others." He looks at me a long time, then takes a note. I let the silence stretch. "The *LA Times* called you a hero. Are you a hero?"

"No. I didn't have a choice."

"Heroes have choices?"

"Something like that."

"It says you saved six teenage girls from being trafficked in the sex trade. By any measure, that is heroic."

"Papers, reporters, they write all colors of crap."

"You didn't rescue the girls?"

"It wasn't that simple."

"Ok." He looks over my file. "*Times* also said you joined the Marines at 16. Lied about your age?"

"They shouldn't have printed that. Personal."

"But it is true? You were in Beirut?"

"I was there."

"Why did you do that?"

"Marines say Washington wants you to go kill, you go."

"The question is, why did you join the Marines in the first place?"

"It was a train out of town, good as any other."

"What about your childhood, parents?"

"Look, Doc, you wanna find out if I will hurt myself or others? Odds are I will. But I'm not crazy. There is a thirteen-year-old girl named Freedom, she's out there in the hands of a pimp. Every moment I sit here she gets farther away from who she was."

"Are you sure about this girl? Could she be a fantasy? Guilt, pain, alcohol and narcotics...do you find it odd that you are searching for Freedom?"

"She is real. Do your fucking homework. Ask detective Rollens."

"Who?"

"Rollens, LAPD detective? She was in the car wreck with me."

"You were alone." The floor started to open under my feet. I sank back into the chair.

"Please, call Detective Lowrie, LAPD, Hollywood Division."

"Is he a friend?"

"Just call him."

Six p.m., no word from Lowrie. Group therapy was a three-ring circus: clowns, ballerinas, lion tamers and me, the human beast. I kept my head down. Turned inside. Tried to sort out the last days. Where the fuck was Rollins? Why had she left me here? Was she real? Was any of this? Maybe I was on the beach and this was a vivid dream. You hang around the nuthouse, you're bound to catch some crazy.

Bobby woke me. I felt half-assed normal. Or sober, rather. Lately the norm was stoned. This actually felt good. The cotton had been swept from my brain. "Mo, you got a visitor."

"Cop?"

"He said you asked for him."

Lowrie had deep bags under his eyes. The man didn't sleep. Instead, he closed cases. Looking me over, he shook his head sadly. "Do me a favor, McGuire, forget my name."

"Good to see you too, old man."

"I had a long talk with the head of Internal Affairs yesterday. Wild guess what it was about?"

"Me?"

"Bingo buffalo. Bastard wants to know why I hang with an outlaw degenerate like you. Told him you were my C.I."

"Buy it?

"Hell if I know."

"How badly am I screwed here?"

"Took down a couple of highway patrol boys. True?"

"I was drunk."

"When aren't you?"

"Now." I held out my hands. They were steady, not a tremor in sight. "Why is I.A. interested in me?"

"You tell me. Horseshit is what this is."

"Do you know a detective named Rollens?"

"Who's he?"

"She. Black, on the short side. Lost her niece." Lowrie thought it over, but shook his head. "Said she knew you. Used your name to get close to me."

"Never heard of her."

There it was. I was well and truly fucked. Rollens, or whoever she was, had played me. The juice I thought I had with the cops was gone. I was an ex-con with two strikes in the middle of a snarling clusterfuck.

I gave Lowrie everything I could remember about Rollens and Freedom. He wanted to know if I thought the girl was really out there.

"My gut says yes. I don't know. Rollens definitely vibed cop, or ex-cop. She's the only string I can see in this rat's nest."

"Do you know why I like you McGuire?"

"Haven't a clue."

"Yeah, neither do I." At least he was smiling when he said it. Lowrie told me he would do some digging into Rollens, look into the vice connection. I thanked him. He shrugged it off. "McGuire?"

"Yeah?"

"Take it easy. Undertow in the city is getting rough."

"What does that mean?"

"Step lightly. Keep your size thirteens off people's chests if you can help it."

When he was gone, I took a long, scalding shower. Switching to ice cold, I felt my skin coming alive. In my room, I did twenty push-ups. I was puffing hard. Was a time I did a hundred just to get my heart rate up. I ran laps around the nurses' station. The crazies watched me pass like a ghost train. The floor was cold under my bare feet, but it was better than trying to run in paper slippers. The blood pumping felt good. After several sit-up reps, I gripped my gut and wondered where the hell it had come from. I guess I knew where and how I had become this hunk of soft flab. Why eluded me. Fuck it. Why was for suckers and bleeding hearts.

Fuck why.

Why was a rearview mirror. Somewhere out there was a bitch who'd set me up. Somewhere was the son of a bitch who killed Angel. Somewhere there might be a little girl being passed around like a Friday night party favor.

Fuck why.

More push-ups. More running. Another long shower. Let the heat loosen my exhausted muscles. It was time to get the hell out of there.

Dr. Miller let me into his office. He had me sit while he finished up some paperwork, then looked up at me.

"You look good, Moses. How do you feel?"

"Better. Ready to go home."

"You know, I think therapy would do you good. You don't have to be in so much pain." He was serious. I didn't laugh. I needed his signature to get free. "Do you know anything about evolution?"

"I stay out of politics."

"Science."

"That too."

"With early humans, the biggest, most brutish male was made the tribe's leader. As hunters and warriors, it made sense. But then agrarian culture came along and society needed cooperation. In that model, three men could join up and take the strongest down. Those who could cooperate, negotiate, became the new leaders. Do you understand what I'm saying?"

"Yes. Maybe it's time I evolve. You could be right." I knew it was bullshit, said it anyway. Down where I live, the brute rules. Cooperation is another way of saying surrender. Tell the motherfuckers holding a teenaged girl you want to negotiate, you wind up in a ditch.

My jeans and t-shirt were torn and bloodstained, but they had thought to wash them. My Docs were a mess, leather jacket torn and scuffed. Hell, guys in Beverly Hills spent beaucoup bucks for this look. The twenty stitches holding my forehead together was the finishing touch.

Lowrie had convinced the highway patrol to drop any assault charges. An insanity defense would have cleared me anyway. I thanked nurse Bobby. He told me I didn't need to come back, I could make it if I would only find a higher power. I thanked him and split before his twelve-step pitch.

I was free for all of twenty feet before they nailed me.

CHAPTER 15

"Give us the room." They drove a couple of doctors and nurses from the break room. Deloris and Carbone. Both men looked like lifetime government employees.

"Do you have ID?" I asked.

"We heard your bullshit story about a fake cop from your loser of an LAPD detective pal." Deloris, the older one, said. He stank of cigarettes and coffee.

Carbone, the younger, sweeter-faced cop handed me his shield. "Sorry about my partner." His shield looked legit.

"Internal Affairs? What the fuck?" That earned me a cuff on the back of my head from Deloris. "I don't work for LAPD, I don't have to say fuck all." I was still bold from the feel-good pills.

"Thousand acres of Federal land two miles from here. Bodies go missing." Deloris said.

Carbone moved between us. "We need your help."

"Fuck off."

Deloris shoved me toward a chair with sudden strength and ferocity. "Sit."

I stepped back, but didn't go down. He looked surprised. He was used to people going down when he pushed. Bullies hate being wrong.

My fist clenched.

"Go ahead, McGuire, swing. Give me a reason to sink you."

"Deloris?"

"Fuck him, Carbone. Fuck. Him. He talks here or we take him, now."

The younger cop shrugged and gave me a weak smile. "You want to tell us what happened, Moses?"

"Starting where?"

"The beginning, dickweed."

"Why are you here?" Deloris shoved me again, harder. I stumbled, righted myself and turned on Carbone. "Son of a bitch touches me again? I'll take his head off and we can speak through my lawyer. Or you will pull a body dump and see what I tell you from the grave. Sack up and deal it, fuck the outcome."

"Nobody is dumping anything. We just want the truth. We hear a story about an LAPD badge in Mexico and military ordinance going off in our county, we investigate."

He wasn't a bad kid, for I.A., so I told him what I knew. A sanitized version of the truth. I started with Rollens coming to Mexico. I omitted killing Xlmen, and the amount of drugs I had been ingesting. I may have painted a less savage picture of how I questioned the pimps. They went through the story again and again. After an hour of going back and forth, Deloris had had enough.

"This is crap, McGuire. Fake cop? You bought it without checking? Crap."

"Her I.D. was real, or good. She dropped a solid name."

"Yeah, fucking Lowrie. Solid piece of shit. Not one thing is right in your fairy tale. Why the hell were those gangbangers after you?"

"I don't know who they are. Truth. We can keep dancing all day and I still won't."

"Screw him, he knows diddly. I say we bust him. Obstruction, or battery of an officer. Plant a gun, whatever. Let him sink under the weight of three strikes. I need a smoke." Carbone waited for Deloris to leave before he spoke.

"You're staring at a life sentence. He will push it if you give him a chance. Me, I don't want that. I get it. A fake detective offered you a get out free card, you jumped. I get it. So you knock a few heads, step on the wrong toes and wham bam here you are. You want a real deal? Tell me the truth about the guys who came after you and I can wipe your record clean, my word."

"This is about the drive-by, right? Why?"

"That and Rollens, or whatever her name is. Bring her in. Help us find out who is trying to blow you up. Do that and maybe I get a judge to clear you."

"Maybe?"

"It is always maybe...when a cop's telling the truth."

"I'll give you that. Ok. Let's wait for bad cop to get back. I don't want to repeat myself." I waited in silence. Carbone tried small talk. Talked about the Dodgers, some bullshit about a pitcher they dropped a fortune on. Like I gave a fuck. Bunch of fat rich men walking around a field that had once been the home of Mexican farmers. Chavez Ravine was stolen to make Dodger Stadium. Poor people lost their homes, then paid heavy to park there and watch rich men play a silly game. So, no, I didn't give a fuck. I let the silence hang.

When Deloris returned, I spoke calm but firm. "Cards up time. You boys got shit on me." If they'd found my drugs or guns, they would have used them against me. "Your threats are bullshit. My people—white people—know I'm here. So fuck your disappearing threats." Neither of them looked happy to see my new resolve. "Here is my deal, take it or I lawyer up. You back off, and I will find who tried to take me out. If I find the bitch who set me up, she's yours. I do either of these things, you wipe the books clean. And I want it in writing before you get zip from me."

"Fuck us and I bury you."

"You'll try."

"No, McGuire, I will sink you."

"We need to know your plans, what's your next move." The serious expression on Carbone's baby face made me smile.

"I'll call when I need something from you." I said and walked out. Deloris may have wanted to knock my head around, but he wanted what I could find out more.

Gregor was leaning against his Chrysler 300. Windows tinted black, rolling 22s. It was an Armenian chariot. Gregor had on his greatcoat, one arm pinned up where he was missing the limb. Rain had blown in and his collar was up. Ray-Bans hid his eyes. "Boss." He nodded like I had just seen him yesterday.

"How'd you know I was here? Lowrie?"

"Who? The cop? No. It was a woman, no name."

"She knew I was getting out now?" I looked around, wondering if I was being watched.

"No. She told me where you were. I called the hospital, nothing nefarious there."

"Nefarious?"

"Come on."

"Nefarious? Word of the day?" He almost smiled. Almost.

We drove across the Valley, headed south down the 101. I told Gregor my real story, leaving nothing out. He nodded when I told him I had taken Xlmen off the boards.

"Little fuck had it coming, and more. Sorry I didn't see it."

"Agreed. He wasn't worth a tenth of one Mikayla."

We were in Glendale when I finished talking. He pulled over on a side street. Through the windshield the swollen LA River was rushing high on its cement banks. Rain danced on the Chrysler's hood.

"Blew a pimp's ear off?"

"Yeah."

"Broke another's foot and kneecapped him?"

"Yes. Leading somewhere with this?"

"Bullshit intel, Boss. You, me, we been tortured. We know, enough pain a man will tell anything, true or not."

"I didn't torture..." I couldn't finish it. He was right. Not one piece of information had been solid. Rollens told me her Vice contacts had seen Freedom on the East LA track. Suspect intel in retrospect. The punk by the river said he had seen Freedom in Titan's car. No proof he ever saw her. Jeremy Greene? He would have said his mother was a man just to get me to end the pain.

Gregor let me do the math. He looked out the window, impassive. Then he spoke, eyes still out the window. "You sure it was military ordinance took you down? Tracers? You can get that on the net."

I thought it over. "I saw a tube out of the back window. I know the sound of an RPG. I'm sure."

"More than a pissed pimp. One more piece don't fit; why is I.A. looking into a gang hit or a fake cop? Both are way off their corner of the LAPD."

"Where the fuck were you when they were interrogating me?"

"Where were you, Boss?" He reached in my breast pocket and found a prescription bottle. Before I could say boo he was out of the car. He sailed the anti-anxiety pills into the rushing current.

"There are going to be some very mellow fish."

"Shit's not funny, Boss. You can't afford to be blurry."

"Agreed." We shook hands in the rain. I meant it. I also knew the value of my word when it came to drugs, so I added, "I'll try."

"All any of us can do, Boss."

In the Chrysler, I lay the photo of Freedom on the dash. It had survived, a bit torn, but still clear as day. Her sweet face looked out at me. Demanding action.

"Think she's real, Boss?"

"That, my little brother, is the question. But, yes, I do." Gregor nodded. No more need be said on that.

He started the car. "You will come to my house, Anya will want to see you."

"We both know that's a lie." If he knew I was right, he didn't show it.

"You should meet the baby." A bit of pride flashed in his steel eyes.

On the way, he took me to The Rack, a discount clothing store in little Armenia. I traded my torn jeans for a pair with big embroidery on the back pockets. Bought a t-shirt with wings painted on the back. None of it was my style, but it fit. They had some aviator sunglasses, Hilfiger or some such bullshit. He tried to get me to trade my stained Docs for a pair of Caterpillars. I drew the line there.

Gregor lives in the foothills of northern Glendale. They tried the Valley, tried to escape their Armenian neighborhood, live in the melting pot. Told me when the baby came they moved back. He had squared it with his former employer, Rafael Hakobian, the local mob boss. Hakobian had no love for the Russian crew we took out. "Our reputation, yours and mine, is strong. Has a value now and then."

"He'll be glad I'm back in town?"

"Doubt it. But won't fuck with us if he can help it."

"Good enough for me."

The house was nice. Not fancy, not up in the money part of the hills. A ranch style, made me expect June and Ward Cleaver to live there instead of a Russian ex-whore and her Armenian thug.

Anya took my breath away. She stood in a bedroom doorway, baby in her arms. Her tall, lithe, dancer's body had rounded with childbirth. Her wild chestnut hair was tamed by a knot in the back. Her sea-green eyes pierced me to the soul. I'd killed a lot of men to save her and her sister. I thought we would be together. I was wrong.

"Moses. Gregor tells me you are back." No warmth.

"It be won't be long."

"Good." Gregor snapped her a look. She waved him off. "What? I am wrong to want my man alive? That is not our life anymore." Gregor tried to hold his cold stare, but his baby gurgled. He took the baby and passed it to me.

"Support his head, like this." The little bugger was warm. Gregor kept a hand on his baby. "His name is Moisse. Russian. Her idea." He nodded to Anya.

"Hoped it would be a memorial."

"Sorry to disappoint." She had to turn away before the smile fully bloomed on her face.

From the kitchen, I heard his mother humming and could smell cabbage cooking. She truly did hate me. Blamed me for her son's injury. Blamed me worse for getting Angel hurt a year ago. I didn't tell her what had happened in the recent accident; if she thought I got Angel killed she would bury a butcher's knife in my chest.

"I should go."

"You will stay for lunch. All of this," Gregor swept a hand around the room, "you gave to us."

"No man, you built this. We still good on the wheels?" He had offered to loan me a car.

He nodded.

The rain had let up for the moment. It was cold but dry when we walked out. In the driveway was a 2001 Mustang 5.0. Not the new, cool retro style, but maybe more honest. It was piped and chipped. Good rubber. The fucker could run. He didn't ask me to return it in the same condition. We both knew odds were slim. Gregor pulled the baby seat out and swept a pacifier and a few toys into it. He looked embarrassed by the state of the car. I smiled. He looked good. Domestic life had softened his features, if only a bit.

I was about to get in when a car pulled to the curb. Nika was in the passenger seat. She was a younger, softer version of her big sister Anya—Anya without all that life had marked her with. I tried lying to myself, saying she wasn't beautiful. I hated myself for it.

The driver was a good-looking all-American boy. Fuck, he even had a letterman jacket. Nika had a cheer dress on. It was like they stepped out of the fifties. They fit the home. They fit her new life.

If my raping her had left a trace it was invisible at this distance. She kissed the boy and bounced out. She took one look at me and flew across the lawn and into my arms. "Moses. When? Gregor didn't tell me." She was hugging me. Kissing my cheek. The boy was out, giving me the nearest he could come to a hard stare. Nika looked at him and laughed. "Steve, come over here and meet my Uncle Moses."

Uncle Moses? Sounded good. I could have bought it, if I didn't know what it had cost us both to be standing on the lawn. The boy reached out his hand. I didn't take it. I eased Nika back. Looked at her. "You look good, kid."

"You don't. Ha, one day you will have to stop your wild ways." Her Russian accent was fading fast. "Even Gregor is settling down. Your turn next?"

"Not in the cards."

"Change the cards. You taught me that."

If only it was that easy. I couldn't stand there any longer pretending we hadn't been where we had. Hadn't hurt the way we had. The gun had been on us. I had no choice in that whorehouse.

If only I believed that.

Gregor handed me the keys. Nika was in the rearview, watching me drive away. The me she saw was a fantasy, a dream that let her sleep at night.

Lucky her.

CHAPTER 16

You are an asshole.

"And you are a dead, one-titted killer." I was driving across LA. I felt like a giant in the driver's seat of the 5.0. My head hit the roof and I had to recline the seat and push it all the way back to fit.

You want to fuck that child.

"Bullshit."

Then why are you jealous of the boy.

"I'm not, wrong again. Just don't trust him. Has that 'I'm a nice guy, wouldn't hurt a fly' look. Seen plenty of those jocks trying to pay for a gang bang at the strip joint."

Moses.

"Yeah?"

Either go back and kill him, or admit you are an asshole with a thing for a teenager.

"Fuck off." I cranked the stereo and the car filled with a kid's song. Something about a baby whale. It drove Mikayla away. After she was gone, I let it play.

Baby beluga in the deep blue sea, swim so wild and you swim so free.

It was oddly calming.

I felt naked without a piece. I knew it was safer for an ex-con to roll clean, but fuck, at least one set of squids wanted to blow my shit up. And two pimps would love to see me splattered. And that didn't include Rollens, if she was still above ground, and whatever deal she did or didn't strike with Sanchez. To quote Eazy-E, "Fuck tha police." Next chance I got, I was packing heavy.

Light fog dropped down, blanketing Silver Lake. A pillow of white surrounded Helen's hillside home, a Frank Lloyd Wright modern cliff hanger. Helen met me at the door. Her Rottweiler pushed past her, stopped, and then cocked his head when he didn't find Angel at my side. Helen arched an eyebrow. I shook my head.

"Oh damn, Mo, I'm so sorry."

"Me too. Someone's gonna pay a mighty price."

"Won't bring her back."

"No, but it will show that her life mattered, wasn't cheap." Her face told me she had no idea what I was talking about.

"This must be the heroic Moses." The woman had short-cropped silver hair and a Scots accent.

"Jules, play nice."

"What?"

"Lady, I'm big, broken and usually impaired. But my needle for sarcasm and dislike is so finely tuned, I hear it when it isn't even said." Kept my face neutral. Scary.

Jules matched my stare for a good sixty seconds then busted up laughing. Made me smile. "I like him."

"I knew you would." Helen forced a cup of coffee and a grilled cheese sandwich on me, slightly burnt, just the way I liked them. I was hungry. Jules hung while we ate then faded to the bedroom when I said I needed solo time with Helen.

"I like her. You did good. Don't fuck it up."

"I will, but I'll enjoy it until I do. Now, business. What do you need?"

"To find Peter, the reporter."

"Screenwriter, now. Big shot stopped taking my calls months ago."

"You got a number?" She tapped her phone and after a moment looked back.

"Been canceled."

"Got an address?"

"Umm, email...Twitter...Facebook...here we go." She wrote out an address in the Hollywood Hills. At the door, I kissed her good-bye, promised to stay in better contact.

"Mo, you should get another pup."

"Yeah, I'll think about it." Angel asked so little of me, and I got her killed. Fuck the bastards who had done it. Fuck me for taking her on this run north.

"No, you won't."

"No, I won't."

"Mo, you can give yourself permission to hang up your guns and live a life. You are a good man. You deserve it. You do. Those Russian girls you rescued? All in high school. None being forced to have sex. You did that. You. Maybe it's time you saved yourself?"

"Tried that in Mexico, shit came looking for me."

"Try harder next time."

"I got to go, Helen."

"I know, a world to save."

"Just one tiny corner of it."

It was dusk when I drove up Beachwood Canyon. The neighborhood was posh, new Hollywood money living in Old World chateaus and faux Tudors. Peter's address was small by the neighborhood standard, maybe only five bedrooms. All the lights were out. Peter had tagged along when I went to war with the Russians in Mexico. It got wet down there, but he held his shit together. The story he wrote from our exploits won him a bunch of awards. Movie deals. He broke a promise and leaked my name. I couldn't complain too bad, he got me the knot of cash that bought me my house down South.

The front path wound past a curving, leaf-covered koi pond. It didn't look like the gardeners had been by in some time. On the front door was a fading eviction notice. I knocked and waited. Heard nothing. Walked around back, where hills dropped to a cliff five feet from the back door. LA stretched out beyond, a carpet of dreams and murder and love and laundry and grocery shopping and panaderías, where puppies once played with little girls and memories and all that other shit that made life.

The sliding door was unlocked so I let myself in. The house was gutted. Anything of any value had been sold. Wire stripped from the walls; at three bucks a pound, copper was worth scrapping. Moving through the house, more of the same. In the kitchen the cupboards were bare. The stove and fridge were gone. I followed the chemical smell of meth and rank sweat to the master suite. In the center of the empty room, Peter sat on a beanbag chair. A skinny waif of a woman was sleeping at his feet. He looked up, sunken face, ashen skin. He didn't seem surprised to see me.

"Moses."

"Yeah, Peter."

"They send you to kill me?"

"Who?"

"Who? Government? Black Ops? Who? Yeah, who?" Sweat was beading liberally on his forehead and upper lip.

"Peter, any chance you can focus?"

"Oh yeah, I'm here big time. I'd offer you a seat but, um... So what you need? Spy shit, killing mobsters, saving girls?"

"Peter." I leaned into his face. His eyes were pinned. "I need some information."

"Ok, wait here. Wait here. Wait here." I sat down with my back against the wall. He disappeared. I heard a shower running. Gave me time to think; never a good thing. Maybe I had chosen the wrong moment to get sober. Seeing Nika had been rough. Was Mikayla right? At some deep level did I want to fuck a child? Did all men? Was I just self-righteous enough to keep that desire buried? And who the fuck was I to think I could do shit to save Freedom? Where the fuck was Rollens?

Peter finally came back. The woman on the floor hadn't moved. He looked two small notches closer to sane. "What, yeah, what do you need Moses?"

"What happened to the forty Gs I told you to give to Jason for the truck?"

"I invested that. Good deal. Points, lots of tits and ass, a real moneymaker."

"Shut up." He stopped talking, but his jaw kept moving. "I need to know who is moving military-grade weapons to gangbangers."

"Fuck yes. Like a Shane Black action flick. Mel Gibson minus the anti-Semitic rants. Updated Taylor Lautner, it is Big Moses. Fast and the—"

I hit the back of his head, trying to get his attention, but wound up knocking him off his feet.

"What the fuck? Ouch. Fucking ouch." He was sprawled on the carpet.

I helped him up. Holding his face toward mine I forced him to focus. "Hypothetically. I'm a gangbanger and I want a rocket launcher. Who do I see?"

"Hell, Mo, grenades, shit like that, are flooding back from the monumental sand trap. Give a banger keys to the locker, some shit's making it home. Who cares? The money is made in resupply, so who gives a fuck where it goes, right? Right?"

"This was high-grade tech. Fired from inside a SUV with almost no backwash."

"Swedish. Crap, yeah. They track shit that can take down planes and crap."

"Who would know how or who's got it?"

"Sunshine."

"Sunshine? What the fuck, Peter? Sunshine?"

"Sunshine. Fuck, follow me." He leads me through the empty kitchen into the garage. It's wall-to-wall file cabinets. In the middle is a computer on a card table. "Yeah, this is, ok..." He bangs away on the keys, and for a moment he looks almost human. Driven, but human. "Here. Oh, you are going to love this woman." He read rapid-fire off the screen. "Rumored to have been a hit man, um woman, um assassin in the seventies, up until late eighties. Resurfaces in ninety-five and is investigated as part of an arms smuggling ring, bust doesn't stick. Two thousand she is investigated for trafficking arms in and out of Africa. Two thousand five she shows up in a congressional investigation into arms-for-hostages. Remember the Reagan deal? Ollie North and that bullshit? She was at least a person of interest, but probably a hell of a lot more. If anyone knows how bangers got hold of ordinance, it would be her." He sat back, spent.

"I need to find her."

"Sure you do. Hell yes, this is what I do." He rallied and typed away. Sat back. Waited. "Mo, you ain't holding are you?"

"No."

"Shit. Yeah, of course not. Right. I know I left a taste upstairs." He started to stand but I gently pushed him back down.

"Your dealer deliver?"

"Used to. Cut me off. If I had cash, different story."

I lay three, hundred-dollar bills on the keyboard. Peter let out a gasp, like a dying man in the desert seeing water, and typed furiously.

"You can score online now?"

"IM, Gmail, ping off the Netherlands...untraceable. Cell phones? Screw 'em. Give me a keyboard and I'm in." He kept rambling but I tuned out. I wondered if I should see if he could score me some Vicodin. Just enough to ease the spooky, empty feeling, enough to get me back to normal. I sat on the floor, leaned back against the cool steel of a filing cabinet, closed my eyes.

I can still feel the gun barrel against my neck. I can remember Nika, how dry it felt entering her. I can see the pain in her eyes. Her eyes. Wide. Resigned. I killed that Russian; hasn't stopped her eyes from haunting me.

"They're making our film."

"What?"

"Duane 'The Rock' Johnson is going to play you. Justin Timberlake is playing me. They got this Hong Kong babe to play Mikayla. Oh yeah, it's set in the Philippines. Russian investors like that better so, bam, location change. We get eighty large—each—if they make it to first day of production. WGA." He pauses to catch his breath. Something beeps and he types furiously. "Bastard tells me to bring the cash to him. Fuck he thinks he is? Mo, got to make a quick run."

I snatch the cash off the desk. "You got to earn it."

"No, I will. See, it takes time. Contacts have to get back, you know?" He couldn't hold my gaze.

"They won't be getting back to you, will they? You burned your contacts. Useless fuck."

"It's not like that. It, well...time, Moses, give me time."

"This Sunshine, she work West Coast?"

"Yes, home base was LA I think."

"Mob work when she was a hitter?"

He pounded the keyboard. "Bingo, but that was a long ass time ago. More time and I'll have an address and a drive-on pass to where she is."

"I'm all out of time. Porsche in your driveway, it run?"

"It better, thing's only four months old. Got it to celebrate the film going. Cash, should have seen the salesman's face. Bam, stack of bills. Credit crunch this."

"Give me the pink."

"The Porsche? No...no."

"Give." He gave. Bitched a lot, but he gave. I left him the cash. I stuffed the pink slip in an envelope and addressed it to Jay's Auto Shop. I put Peter's address as a return, and for the name I put "M" and a drawing of a square.

It was time to talk to The Pope, Don Gallico. He was the head of the LA mob. They were a weak family but they still had juice, or I hoped they did. I had run errands, done some collections for him when I was a kid. Me and the other junior mobsters always called him The Pope, and his lieutenants we called the cardinals. Never to their faces. If anyone knew where to find an arms dealer in LA, it was The Pope.

He operated out of Figueroa's, a small Italian restaurant and bakery in the Los Feliz area. When I entered, I was met by a gray-haired thug. "Mo, how's it hanging?"

"Low. Mr. Gallico around."

"Where else would he be?"

"A crypt?"

He didn't smile, even a little bit. "Heard you was in Mexico."

"Came back."

"Why's that?"

99

"Missed you. Can I go back?" He had me raise my hands, did a pat down. Found nothing. Hell, I didn't even have a lock-blade. Would have to change that sooner than later.

Don Gallico sat at his usual table, drinking a tall glass of milk. He had tubes running out of his nose to an oxygen tank. A nurse in a starched white uniform sat beside him reading a paperback.

"Shelly, this is Moses McGuire. A famous man-killer." He quacked through a buzzing cylinder he pressed to what was left of his vocal cords. The nurse nodded but didn't look up from her book. "Moses, who have you come to ask my permission to kill today?" In years past he spoke in code, always afraid of a wire. Time had made him either bold or stupid.

"I'm looking for someone."

"Of course you are. Anthony," he called to the kitchen, "get Moses a bowl of soup." You never refuse a meal with Don Gallico. The room was largely empty. It was a relic of better times. The Pope looked around the room; two old men sat drinking coffee. "Not like back in the day, right, Moses? I ran this town. Tell Shelly, tell her I ran this whole town."

"He did, he no shit ran Los Angeles." She looked up, smiled at me, then went back to reading.

"Those was the days. When I made my bones? We had Frank the Voice. Fuck pads all over town. We had class in those days. Never sold drugs, left that to the niggers. I miss those times, know what I mean, Mo?"

"Good old guinea days? No drugs, but you never shied away from prostitution, right?"

"Class kid. Girls, loans, numbers, none of that drug-drive-by-backward-baseball crap."

"No, you just sold young girl's innocence for five bucks a shot in back rooms and alleyways. Pure class, you old guinea prick."

He looked like his head was going to explode. He sputtered, trying to form words. From the door, Bobby the aged thug started to move on me. I wrapped my hand around a fork. Focused on the Pope's throat. Bobby left his hand resting on the automatic in his belt, but stopped moving.

The Pope looked from Bobby to me to the nurse and smiled. "Don't grow old, kid."

"I'm doing my best not to."

He let out a rattling laugh. "Yes, you are." The laugh turned into a coughing fit. The nurse handed him a tissue. Blood flecked his phlegm. He finally looked up. His eyes went hard. I knew he hated me seeing him like this. His pride made him dangerous. I'd hate to get shot so he could prove he still had his balls intact. A gray-haired waiter broke the tension when he set a bowl before me. Vegetables in chicken broth. It was good, fresh, healthy tasting.

"Mangia, che ti passa. Doctor has me off the sausages, cheese, butter. Life, huh?"

"Life."

"They say you took out those Russians, cleaned house, no one here or in Mexico was left standing. They say you even took out an Israeli defense team."

"They say a lot of things."

"You should have stayed with me, kid. We could have owned this town."

"From where I was sitting, it looked like you did." He smiled at that one. He was strolling down a bloody memory lane.

"True. Our friend from Chicago convinced the families to leave you alone. As long as you weren't killing Italians, who cared?"

"How is he?" Leo was a mob fixer. He saved my life and I, in turn, had kept him out of jail.

"Leo, is Leo. Impeccable. They gave him LA." The old man looked off into the near distance, starting to lose focus.

"Mr. Gallico, I'm looking for a girl. She was kidnapped. I think you can help me."

He didn't look up.

"I'm looking for a gun dealer named Sunshine."

"That moolie bitch been a thorn in my side since she was a kid." His face flushed. "In the seventies, she took a couple of very good earners off the board. Not that I didn't use her as a hitter when I needed it clean. You wanted someone killed in nigger town, or anywhere else, she was your man."

"I need to find her."

"Why would you want that? She's washed out."

"She's the only lead I have. Unless you know who's been giving bangers rocket launchers."

"Rocket launchers? It is the Wild West out there. Crews coming up from El Salvador are going to make people wish Italians still ran things." He was talking more to himself than to me.

"Mr. Gallico, I need to find Sunshine."

"Yes, you do." He scrawled an address and passed it to me. He looked confused. "Anthony, get Moses a bowl of soup." If the waiter was confused by this, he didn't show it. He replaced my almost full bowl with a fresh one. I ate it.

I pulled the 5.0 into traffic and headed for Compton. The old man gave me an address, beyond that I was on my own. An older Chevy Malibu was following me from two or three cars back. I wasn't sure how long they had been on me. Not good. To stop noticing who was behind you was a quick way to end up dead.

CHAPTER 17

I was doing over a hundred when I exited the 101 at Stadium Way, up on two wheels and sliding. The Malibu followed me. Their tires were smoking hard, but keeping stuck on me. The signs pointed toward Dodger Stadium. I kept the gas pedal nailed down. Rounding a sweeper, I saw what I was hunting for. LAPD Police Academy. I hammered the brakes and went from sixty to thirty fast. The Malibu almost rear-ended me. The driver was an olive-skinned veterano, do-rag. I could almost read the tattoo on his neck. His passenger was a teenage Latino banger.

I slid into the police academy's visitors' parking lot. They didn't follow me, so I guessed they weren't undercover cops. Titan had a whole stack of reasons to want me in a casket. If these cats had been black, I'd have known why they wanted me dead. Hell, Russians, Italians, Armenians, they all wanted me dead. But other than the Ensenada crew, I couldn't think of any Latino who wanted me dead. Maybe Xlmen had familia in Los Angeles.

Raffi was singing "Shake My Sillies Out" under the low rumble of the Mustang's custom pipes. I waited for the verse to end then barreled ass out of there. By the time I hit the 101 I was relatively sure I'd shaken the Malibu. Rain started coming down, turning the windshield into a colorful smear dotted with ruby flashes of brake lights. The 5.0 had good rubber and clean wipers. Gregor bought it for Nika, he was teaching her to drive, so I knew it was safe.

Raffi was killing me with his jolly tunes so I switched to the radio and was confronted by thumping hip hop. I turned it off and listened to the rhythm of the wipers. The address The Pope gave me for Sunshine was in Culver City, at the base of Baldwin Hills.

The building was a scarred warehouse in an industrial neighborhood in that no man's land stuck between Compton's poverty and West LA billionaires. It was after seven, streetlights painted the slick asphalt. The factory buildings lining the road were all closed for the night. The only parked cars looked like they hadn't moved in a long time. I circled the warehouse twice to be sure there weren't any surprises.

All was quiet.

I parked and moved up to the front door. The windows were blacked out. I raised my hand to knock.

The door snapped open and a young man stabbed a revolver barrel into my cheek. "Wrong fucking door, old man."

"Pull the trigger." I was relaxed. "Or don't." He clicked the hammer back. "Son, you've been watching too many movies. If you want to kill a man, cock it before opening the door."

"Fuck you, bitch." He was sweating, but he wasn't squeezing the trigger.

"Son?"

"I ain't your son."

"Nope. It's time to decide. Drop me, or step aside."

"Kenny," a woman called from the shadows.

"I got this handled, Miss S."

She rolled her wheelchair into the light. She had a beautiful face, flawless coffee and cream skin. I knew she was in her fifties, but only her eyes showed her age. They were cold. No, more than cold, they were world-weary. I knew that look; it stared back at me in the mirror every morning. A quilt covered her shoulders and lap. Her right hand was under the quilt, holding a piece no doubt.

"Kenny, put the gun away before Mr. McGuire rips your hand off." Kenny eased up, then let his hand fall to his side, still ready to pull it up. "Now step out of the way. Mr. McGuire, please come in out of the rain."

Kenny finally cleared the doorway. I rubbed my cheek where the barrel had been. I shook the water off my leather. "Sunshine?"

"Join me for a drink?" She turned the chair around, expecting me to follow. I did.

"Mr. Gallico's people call you?"

"Who?" She seemed surprised to hear The Pope's name. Kenny slid back a thick steel door and we entered a warm, windowless office. It was a combination of rich leather couches, club chairs, an antique coffee table, a bookcase filled with leather bound books and high-tech computer workstations. Video monitors showed the neighborhood surrounding us.

"Macallan, right?" She stopped in front of an oak bar.

"Neat."

"Is there any other way?"

"Not in my opinion. I saw kid showing off order it with Coke."

"Did you shoot him?"

"Nope. Should have."

"Yes, you should have." She poured a good three fingers into a crystal tumbler. Kenny settled at one of the computers. The revolver was on the desk beside his hand.

"Why are you here, Mr. McGuire?"

"How do you know me? I know we never met, some things a man doesn't forget."

She smiled very slightly. "You don't flatter, do you?"

"No, I don't." She was the kind of stunner you could have seen crossing a street just once and never forget. "How?"

"Yeah, baby, how do I know you? Right? You are one of my heroes. Aren't too many big old Vikings running around this hood after dark."

I took a healthy slug of whiskey. Tried not to look half as confused as I felt.

"What you did to those flesh traffickers in Ensenada was pure gold. We could have made quite a team back in the day."

"Except I was in the joint and you were working for the mob."

"Gallico, he gave you my address? Man either trusts you or you had a gun on his junk."

I took another swallow. She was enjoying holding all the cards. "Let's say he trusts me. Or that it doesn't matter one way or the other. Someone fired an RPG at me, from inside a car. The blowback didn't rip out the door behind him." That got Sunshine's attention, not that she showed it much. "They also used a tracer round, but it was the RPG that got my attention."

"How the fuck did you survive?" Kenny had been listening in.

"It's rude to eavesdrop, son." Even from across the room I saw him tense at being called son again. Back to Sunshine I said, "Luck, I guess." I thought about Angel, dead. Luck? It was anything but that.

"Luck? More likely operator error. Surprising. An AT4-CS, close quarters urban RPG. Limited backblast." There was a spark in her eyes as she talked about it. "Sexy motherfucker. Simple, any grunt can use it. Point, shoot and throw away. You must have been a very bad man to have someone willing to spread the green to kill you. Who have you been pissing on?"

"That's what I'm here to find out. Who would have the juice to get one of these?"

"You want me to tell you if I sold any. That's the reason you're here, right?"

"That's about it."

"You are a fine-looking man. I still had working legs, I might wrap them around you and see if we could break some furniture. But I don't. So just what the fuck is in it for me?" Hearing the edge in her voice, Kenny moved his hand onto the revolver. He was watching my refection in the monitor in front of him.

"Lady, I got nothing. I'm miles in over my head and dropping fast. Anyone who helps me is guaranteed to be paid back with trouble. I'm also a thirteen-year-old girl's only hope. She was grabbed in Crenshaw. I think she's being pimped out."

"Why her? Why this little girl? Toss a rock and you'll hit some baby being forced to suck a dick she don't want to. Why this one?"

"Freedom. That's her name, Freedom. I know her name. I promised I'd get her home. No more complicated than that. Gave my word." I shrugged and stared into my empty tumbler. Sunshine closed her eyes and looked like she was running some tough calculation. She opened her eyes and looked at me from my boots to my face.

"Right answer, McGuire." She tossed me a smile. It was genuine, something stirred. I looked at her full lips, plump and sexy, better looking for her lack of lipstick, dry with soft cracks that made me want to kiss them.

"McGuire?"

"Yes?"

"We are not going to be hitting skins any time soon." She looked down at her immobile lap for proof. I wanted to say that wasn't what I was thinking. I wanted to say I left my sex drive in a shitty hacienda above Ensenada. I wanted to tell her I was as numb as her legs. I wanted all that to be true.

I drank another whiskey while she went to work, sliding between three computers. Over her shoulder she asked me to repeat everything that had happened since leaving Mexico. She called up a photo of me, a mug shot. She showed me a picture taken with a red light camera two blocks from her warehouse. She told me she had face recognition software, beta, but three generations beyond Homeland Security. "Kenny's broken into more databases than I can remember. NSA, Homeland, FBI— name it, he's up in it."

Kenny looked over at me, almost smiling. I raised my glass to him.

"Fuck you, old man. Jury's way the fuck out on you."

"Always is." I shot him a playful wink. He frowned and went back to typing.

"He was being followed, but they backed off once he hit the blocks," Kenny said, not taking his eyes of a display.

"They either knew there is only one way in and out," Sunshine was mulling, speaking to herself mostly, "or they are players and know we have eyes on the blocks. You forgot to tell me?"

"Figured it was his motherfucking problem, long as they didn't roll on our street. Fuck 'em."

"Was it a Chevy Malibu, maybe mid 70s?" I asked.

"Sounds right." If Kenny knew more, he wasn't sharing.

I was three more whiskeys to the good when Sunshine spun her chair around and rolled over to me. "Ok, big man, here's how it looks. Bitch is, this is at best an educated guess, nothing solid. We straight on that?"

"Straight. I shouldn't take heads based on this intel."

"Exactly. You know Mara Salvatrucha? MS-13?"

"I hear it's best to stay clear of those crazies. Hear that machetes are their weapon of choice."

"Whatever you heard, times ten, no shit. When we came up, we had Crips and Bloods to deal with. Good old days. Really. Mara Salvatrucha, El Salvadorian immigrants, got tired of being kicked around. If they wanted to survive they needed to make up for body count with brutality. These cats put Crip heads on spikes in their mommas' front yards. They burned their enemies alive. Old school Inquisition shit."

She took a long drink of Pellegrino then launched back in. "Jump thirty years down the road, they make the Mafia look like kindergartners. They control more territory in SoCal than any other gang. They are in forty-seven states, Canada and Central America. Suddenly the Feds are all over stopping them. Problem is, they work like Al Qaeda cells. These motherfuckers have no real overriding power structure. They have Councils, but it doesn't connect to a head. History lesson over."

Another deep drink of mineral water. "Now," she said, "the Middle East wars have been like opening an arms superstore for these evil bastards. If I was still a player, I would never sell to MS-13. They want it all and they may make it. Drugs, protection and prostitution. But they don't need me. The military is grinding up poor boys. Rich ain't going, powerful ain't going, educated ain't going. That leaves ghetto princes. Motherfuckers with nothing to lose and everything to gain by grabbing what they can."

My eyes were glassing. "Too much information, no closer to who is trying to kill me."

"Why? That's the key. Why leads to who."

"Buddhist monk? This a koan I'm supposed to spend years thinking about?"

"Sorry, this is what I do now. I sell possible futures and motivational branching lines. Sexy, right? I started as a stripper, and this is where that line led."

Truth? She was sexy as hell. On fire, passionate, when she spoke.

"Done." Kenny dropped a freshly printed map of LA. It had big stars with notes like *Took pimp's ear here* and *Crippled soldier here.* He had overlaid it with known MS-13 turf. Sunshine looked over the map, gave Kenny a nod and small smile. He bounced back to his computer as if she'd given him a medal.

"So, big man, this is the best intel we got. Now, what is your plan? Hit me with it."

"I'll go after the pimps I saw before and find out if any of them draw heat. If they do, I will kill every motherfucker who comes after me until I get to Freedom."

"Hmmm." She looked me over once more. "What a shame. Fine men are rare. You are going to stake yourself out like a goat, and you are going to be the hunter?"

"I'll have back up."

"It won't be enough."

"You're sure?"

"Doesn't matter who you bring, it won't be enough."

She slipped the map into a military case. We left Kenny pounding keys. He didn't look up as we closed the middle door. At the front door, Sunshine slipped me a number.

"Dead drop. Leave a message if you need...want. Hell."

"Goodnight, Sunshine."

"Goodnight, Mr. McGuire." She leaned forward.

"Moses." I leaned in. I was planning to kiss her cheek. She turned. Our lips met. Neither pulled back. Her lips were as soft and full as I had imagined. We pressed semi-closed lips together. Slowly, she reached her arms up around my neck, pulling me closer. She opened her lips. Her small tongue darted against mine. My hands looked like giant mitts on either side of her face. I was lost in the kiss. Nothing else was out there. For a brief moment, the constant pain went away. After almost forever, she pulled away. Her eyes looked soft, slightly unfocused. From under the quilt she handed me a snub-nosed Ruger .454 Casull.

"Survive, Moses."

"I'll do my best."

CHAPTER 18

The rain settled in for the long haul, smearing my windshield and dimming the streetlights to useless. I rolled slow around two corners, one more and I'd be out of the box and onto the main street. I moved to the curb and turned the Mustang off. It was registered to Gregor, so I had to be careful not to bring my shit back to his house. His loyalty had cost him an arm. I wanted to keep it at that. My normal M.O. would be to lead a tail into an industrial neighborhood in Northeast LA. Places where I knew all the streets, blind alleys and best places to dump a body if it went that way.

I pulled on a balaclava, for warmth and the CCTV that now blankets Los Angeles. Decades of gangland killings nobody gave a shit, but post 9/11 the surveillance cameras started going up. Fuck brown on brown violence, a terrorist could kill some pale citizens, so action needed to be taken. We weren't up to UK standards yet, but it was coming.

Hoody up. Popping my collar, I pushed against the wall. A hundred feet away I could see the cul-de-sac exit. Ten feet ahead of me sat the Chevy Malibu. Fog pumped from the dual exhaust. I dropped to the deck, cold water soaking my clothes. Crawling in the gutter, I moved along the Chevy. The driver's window was cracked open, letting the sweet smell of mota drift out. They were listening to Cafe Tacuba's "Desperté." Mellow music to kill by. Adolpho's son turned me on to them. Good stuff. No Clash, but it had heart.

The Ruger was in my hand when I stood in front of the Chevy. I pressed it onto the hood and pulled the trigger. The .454 Casull roared, bellowing flame. I fought to keep the revolver from flipping into the night. It punched a hole the size of a quarter into the hood, scorching the paint around it. Gears screeched and screamed as the engine tore itself apart. I fired a second round into the windshield. The concussion sent a million chunks of glass spilling back. It tore a three-inch hole through the seat before ripping out through the trunk. The safety glass bloodied up the bangers pretty good, but they showed good form, not a wail or a moan.

"Whatever gun you hoped to go for, don't."

"I'm going to lose my eye." Blood was running down the veterano's left cheek.

"Looks like it, but ya never know."

"You going to kill us?" The kid's voice was trembling.

"Yes, if I don't hear what I need to. Who do you work for?"

The veterano wiped blood on to a handkerchief. "You don't hire guys like us if you expect them to talk." His voice was soft, pure ghetto badass. He wasn't fronting, just stating facts.

"Everybody talks," I said. "Sooner or later. How about you, kid. Wanna play see how many parts we can remove before you open up?" The kid looked at me, then at the veterano. His lips went firm.

I dragged the veterano to the rear of the car, pat-searched him, zip-tied his wrists and tossed him into the trunk, locked it and tossed the keys into the rain.

I dragged the kid out, laid him spread-eagle, belly down on the hood of the Chevy. I ripped his pants down around his ankles. Partly to freak him, partly to fuck him up if he tried to run. "Move and I'll kill you."

I sat in the Chevy. With the windshield gone, it was only slightly dryer than the street. I searched the glove box, found the registration. It was good, well printed but a fake. Taped under the dash was the real Mexican registration. I slit the headliner. Three bundles of US cash, Mexican documents, even two driver's licenses tumbled down. I matched the first driver's license with the kid on the hood. Roberto Orizaga was starting to panic. Couldn't see if he was sweating in the rain, but he was starting tremble. Opening a manila envelope, I found a picture of me and Rollens taken on the beach in Ensenada. Fuck. I near ripped the car door off getting out. I swung my fist, connecting with Orizaga's tighty-whities and the junk inside them. He started to puke. I grabbed his hair, pulled him up, then slammed his face into the Malibu's hood. Blood from his flattened nose mixed with his vomit. I was ready to slam him down again when a gun barrel pressed into my back.

"Release him."

"I have to stop putting people in trunks. Always works in the movies."

"Don't feel bad, we all see the same movies. Put releases in. Now let him go."

I did. Orizaga grabbed the Ruger from my belt, aimed it at me. He stepped back, got his feet tangled in his pants and almost took my face off when he fell. The muzzle blast singed the hair above my ear.

Gálvez, the veterano, looked no worse for his time in the trunk. "On your knees. Laced fingers." It sounded garbled and thick after the blast.

I did as told. Gravel dug into my knees. He waited until his young partner was standing up, pants secured and the Ruger aimed at my chest. Gálvez ripped the balaclava off my head. He snapped a picture with his phone, then rested the barrel of his gun against the back of my skull while he punched numbers into it. He spoke in fast hushed Spanish, but I was sure I heard Señor Sanchez mentioned. No good ever came from that man's name.

Then we waited. Gálvez kept the phone to his ear and his piece resting on my neck. "McGuire? Catholic?"

"Atheist."

"Maybe agnostic?"

"I'm fairly sure the son of a bitch don't exist."

"Fairly sure? Agnostic."

"This leading somewhere?"

"I'm just killing time, Irish. Waiting for the big jefe. He either say kill you, kill you slow, or maybe just fuck you up and leave you broken."

"Any chance take me out for a quick dinner and let me go?"

"No, pretty sure that's not an option. Me, I believe our heavenly father lets nothing happen that is not in his plan."

"You think it's in his plan for me to drop tonight?"

"Yes, I do."

This was it then. The moment. The one that most fear. Fuck it. If it was time to kiss this mess goodbye, so the fuck be it. "Do me a favor, don't let this pussy do it. Way his hand is shaking he'll blow out my kidney and leave me to bleed out." Orizaga's face tightened. "You see the way he went all bitch when I nutted him? Bitch in Español? Puta?" The kid took aim at my head. He was ready to prove himself regardless of his boss's orders. "Dude, your boy is about to go way off the script."

Orizaga's finger was trembling on the trigger. The bullet took him at the base of his skull, clicked out his lights before he even heard the shot.

Gálvez turned to look for the shooter. The subsonic round entered below his left cheek, exiting low in the back of his skull. I was sure he never felt it. If he was right, he was at the pearly gates before he even knew what hit him. If I was right, he simply stopped breathing.

The rain had turned to mist, proving nothing in LA is constant. Nothing but pain and death, which both seemed pretty damn constant. I looked to the buildings that made up the cul-de-sac. Half a mile across the rooftops, a hydraulic crow's nest stood on the roof of Sunshine's warehouse. It was dropping from sight fast. I couldn't see the shooter, but I'd bet big time she had soft, full lips.

I picked Gálvez's cell up from the gutter. It was silent. Whoever he had been talking to was long clicked off. Headlights swept across me and I grabbed for the gun Gálvez had dropped. The lights swung clear and I saw a tow truck, Sal's Service Station written on its rusted side along with a phone number I was sure was a dead-end. Kenny was behind the wheel. He backed up to the Chevy and started hooking it up.

He said nothing to me.

I said nothing to him.

I collected the Mexicans' papers, both fake and legit, and their firearms. Kenny was winching the front of the car when I dropped the bodies into the trunk.

"Any chance you can find out who he was talking to?" I handed him Gálvez's cell.

"Everything leaves a trail, everything. But this here will lead to a burner and a dead-end." He dropped the phone back into my hand. "From here on, stay clear of Sunshine."

"That an order?"

"No, a request. She's had it tough. Pays heavily for every trigger pull."

"Yes...thank you."

"Don't. McGuire, everything I do from here on is to keep you off her front porch." He turned away and drove the rig into the cul-de-sac. I was sure by dawn the only thing left of the Mexicans would be a whiff of acid.

Across the LA basin the clouds were gone, leaving stars and long vistas. Kenny was right. If I gave a damn about Sunshine, or any woman, best I could do was put fifty miles of hard road between her and me.

CHAPTER 19

Lil' Diamond sat in the back of the convertible, German luxury car. Frankie had told her the brand but it didn't stick. She was blazing on a Xanax and a joint. Zero was driving. Amethyst sat on one side of Lil' Diamond, Frankie on her other side. He was an old man, forty at least. She'd fucked men plenty older and uglier. He wore a sharp suit and a Sam Jackson Kangol, backward. His smile made her feel warm.

"Amethyst tells me you doing real good. Says you're a fast learner. Here, I got this for you." Frankie nodded at Amethyst, who then gave a small box to Lil' Diamond.

"You didn't need do that."

"Just the beginning, Lil' Diamond. Down payment on the good life you will be living. You do what you told, you be swimming in chinchilla."

When the child opened the box, she found a small square-cut golden "LD." Filled with diamond chips, it sparkled wildly. "It's for Lil' Diamond, our baby princess." Frankie hung the pendant on a gold rope chain. After he closed the clasp he let his hand rest on her cheek. "I know you had it rough. Zero and the boys is a tough bunch a street dogs. But that's over. Any one hurts you again, you tell me and I will fire them up. Got it, Princess?" He gave her a chaste kiss on the cheek.

"Thank you, sir."

"Not sir. Daddy or Frankie, never sir." Behind the wheel, Zero tried to keep his face flat. If he or any of the men didn't call Frankie "Sir" they got ass whupped.

Lil' Diamond watched her pendant reflecting in the side window. She had never owned any jewelry, let alone diamonds and gold. She still might kill Zero and his crew, but not Frankie. "Thank you, Daddy."

"See, I told you she was a good one."

Frankie beamed at Amethyst. "You brung her up right."

Zero took a left, fast. This bullshit was almost over.

"Slow down, bitch." Frankie slapped the back of Zero's head.

"Sorry, sir. It's just...well...fuck you hard in the ass, old man." The car bounced into an auto painting shop. In a blink, the door slid closed behind them. Two young Latino men aimed cut-down 12 gauges at Frankie and the girls. Mostly at Frankie, not that it would make a difference. They pulled and the spread would kill all three in the backseat.

"Who the fuck?" Frankie looking like he might explode.

"Zacarías." He was early twenties. Scars and tattoos covered his face, MS-13 on his cheeks, looked like a skeleton. "Yeah, you know me."

"Ain't we a few miles outside your set?" Frankie was holding it together.

"You know shit. My boy reached out, you refused."

"Nothing personal, brother. I stay wide clear of the gang and stay in the game."

"Zero," Zacarías nodded at him, "you done good. We keeping these two girls?"

"Ask 'em. I bet yes though."

Zacarías took out a nine-inch knife, pointed it at each girl. Frankie started to slip his hand into his jacket. "You go for that gun and you will die slow. Two days. No good."

Frankie let his hand go limp. "What do we do from here?"

"Do you know what Zacarías means? He who God remembers. You think God remembers you?"

The knife moved too fast to see. It dipped into Frankie's neck above the collarbone, almost no blood. Frankie slumped over.

Freedom slowed it down in her head: Zacarías had pierced the left lung, then hit the heart. Frankie bled out inside his chest cavity. She remembered a dream. Remembered medical high school. Looking at Frankie's slumped over corpse, she cared, but not a lot.

The man with the scary tattoos and knife skills smiled at her. He ran his thumb over the dead pimp's wound, coating it in blood. He then placed a cross in blood on Freedom's forehead. "Madre a mantenerse a salvo."

CHAPTER 20

"I bought this for you. Well, Gregor did. His money, my idea." Nika held out an iPod, flat black, cool and clean.

It had taken me two hours to drive across town. I looped around, being damn sure I wasn't followed. I'd brought enough pain to this family, didn't need any more waking me at night.

I'd called Detective Lowrie, left a message. We were sitting in Gregor's garage, waiting. He had converted it into an office of sorts. He had a desk, a computer, filing cabinets. Tools hung from pegboard above a workbench. A gun safe took up much of one corner. In the center of the room were the white patio table and plastic chairs we were sitting in.

Gregor motioned with his chin at the iPod. "I told her you would never learn to use it."

Nika leaned over my shoulder. "It's easy. Push this button to open iTunes." I could feel her warmth against my skin. I fumbled with the small device. My fingers felt huge and clumsy. "No, Moses, push on the music icon, see?" She touched my hand, moving it over the screen.

"Where's your boyfriend?"

"He's not my boyfriend."

"No?"

"No." She looked into my eyes, playfully batting her lashes.

"Seemed like a nice guy."

"He is, but...I don't know." On the iPod, a play list appeared. "I loaded in a bunch of bands Gregor said you like. And one new one, Admiral Fallow, they're from Scotland. I know you like The Pogues and The Clash. You may hate them." Her finger tapped the screen. "There, that track."

I could see the title, "Old Fools."

"It made me think of you."

From the house, Anya called Nika, who rolled her eyes.

"Don't." Gregor said "Give your sister respect."

"Whatever." Nika gave me a kiss on the cheek. "Goodnight, Moses." And she bounced off into the house. I looked at the iPod to keep from having to look at Gregor.

"You know, you are her hero."

"That's a mistake."

"She compares boys she meets to you."

"Teach her the truth."

"Can't. I agree with her. Look, Boss, what happened in Mexico, you did what you did, brought her home. Time to let it go."

But Gregor wasn't there, didn't see the Russian pimp pushing down on me, forcing me to enter her. I could say he would have killed us both if I hadn't done it. Could say there was no other way out. Could say a lot of crap. Didn't mean much at four in the morning when the truth hit home.

He sipped his muddy Armenian coffee. "Boss, remember how we met?"

"I broke your nose on the hood of a car." He'd been muscle for a wannabe gangster running a protection racket at the strip joint I bounced at. "I pointed a nine at you. Crazy bastard, you looked ready to eat a bullet then rip my head off."

"I was. In church tonight, I saw that moment." He stared into space. "Bad day. But without it, no hiring me. No firefight in NoCal. No meeting Anya. No saving Nika. No son. No life."

"You look happy."

"I am. Blink and this could crumble, but somehow I have faith it won't." He shrugged, done talking. We sat drinking our warm brew in comfortable silence. We had been to war more than once, and for all it had cost us, we had survived, that much was true. Price paid.

Later, Gregor told me he still felt his missing arm, that his brain couldn't fully grasp it was gone. Angel was like that. I found myself starting to call her name before remembering she wasn't there anymore. Kelly, the woman who had given me Angel, was like that. I had loved her, and still saw her out of the corner of my eye on a crowded street. Sometimes I even had a phantom childhood, one where mom wasn't a monster driven by equal parts booze and Bible. Where my brother hadn't left when I was sixteen, leaving me to steal his ID and join the marines. Hadn't learned to kill and to live with it.

Gregor told me the hospital wanted him to wear a prosthetic arm. Anya hoped he would, it would make him look more normal. But it would be useless. For show. He turned them down. Guys like us wore our scars for all to see. Not as badges of honor, but as warning to our enemies of how far we were willing to go.

It was after ten when Lowrie called back. He sounded weary as ever. "Rollens is a ghost. Never worked LAPD, the Sheriffs, no one. Lucky for you I have OCD, least that's what the department shrink tells me. I did some digging, deep. I found a woman with Rollens as her maiden name. Husband was an LAPD detective, then moved to DEA in San Diego, killed in the line of duty in...Mexico."

"Coincidence?"

"Bullshit, right? Same last name? I don't have a picture of the widow, but she ticks all the boxes."

"Don't tell the IA boys yet."

"Screw those pricks. They are on my need to know nothing list."

"You got any clue what's going on? Anything?"

"Nope, kid, all I see is how dicked you are."

He gave me Rollens's last known address. I thanked him, he grumbled and hung up. I owed him, but doubted he'd ever call in the marker.

As I climbed into a cab, Gregor tossed me a cell phone. "What's this?"

"Burner. Time to step into the twenty-first century." He was right. Pay phones had disappeared, landlines were rare. First an iPod, now this. Evolve or die, that's what the shrink said. Not that these were mutually exclusive ideas.

Gregor had the grace not to ask where I was going. I didn't tell him about the dead Mexicans or Sunshine's assessment that I was being hunted by MS-13. I carried my own water and hoped what he didn't know couldn't hurt him.

For once, Jason was happy to see me. "Dude, that newspaper guy was a mess. Wept. I mean snot running down his chin wept when I hooked up the Porsche."

"We square?"

"More than."

"Good, I need wheels." His smile dropped.

"Of course you do. One-man demolition derby. What kind of car you want to fuck up this time?"

"Fast. American." He bitched about the value hike in domestic muscle cars. He whined and moaned, but when he showed me the '67 Tempest he looked as proud as any papa.

"Bear-Tex disc brakes, Morrison suspension, rack. Has the original 326, four-barrel. Blue printed. Four hundred ponies at the rear, before nitrous, which you won't be using or you might blow this engine up. Tremec manual 5-speed, Hurst shifter." It was a gearhead's wet dream. When I was a kid I would have been drooling along with him. Now I just cared if it would rock and roll.

"Lucky it's a four door. All the twos have been butchered into GTO clones. Looks good, right?" The paint was faded and airbrushed to look like it was rusting out. The seats were more duct tape than vinyl. The dash was cracked. The trim was either missing or pitted beyond recognition.

"Looks perfect." He gave me a rash of shit about its supposed value, told me I'd owe him twenty large if I trashed it. But his heart wasn't really in it. Odds were squarely on me turning his classic into scrap metal, but he knew I'd make him whole sooner or later.

It was three a.m. when I hit Burbank. I parked across the street from Rollens's last known address. The salmon-colored apartment building was ten years past needing a new paint job. Admiral Fallow was in my earbuds. Nika was right; I liked their sound. Peaceful. Wouldn't go to war with it, but maybe not everything was a war. *Cry from the bedroom, spend your time wishing back an act that is thankless.* Fuck, that nailed me.

There was also a sexual older/younger element to the song, made me worry. Straight-up, Mikayla was half right. I felt proud of how Nika looked at me. Hated myself, but I found her touch on my hand electric.

Idiot, second floor.

"Were you this rude when you were alive?"

Fucked if I know. I think you made me up.

125

That is what the shrink would have said if I'd told him I was in a car arguing the existence of a dead assassin with her ghost.

On the second floor, number twenty-four, nothing moved. I waited another ten minutes before heading in. The camera above the security gate hung uselessly down on torn cables. I found Rollens's shitty Honda in the parking lot. Climbing up onto her rear balcony, I stepped over a hibachi. The sliding glass door's lock took some gentle prying before it popped. I pulled the monster Ruger, cocked the hammer and moved in past the faded curtain.

As my eyes adjusted, the 1970s appeared from the shadows. Shag carpet. Popcorn ceiling. Harvest gold appliances. This was no retro cool choice. This was detritus of a life unpaid.

On a low sofa, Rollens was snoring. She was dressed only in a slightly too big, and very faded, San Diego Chargers t-shirt. For a short woman, she had a great set of legs. Within arm's reach on a coffee table were a Glock and a bottle of Vicodin. Like an old friend, the white pills called. Just one. What harm could one do me? I picked up the Glock instead.

Her eyes fluttered into focus as I pressed the .454 Casull between them. She was dope-slow, her words slurred. "What the...McGuire, hell you doing?"

"Focus. Your lies got my dog killed. No more bullshit or pow and I walk away."

"Ok. Wait." She slowly pushed the revolver off her face. I let her. I could always shoot her later. "Hold on, let me think." She sat up. Her face was covered in cuts and bruises, an ace bandage held her left arm pinned to her side. "Your bitch," she indicated with her head, "is in the bedroom."

"What?"

"That fucking horse."

I cleared the room in two steps. Angel lay on the bed. She wasn't moving, but she was warm when I knelt and rested my hand on her side. Slowly her chest rose as she inhaled.

"I gave her a Vicodin." Rollens was leaning on the door jamb.

"What?'

"She was a wreck."

Angel lifted her head. Her left eye was missing, the lid sewn shut. One ear was shortened and taped up. Seeing me, her tail gently slapped the bed. She struggled to rise, but hadn't the strength. I leaned in, let her nuzzle my face.

"Are you crying, McGuire?" Rollens's voice was full of disdain.

Rollens told me she'd served as a medic in the National Guards, and she'd stitched Angel up. After the accident, she dragged Angel out of the car. She got the guns and was going back for me when the rollers showed. That was what she said. "My niece, she is real. I lied about being on the force. I *was*. Now, more like freelancing." We were drinking Folgers instant coffee.

"Stop. You never were a cop. Married to one, he died in Mexico." Her eyes went rabbit in the headlights. "You saved my dog, that buys you the right to talk. Bullshit me, you're a grease stain on the carpet and I'm in the wind."

She looked confused, fought to reorder her lies without fully knowing what I knew. Her eyes looked everywhere but into mine. "This coffee sucks. How many spoons did you put in?" she asked.

"Three. You're stalling. It takes no time to come up with the truth." I dropped all the shells save one from the Ruger. Snapping the cylinder shut, I gave it a spin. "Ever seen *The Deer Hunter*?"

"What?" Her eyes were pinned on the revolver.

"*The Deer Hunter.* 'Di di mau.' No?" I pushed the barrel against my temple and pulled the trigger. The hammer fell heavy on an empty chamber. "Your turn."

"You're fucking crazy, McGuire."

"No, I have been certified sane and not a danger to myself or others. Truth or dare, choose." I put the gun down in front of her. She let out a weak laugh. She picked up the gun. Almost had it to her head, set it back on the table.

"I was a social worker. Got fired when I ran over a pimp who was threatening one of my girls."

"Bullshit."

"It's the truth. When Bobby, my husband, went to work for the DEA, I...I was a social worker."

"You're trying to roll the dice on what I know and don't know. Big mistake."

"No, I'm not."

"Mexico? Sanchez?" Her eyes twitched, almost imperceptibly. I grabbed the Ruger, pointed at her face and pulled. Another dead chamber.

"What fuck, McGuire? I'm talking."

"Not fast enough." I thumbed the hammer back.

"Ok, I wasn't ever a cop. My stepdad was, my husband was. I used his old badge, made the fake ID at a copy shop."

"Mexico?"

"My husband's old partner in the DEA, he got me in contact with Sanchez. Sanchez is working with them. I needed him to get to you." Part of that was true. Badge or no, nothing got done in Ensenada without Senior Sanchez's nod. She told me growing up with a cop she learned to handle a gun. Said the bit in the National Guard was real.

"As a social worker, I saw what happened to girls in the life. The part about running over a pimp? That was real. Freedom? She is real. When she disappeared I panicked. An old friend on the force, she told me about you, about Lowrie. Would you have helped me if I told you the truth?"

"We'll never know." Standing, I put my back to her. Poured what was left of my coffee down the kitchen drain. "You're right, tastes like shit."

"Do you believe me now."

"Does it matter?"

"Not if you find Freedom."

I nodded. That was true. I picked up the Ruger, opening the cylinder. I let her see the bullet in the chamber. It was important for her to be clear I wasn't fucking around. If she was impressed, it didn't show.

"Can I get dressed now?"

I nodded, stepped onto the balcony and dialed.

"Hello, Moses." Sunshine picked up on the first ring. "Couldn't go seven hours without hearing my sexy voice?"

"Something like that. How'd you know it was me?"

"You're the only one has this number."

"My own personal Batphone?"

"Don't get too engorged big guy, numbers are cheap, free actually." She let out a husky laugh. She sounded good, tired but good.

"You get any sleep?"

"I'm in bed right now, all tucked under a quilt my grand mammy made me. Feather pillow." She was filling my head with pictures and she knew it. Not that I minded. "Wanna join me? You know you do." Nothing I would rather do.

"Rain check." I went for smooth indifference.

"Fuck you, McGuire, you know you want me."

"Fact. But right now, I need an address. Pimp named Titan, works girls out of Capone's, a strip joint in the Valley."

She let out a long sigh, "Fine, give me ten minutes I'll text it to you. Anything else? Coffee, latte, quick hand job in the back seat?" I could hear the smile in her voice.

"Woman, you're making it hard to get to work."

"Long as I'm making it hard." She had all the flirt of a seasoned pro, yet it felt real. Maybe she was better at the game than most. But why hustle me? Then again, why not hustle me? I didn't know the game I was stumbling along in, let alone who the players were.

"I need intel." I looked through the sliding glass door. I was alone. "Name's Evelyn Rollens, widow of Robert Mayers, LAPD slash DEA."

"Widow? Sexy. She your squeeze?" The pout came through in her voice.

"You care?"

"Not really." She laughed. Quick. Real. "I do care how you are going to pay for this information."

"You tell me."

"Goodwill, and you owe me. Godfather style."

"Works for me." I hung up before she could say another word.

Her too? Mikayla was leaning against the Formica counter. *You want to fuck her?*

"All of them. But, yes, her too. Maybe her most."

"What?" Rollens called from the bedroom.

"Nothing."

And her? Mikayla lifted her chin in the direction of the bedroom. *Why?*

"Maybe she... fucked if I know."

Mikayla was shaking her head sadly, then she was gone.

Rollens came out of the bedroom dressed in jeans and a hoody draped out of a leather blazer. She did look good. She pulled my duffle from a closet. Shotgun, 1911, boxes of ammo, what clothes I owned.

I pulled on a clean Clash t-shirt and we were ready to rumble.

CHAPTER 21

"This is Helen. If you are calling for me or Jules, we can't come to the phone because we are fucking, or reading, or screening your call." Even her voice sounded happy. I called twice before giving up and heading toward Gregor's.

Somewhere down the Hollywood Freeway, a tremor started in my hip. I couldn't figure out if I was having the DTs or withdrawal from the Vicodin. The vibration was joined by a low buzzing noise.

"You gonna answer that?" Rollens asked.

My new cell phone was buzzing away in my pocket. I pulled over and tried to figure out which damn buttons to push.

"Give me that, McGuire."

"I got it," I lied, not sure why. My fingers felt like massive sausages on the small touch screen. Finally, a text appeared. It was from Sunshine, an address in the Valley and a note that said, BE CAREFUL OF THE OTHER QUESTION. DIGGING DEEPER. No cute salutations. No xoxo. All business. Clear. Solid intel. I wondered if Kenny had sent it.

"We good?" Rollens asked.

"Old contact, sent me Titan's address."

"Then let's go nail the son of a bitch." Her face was hard, locked looking out the windshield. I wondered about the wisdom of giving her back the Glock. It was too late now.

I dropped Rollens at a Chevron station down the hill from Gregor's home. She didn't need to know how to find my people.

Gregor had to keep his mother from burying a butcher knife in my back when she saw Angel in my arms. She shouted in Russian.

"She said you don't deserve the dog. Says you're a careless son of a bitch," Gregor translated.

"Yeah, got that."

"She's wrong."

"No, she's not. Least not about my mother." He was about to say more. "Lighten up, she loves the dog and that's a good thing." After all we'd seen and done, that he worried his mother might hurt my feelings made me smile.

Gregor made Angel a bed in his mother's room. As I lay her down she gave me a dopey lick then fell back asleep.

As I was leaving, Anya came out, baby at her breast. Rumpled, tired, in a bathrobe, childbirth had softened her dancer's body, adding a softness to her curves. She was stunning. She could still raise my pulse, probably always would. She saw me and her eyes went to ice. She handed the child to Gregor. "I need to speak to Moses, alone." He didn't ask. Took his son and walked into the house.

"He is a good man. My Man. You must leave him, us, out of whatever this is you are in. You saved my sister. You saved me. We will never forget you. But my son needs a father. I need a husband. Do you understand?"

"Yes." I did. Gregor did his tour and then some. It was time for him to live in the world. Anya might have once cared about me, or maybe it had all been a scam to get me to rescue Nika. Didn't matter. She was Gregor's woman now. He'd been fighting a war without end since he was a kid in Eastern Europe. He deserved a fierce woman, a warm family, peace. I hoped I could keep him clear of the shitstorm I was stirring up. I also knew he was a soldier and would make up his own mind.

Dark clouds hid the rising sun when I picked Rollens up. Mist haloed the gas station sign. I dropped a hundred plus to fill up the Tempest. Jason had expanded the gas tank, pushing it up into the trunk. It now held twenty-four gallons. She was a thirsty beast, but worth every gallon.

Hitting the 101, I opened up the engine. The Quadrajet carb sang. Dual pipes rumbled. She sank down onto her racing suspension, fixed to the asphalt as if by magnetic force. I could learn to love this car. I really hoped I could keep her from a fiery death. Doubted I could, hoped nonetheless. An old AA guy in lockdown at Pelican Bay once told me, "Hope is just disappointment delayed." I was drunk on pruno at the time so I didn't pay him much mind. Knew he was right, just didn't see the strength of dwelling on the obvious.

"You have a new plan?" Rollens asked as we headed into the Valley.

"Same plan, smarter execution." I slipped in my earbuds and turned up "Tommy Gun." Strummer and the boys drowned out any objections Rollens had.

The address was a condo off Woodman Blvd. Parked across and a block down the street, we drank bitter gas station coffee. Rollens had a military spotter's scope and we took turns watching. A cab pulled up and a tired looking woman stumbled out. Sexy dress now stained and rumpled, makeup mostly gone leaving only faint smears of color, she carried her stilettos, bare feet swollen and red in patches where the cheap shoes rubbed. If johns could see what their dolls looked like at eight a.m. after a hard night of being pumped, they might think again...but I doubt it.

A second cab arrived. The two girls getting out didn't speak. They paid the cabbie and walked toward the condo. The whole deal reminded me of a strip club after last call, when the lights came up, the glamor gone, evidence of shabby sex and broken hopes littering the floor. The men's room trash can overflowing with condoms. Money traded for making a man come and forget his life. A whore's promise. Seconds after you bust a nut the self-loathing rolls back in, washing away any semblance of romance. Nothing more romantic than a man wanting pussy, nothing more cynical than a man who just got some.

The wilting flowers punched a code in the security gate and disappeared into the complex. It was three two-story condos with shared walls. Behind the gate a small common lawn ran the length of the property. There was underground, gated parking. It was upscale. Not lawyer or stockbroker rich, but definitely upscale.

After a full hour, only six girls. Always the same, tired, used-up look. I knew after a day's sleep, a shower and the soft lights of a strip club, they would be beautiful sirens. Even in hard times they had to break a grand a night. I'm no mathematician, but any way you count it Titan was banking large.

"Looks like he owns all three houses." Rollens passed me the scope. "They enter number one, down on the end. After a few minutes they leave. Four have gone into number two. Two into number three. Are you writing this down?"

"Nope." Cops wrote facts down, building a case. Cons, we wrote nothing down. Why help them bust us.

The last vehicle to show was a black Escalade. Three of the strippers from Capone's stepped out. The girl who promised me the prettiest pussy in town was holding hands with the girl she had been laughing at. As the SUV waited for the underground parking gate to open, I saw the driver. It was my good friend Jeremy, a.k.a Atlas. "Stay put," I told Rollens and was moving before she could give me any bullshit. I ran low, keeping parked cars between me and the Escalade. I followed it down, the gate scraping against the cement as it locked behind us.

"Hey, buddy." I was glad to see he was still above ground. One less ghost to come calling.

"That motherfucking...no, damn no." His eyes searched for any way away from me.

"How are you, Jeremy?" His leg encased in a plastic brace, he leaned against the truck for support. His face was puffy, the bruises faded to yellow. Seeing no escape, he got angry.

"The fuck you want? Wanna break my arm? Shoot my other leg? Do it."

"I got a little crazy."

"Fuck you. Crazy? You sober, come to make bullshit amends?"

"Not even close. You lied to me."

"No shit. That's why I'm still alive. Titan don't truck snitch bitches."

"How did he take me torching his tug joint?"

"Ha. Yeah, that shit was funny." He was smiling. "That shit wasn't his."

"Who owned it?"

"Fuck I know? Some Chinese. You needed an address, I gave you one."

"Fair enough. Now it's time I meet Titan."

"Oh yeah, like that shit is happening. Fuck you."

I pulled back my leather jacket, showing him the Ruger stuffed in my waistband.

"Titan, or we go another couple of rounds."

"Fuck it. Stupid white monster. Your size gonna protect you? Shit." I heard the distinctive ratchet of an automatic being charged behind me. "Video monitoring, dumb motherfucker." Seems Jeremy kept me talking just long enough for reinforcements to arrive.

"Pat him down." The voice at my back was deep and hard. Jeremy took the Ruger from my belt. I towered over him. He didn't care. Swinging up, he slapped me with the heavy revolver. Blood sprayed from my cheek and I heard bone crack. I stumbled, didn't go down. Wanted to. His second blow split my lower lip against my teeth. Blood rolled down my chin.

"On your motherfucking knees, bitch." He pointed the .454 at my gut. I did not want to spend my life shitting into a bag. I did as told. I looked for some smartass comeback.

"We even yet?" was the best I could manage.

"Not even in the neighborhood of even." He raised his hand to strike again.

"Enough." The deep voice spoke and Jeremy lowered his arm.

Jeremy gave me his hardest eyes. "This ain't over." He was young, didn't know it was never over.

"Is this the man beat you down?" Titan was young and handsome in a clean-shaven, preppy way. His skin was light, freckled, what we used to call high yella. A fitted cardigan covered his muscular chest. Gym trained, not crazy prison buff. The condo was nice. A few too many statues and paintings of Greece, but nice.

"To be fair, he did hit me with a baseball bat first." I was on the floor, my hands tied behind my back. Blood was running down my cheek and chin, disappearing into my Clash t-shirt.

"Where's your partner, Pam Grier looking lady?" I shrugged. Titan looked at a big guy in a sleeveless shirt. He was the real muscle in the room. He nailed my chest with a size fourteen Timberland. I flopped back, wondering if the concussion had stopped my heart. It burned as air flooded back into my lungs. Dead couldn't hurt like this, so I was betting on alive.

"Titan ax you a question."

"Yes... he...did." I pulled myself up to a sitting position. "Pam Grier?" I smiled.

"Yes, a dirty, gold Pontiac. Who is she?" Titan was cool, at peace, spooky almost.

"I Love Pam Grier. Foxy Brown, forget about it, right? Not sure Jackie Brown was as good—"

The Timberland kicked my lower spine. I fell face-first, no hands to break the fall, onto the hardwood floor. Titan moved closer. I could smell his cologne. Could see tasseled loafers that cost more than everything I owned. Not that that was saying much.

"Coeus. He has a heavy hand, or boot. You have two, three blows before he is bound to rupture something. You aren't spitting blood are you?" I just stared at him. "Good. I find the idea of a kicking a man until internal organs fail distasteful."

"She's just a lady, an aunt. She paid me to find her niece."

Titan smiled, seemed to control the giant named Coeus with simple eye flicks. I was lifted into a chair and the rope around my wrists was cut. Blood screamed as it ran back into my hands. Pins and needles? This was nails and rusty screws. The room had a large desk, behind which Titan regained his seat. On the desk was a computer, stacks of ledgers, papers and a copy of the Wall Street Journal. I got the feeling it wasn't a prop.

"You are no less close to slipping off this mortal coil, we clear?"

"Yeah, clear."

"This aunty, she coming back?"

"Doubt it."

"Then you are very deeply screwed. The car yours?"

"It was."

"It's a piece of shit."

"But it's paid for."

"So is the steak I ate for dinner, and now it's a piece of shit."

"Point taken."

Titan snapped his fingers and held out his hand palm up. Jeremy moved clumsily and gave him the Ruger. "Did you come here to kill me, or are you looking for suicide by pimp?"

"Neither. I'm looking for a girl. She's lost. Not in the life, got snatched. Rumor is you have her."

"Rumored where?"

"Doesn't matter. I'm tired, my face hurts, my guts hurt, back hurts. I need to see a dentist, and to cap it all off, cherry on this cum pie, is... it's boring." The preppy pimp's face was tight as a drum. "Boy, do you have any interest in seeing another sunset?" I had his attention.

"Boy? That is bold. Please..." He rippled his fingers, encouraging me to continue.

"The kidnapped girl, her aunt was LAPD. Mistake one. Witness saw the girl in your Escalade downtown, that's two. But the big bitch, one that is going to put your ass down, is when you used a rocket launcher to try and take me out. That shit got some very powerful, very outside of oversight cops looking for you."

"I did what?"

"Want to play dumb? Really?"

He looked at me, then out the window. The street was coming to life with squares heading off to jobs that didn't require packing guns or threatening pimps.

"They know I'm here. The girl's aunt will tell them. Odds are I will be dead before they haul ass here, but this? All this? It goes away, and you go from Titan to some AB's prison punk."

"Get Athena." Coeus was gone and back in less than a minute. Athena was a tall, leggy woman with a tight dress, neckline cut to her belly button. Her breasts were unnaturally perky, fake but fine work. As a titty bar bouncer I'd seen my share of tits, and hers were real works of art. Funny, death staring a man in the face and he takes time to notice breasts. Just proves the power of flesh.

"Athena, I ever rape a girl?"

"You crazy, baby?"

"Man here called me a gorilla pimp, said I been dragging girls off the street."

"That's bullshit, Daddy." She shot me a hard stare. "A man can't steal what is freely given, Titan taught me that. You run him down I will cut you."

"Easy, Athena, no need killing over a mistake. Send in Eos."

"Sure, Daddy. Are we good?"

"We are golden, now go on." I watched her swish out and wondered what hold he had on her. Her affection looked and felt real. Eos was another stunner, same perfect tits created by the same doctor. She gave the same praise of Titan and his loving ways. It was all one big, happy family. He took care of them, and they took care of him.

Hera, his bottom girl, was older than the rest. She was diamond hard. She'd been with Titan from the jump. She slept in his bed. She was the queen to his king. She was the one the other women feared. "I don't know who has been filling your

139

head with malicious defamation, but it is bullshit. My man is a good man. Do you know whose name is on the deed here? Mine. Mine. You think he do that if he was a rapist thug."

After Hera left, Titan sent Coeus and Jeremy out. He fired up a fat joint, didn't offer me any. It smelled rich and sweet as a woman's love.

"Moses. The prophet, the seer. Tell me what my future looks like."

"Fucked. Unless I walk out of here."

"Hmmm, I have shown you my world. I suspect you know I wouldn't do that if I was going to take your head. You think I took this girl?"

"Honestly, I don't give a rat's ass. Dress this up any way you like, but you make money off those ladies' pain. No baby ever woke up and said, 'I wanna suck a stranger's dick and give my cash to some punk with a stupid Greek monster's name.' Given a chance, I'd burn your shit to the ground, leave you king of an ash pile."

He released a stream of golden smoke, eyes cold and deadly. "Motherfucker. In my house? Talk to me like that in my house? You want to die? I call Coeus and he won't stop stomping this time."

"Cut the bullshit, tough-but-loving-pimp act. You're a kid, and this game just got adult real fast." Eyes locked on his, I picked up the Ruger and slipped it in my belt. "You don't have the juice to come after me with military ordinance. Timeline says you called them in. Who?"

"Who? Fuck you. Who?" He was genuinely confused, and it wasn't the pot.

"Then it was your boy, Jeremy. Only way it plays. Did Jeremy tell you about the tug and rub joint I torched? Didn't, did he? He told someone, because they came after me."

Titan took a long drag off his joint, held it in. Old school. When he finally released it his decision was made.

"Came up together. Solid. Weak, but solid. Fuck." He yelled into his cell phone for Coeus and Jeremy to get their asses in there. In a blink Coeus was though the door. The 9mm looked like a toy in his hand.

"Where is Jeremy?"

"Said you wanted him to make a drop."

"How much?"

"All." The gravity hit Coeus, his eyes cast down. "I'll go after him."

"Where? Where the fuck will you go after him? Get the fuck out of here. Out." He looked me over, slowly. "You are one fucked up old white man."

"No lie."

"And you are my only chance of seeing my cash."

"Looks that way too."

"Fuck you. Hundred and fifty large. Ten percent you get it back. Twenty you bring me that treacherous bastard."

I nodded. Didn't agree, just nodded my acknowledgment of the offer.

"You gonna call off the cops?"

I punched in Rollens's number. It buzzed and buzzed. Finally I got her voicemail cheerfully asking me to leave a message, when the room exploded in shards of glass, plaster chunks, wood and blood.

CHAPTER 22

Silence. Smoke. Coeus crawled back, broken, pistol still in his hand. The front window and a healthy section of wall were missing. The desk had me pinned down, had taken most of the blast. A 4x4 chained to the front gate leapt forward, ripped it out. Sparks flew as it scraped the parked cars and cement. Two white panel vans skidded in. Six men in black jumpsuits and ski masks ran toward the condo. They were precise, clean, military.

I curled up as small as possible, not that easy at my size, but I tried. I pulled a shattered chair and painting over myself and gripped the Ruger. I could see the room through a crack in the oak desk. Two men leapt into the room, rolled and came up sweeping with machine pistols. Coeus tried to raise his 9mm. A machete swung down severing his hand at the wrist. Blood sprayed. The soldier in black didn't move out of the way. The second blow sheered off Coeus's other hand. Next went one leg at the knee, then the other. It was so fast and clean that Coeus didn't bleed out. He was alive when they took his head off.

Past this horror show, men were herding freaked-out hookers into the vans. They all had their arms tied behind their backs. Some of them were bleeding.

A soldier moved toward me, looking at the pile of debris and the desk. I took shallow breaths. His partner found Titan covered in plaster from where a section of ceiling had fallen on him. He pulled Titan up by the shoulders. The man near me turned to look at the funny black man in whiteface.

I roared like a bear when I rose up, lifting the desk off my back. From three feet the Ruger blew a hole big enough to take a section of his spine clean off. The man crumpled on his useless legs. The second shot hit the soldier holding Titan, his ski mask turned to bloody pulp. Red splashed on white. The pimp was modern art carnage. I screamed. He didn't listen. He was mentally gone. I lifted him over my shoulder and ran deeper into the condo. My plan was to keep running and killing until I was free or dead. I made it up a flight of stairs and across a hallway before the shot hit me.

A shotgun blast from behind lifted me up and tossed me onto a silk covered bed. The buckshot made a mess of Titan's torso and head. I rolled across the bed and placed a .454 slug into the shooter's flack vest. It may have been Kevlar, but it did nothing to keep the punch from driving him off the landing and out into space. Deaf as I was, I never heard him land, but my guess is it was wet.

Titan was staring into another world. I threw a vanity stool through the window and was gone. The roof wasn't pitched very steep. Thank the lack of snow for that. I ran across the three we assumed were Titan's. A gap of eight plus feet stood between me and the next set of condos. I really wished I'd practiced long jump in high school instead of getting stoned, but then you never really know what skills you will need until you need them.

Giving myself a good run-up, I leapt into space. Even as I left the roof, I knew I was fucked. Not even close. I fell into a bougainvillea-covered lattice. Splinters and thorns tore my clothes and flesh. A plastic picnic table scrubbed what was left of my momentum. Lying looking up at the blue sky, it occurred to me this right here might be a good fucking time to call it quits. All my life people had been trying to kill me. Hell, I'd done the best I could to kill myself. Why not let this moment be it?

Pussy.
"Easy for you to say, you dead Russian bitch."
Ukrainian. They have that girl. They must die.
"And the next?"
They die too. All until you.

As she drifted away I heard sirens coming. Weak, but building. Would drive off the kill squad. It would bring cops. I'd spend my life in a cage. Death I could take. Not a cage. Been there. It sucked. Wasn't going back.

It wasn't pretty or graceful, but I climbed over the dumpsters behind the condos. I stuck to back alleys. When I found a vacant lot I rolled in the dust, then the bloodstains just looked like I was in serious need of a bath. I finally found the Pontiac, no Rollens. Cops rolled the streets. I was seriously fucked.

CHAPTER 23

"I knew you'd be back."

I was soaking in a tub with water that had turned a deep brownish red. Sunshine rolled in. She let her eyes roam over my body, shamelessly.

"I was out of options."

"That is bullshit, darling. Man like you always has options. You chose me. Either that or you don't care if you bring this heat down on me."

"It wasn't—"

"Hush. Or you knew I could handle whatever bullshit came down the road. Or, and I like this one, you missed me. Had to see me again." Rolling behind me, she shampooed my hair, massaging my scalp. I could feel her hands slipping slowly through my carefully constructed defenses. She traced a finger over a scar running across my skull. She stroked the scar splitting my eyebrow. She lifted the Saint Jude medal.

"Patron saint of lost causes," I said. "Friend in Mexico gave it to me."

"And how has it been working?"

I gave her a good looking over. "Pretty damn well."

Her finger followed the bullet scars that ran down under the water. She was leaning in, giving me an ample view down her silk nightgown. Her breasts were full. They sagged a bit with age, and that made them all the sexier. I'd had my fill of perky fake tits; she was real.

"You can touch me," she said, her voice husky with building lust. Cupping her breast in my hand, I let my thumb trace a circle around her deep brown areola. Brushing over her nipple it plumped, responsive to my touch. As it swelled she let out a small groan. "Take me to bed." It was an order, a request, a question. I stood and let the dirty water drip off me. I took the handheld showerhead and washed the last of the blood and dirt off. She didn't take her eyes off my erection.

"I don't know..." I looked at her, lovely, and the chair that held her.

"How? We'll work it out. Lean down." She wrapped her arms around my neck and I lifted her up into my arms. She was light. I ran my arm under her knees. Time had atrophied her legs. She let her neck rest on my mine, whispering, "you could be the one, Mr. McGuire."

"One?"

"Yeah." She had me set her on the bed. I helped her out of the nightgown. I stood back and just took her in. She was a full-grown woman, strongly built. Her shoulders were defined by thick muscles dropping down to soft breasts. A jagged scar bisected her belly, pale against her dark skin. It had been a long time since I had let myself feel lust. Looking at her, it felt clean, the correct response to this beauty.

"Pull the comforter up."

"I'm enjoying the view."

"I can see that." She looked down at her unmoving legs. "They used to break men's hearts." I wanted to say something about how they looked good to me, but we both would have seen the lie. She made me want to play it straight. I started to cover her.

"No, stop. We gonna start this, let's do it clean, up front."

"You about to tell me you aren't into guys?"

"No, I been with women, but I like dick just fine. I want you to look at this. On her lower abdomen was a small mound with a two-inch opening in the center, a colostomy bag attached. "It's called a stoma." She had tattooed sunrays around it, making body art out of her pain.

I started to speak, having no idea what to say. The bag needed changing. She showed me how to help her. I got her cleaned, new bag in place.

"If you want to run for the door, I get it."

"Why the fuck would I make a stupid move like that?" I kissed her forehead. Her lips. Her belly. The tattoo around her stoma.

She pulled herself up to sit against the bed's backboard, near the edge. "Come here. No, standing. Yeah, like that." I stood facing her. She took my cock and stroked it. Softly, she licked the tip. Grabbing my ass, she pulled me deep into her mouth. She gagged but kept going. I grabbed her hair. I pulled her onto me harder and faster, could feel the pressure building. I held back as long as I could. In a rush I came. It had been so long. So long. My knees went weak. She was grinning up at me, lips still suckling. I started to cry and laugh and moan. Somewhere deep in my chest a cage opened and the pain I felt for what I'd done to Nika started to flutter away.

I curled up behind Sunshine, moving her legs so that I could spoon her. We didn't speak. We were past that. An hour later I was woken by an erection. I pressed against her, she murmured softly. Reaching back, she stroked me slick with a lube filled hand and guided me toward her vulva. Softly I pushed into her, her muscles tightened around me. Gripping her hips, I pushed harder and faster. She reached down and worked her fingers across her clit. She came screaming bloody murder. She clawed at my wrist, drew blood. I came, my screams matching hers.

In the morning, we woke sticky and wrapped in each other's arms. Her face was softer than I had ever seen it. I kissed her full lips. Kissed her again. Kissed her like we had nothing else that needed doing. On my elbows, I looked down at her.

"Moses?"

"Sunshine."

"If this was a raging blood's up after battle fuck—"

"It wasn't."

"Shut up. If that is what it was, or a novelty fuck, or pity fuck—"

"It wasn't, Sunshine."

"I'm warning you, so pay close attention. If it was, I will kill you like a wild dog. Kill you and never look back."

"That is the best thing anyone ever said to me."

"How is that?"

"Just is, I guess." All my life people, even my mother, that drunken Jesus-loving bitch, wanted me gone. My big brother split for Texas and left me alone. Women only wanted me around as long as they needed protecting. I guess Gregor wanted me around. Mikayla had, in her way. But none of them, not one, had ever wanted me bad enough to kill me if I left.

Taking her face in my hands I kissed her deeply. I used my knees to spread her legs. I took a hand off her face and used it to tilt her pelvis up. My lips never left hers. My eyes never left hers. I was claiming her. I was owning her. I was making it clear with every thrust that she was mine.

An hour later we were bathed and eating breakfast. Corned beef hash and greens that Kenny whipped up. He gave me the stink eye and scowled every time Sunshine and I laughed.

"While you two were..."

"Fucking. We were fucking," Sunshine said.

"Yeah, I heard. While you was fucking, I been monitoring all feeds. The shootout at the pimp's crib hit Van Nuys PD. Cars rolled and then it went dead silent. News is reporting a gas main blew up. No fatalities. Footage of frightened residents in front of the pimp's place weeping about lost family photos."

"Who is cleaning for them?"

"Internal LAPD, looks like. Our backup is the only feed left that proves it ever happened. They even wiped the 911 database. There's a ten-minute gap in their timelines."

I looked from one to the other, getting no clearer on what all this meant.

"Moses? You ever hear how they killed Malcolm X, the Kennedy brothers?" Sunshine asked.

"No."

"No, of course he didn't," Kenny jumped in. "That was old tech. Rowboat, oxcart bullshit. Now they can rewrite the narrative in minutes. Hell, they can rewrite it while you are watching and make you believe it. Fuck Chris Angel, David Copperfield. Disappear a 747? How about a city block and an African National Congress."

"Ok, got it. These are smart, tricky bastards who make shit disappear. How the fuck does this wind up at my doorstep?"

"That, white man, is the sixteen million dollar question."

"CIA? Homeland? Who else has this?" I swept my hand over Kenny's workstation.

"Anyone with money. LAPD don't have the cash for new cars, I doubt they did it."

"Kenny, what do I tell you?" Sunshine sounded like stern schoolteacher. A really smoking-hot schoolteacher.

"Making assumptions before the facts are in screws the investigation."

"That's the one. Los Angeles city budget was $6.9 billion last year."

"That's a lot of cheese. Rats?" They were locked in on each other. Clearly this process was honed by time and practice. I was starting to feel like a fifth wheel, when from nowhere a perky little electronic song started playing. They both looked at me. I looked at them. The song went on.

"You gonna get that, baby?"

"What?"

"Your phone."

She was right, the sound was coming from my pocket. By the time I figured out how to get it to work it had gone dead. Lowrie's number was flashing.

"Where the fuck are you, McGuire?"

"Good morning, Detective."

"No, it is not. Get your ass to the normal meeting place. Now." He hung up.

The meeting place was a Denny's in Hollywood. Why so cryptic wasn't clear, but at this moment acting paranoid seemed like a bright plan. I told Sunshine I had to roll. She took my phone and switched some cards out. She punched a number into her phone and mine started playing Parliament's "I Call My Baby Pussycat."

"You hear that, get your fine self back here. No shit, baby. You get back." I kissed her, told her I would. Promised to call when I knew what was what.

Kenny dropped a Kevlar vest, a riot gun, ammo for it and the Ruger on the table. "I put a tracker in both the car and the Ruger. We'll keep eyes on you best we can."

"Sweet, kid, almost sounds like you care."

"I don't. But you make her happy, so don't die."

"Do my best." We both knew my best wouldn't be enough, not by a long shot. He gave me that subtle tough guy nod that is supposed to mean we get each other. I gave him the thousand-yard stare that said he had no fucking clue where I had been or where I was going.

CHAPTER 24

The Tempest felt good. Hell, all things considered I felt good. Had crazy-fine fucking. Slept without the dead haunting me. Ate well. Was drug free and sober. I had the iPod Nika gave me blasting U2. What wasn't to like? Yes, some psycho paramilitary freaks were trying to take me off the boards, LAPD was after my ass, and I was one strike away from doing the bitch. But the clouds had blown away, rain leaving the air crisp. The Hollywood Hills looked as inviting and friendly as a postcard. The same couldn't be said for Lowrie's face. He was ashen, eyes bloodshot to brick red, bags near black. All this I'd seen before. It was the stink of tobacco and defeat that was new.

"Where were you last night?" I was still walking when he asked.

"Where do you think I was? That's the real question. Where?"

"No bullshit, McGuire, zero. Talk here or at the house. Cuffs are optional."

I held up a mug, motioning the waitress for coffee. Lowrie shook his head and she backed off. "I spent the night balls deep in fun, and no I won't give you her name."

"How about yesterday morning, seven a.m.?"

"That depends on who you ask, doesn't it?"

"Don't fucking riddle me, McGuire. Way past taking crap from anyone." His eyes were glassy. It was almost as if he had been crying, but he didn't cry.

"Truth is really fucking flexible right now. I was in a pimp named Titan's crib. We were hit by a tactical team. Brutal bloody, took heads. I made it out. Killed two, maybe a third. But twenty minutes later it's reported as a gas explosion. So you tell me where the fuck I was, because I'd just be guessing if I told you."

He nodded his head as if I'd confirmed something, stood, dropped a bill and walked out. Leaning on the back of his unmarked Impala, he shook out a pack of Camel Straights. I must have given him a look.

"You gonna judge me, McGuire?"

"Nope, wondering why is all."

"That shit in my gut? Big old C. Maybe a year. Until today, I cared."

"Today?"

"They found your friend, one you called Rollens?"

"Yeah?"

"Dumped up on Angeles Crest."

"Fuck."

"Maybe you want a cigarette?" He handed it over, not really asking, and flamed it. Burned like hell. I didn't care. I knew no good news was coming.

"How?"

"Chopped her up with machetes. They're sending someone a message. Any idea who?"

"No. Who's the they? Who did this shit?"

"Clueless, no witnesses. What aren't you telling me?"

"Got nothing, Lowrie. I'm still not even sure who she was."

"They knew her. This was personal, or we have monsters on the street." He spoke slowly, flat, giving no fact any more weight than another. "They ripped her open. Shattered her pubis, tore up until they hit her sternum. M.E. figured she was alive when they choked her on her own intestines. They nailed her shield, her husband's I guess, to her forehead with a ten-penny nail. Wanted us to know they thought she was a cop and they didn't give a fuck. Never seen anything like it. No one has." He fired a fresh smoke. I joined him without giving it a thought. We stood in that cheerful afternoon, two men smoking. Each trapped deep in our heads.

"Her apartment?"

"Sanitized. Not even a toothbrush."

"So what now, she disappears? That the fucking deal? Lowrie, toss me a line here. What the fuck?"

"They will discover her car tomorrow, maybe the next day. A bereaved widow. Alcoholic. Drank too much and the mountain took her out."

"Fuck that."

"Then stop them." He passed me a thick case file. Without a look back he was in the Impala, driving away.

In the Tempest, I spilled out the crime scene photos of Rollens. I wanted to puke. Instead I punched the driver's side window. The Lexan didn't crack but it hurt like hell.

Peter looked worse than before, a rattling ball of nervous energy. His cheeks had deep scabs. He barely recognized me. On the deck of his expensive cantilevered home was a cold hot tub. Peter screamed when he hit the water. I held him under, let him up. He screamed, I pushed him down. This dance took about twenty dunks until he stopped fighting. I forced a cup of Bacardi 151 down his throat. I needed to bring him down, if only a notch or two.

Leaning against the tub, I sparked a butt, blew out a stream of smoke. This was a stupid plan.

"Mo? What the fuck, Mo?" Peter was chattering and wild-eyed, but he was focused on me. That was a start. I found a pill bottle with some bud in it. I had no idea how long he had been tweaking. The pot would get his appetite up. Booze. Pot. Food. A perfect plan.

By the time he'd done a healthy bowl and a mug of half 151 and half hot water with lemon he was hungry enough to eat most of the al pastor burrito I brought him. The house was now completely empty. Only his garage full of steel filing cabinets and a card table with an old laptop was left. A bare neon tube and two folding chairs completed the look. I found a roll of tape and put up the 8X10s of Rollens's body. I slapped each shot up hard enough to dent the cabinets.

"I knew her." Her severed hand went up. "She saved Angel's life." A close-up of her peeled-back scalp, almost detached from the occipital area. "While on the job she ran over a pimp to protect one of her girls." Her body split open, intestines stuffed down her throat. "The men who did this have her niece." I put my picture of Freedom on the board. "LAPD, or higher, is going to make this disappear. She will become just another drunk driver who shouldn't have been driving up in the mountains."

Peter was silent for a long time. He opened the police file on his desk and started reading. "Where did you get this?"

"A solid cop."

"Will he go on record?"

"Doubt it."

"Fuck, fuck, fuckity fuck fuck. Fuck. No, really, fuck. Backdoor bullshit. Fuck. No budget? Fuck. This, this right here is what happens. This." If I didn't know him, I would be sure he was having a seizure or an episode of Tourette's as he attacked the keyboard mumbling a string of fucks.

"Peter, over here. Look here, my eyes. Good. I need to know, can you can get this on the wire?"

"Wire? Fuck yes, goddamn front page *LA Times*. Tweet stream. Wired stream. Mainline mainstream."

"That a yes?"

"Fuck yes."

He promised as soon as he hit send he would be in the wind. I gave him my number and told him to stay the fuck out of sight.

I was down the hill and almost on the freeway when I spun the Tempest and headed back. Peter was just where I left him, typing away. I told him to get what he needed. That took less than a minute. I grabbed the file and Rollens's photos and we were gone.

When I pulled off the sweatshirt I'd covered Peter's eyes with, he was standing in Kenny's control center. "Well, fuck me. When did you get a Batcave?"

"You really think we need one more brain-fucked white man up here?"

"Kenny, this Peter. Peter Brixon of the—"

"*LA Times, LA Weekly*. Broke the Walmart/City Council payola story. I'm a big fan." Kenny changed instantly. He led Peter to a desk. The pride infusion was almost enough to mitigate Peter's chemical withdrawal crash.

"Soon as he gets the story written, pump him full of tranqs and put him down for at least twelve hours. He's a junkie, don't let him leave." I knew Kenny would keep his hero safe. I left them geeking out over information streams.

I found Sunshine in a canvas rig that lowered her into a whirlpool. She looked tired, slumped in the steam. When she saw me she pulled herself up, smiling. "Baby, thought you was out meeting with your cop friend."

"Done. You OK?"

"Oh, baby, I have never been better. Maybe before that bullet clipped my spine...no, not even then. I'm just a bit beat.

You a rough rider, big man." Her smirk convinced me to drop it.

Squatting next to her, I told her all that had gone down. Told her how Rollens died. "I'm going to find who did this."

"Big man, you don't even know who or why."

"I'm going to find out. Can Kenny get me clean papers and reg? I need to go to Mexico."

"He started making you a clean identity this morning. You going to tell me why Mexico?"

"I have to see a man. I think he hired Rollens to get to me. The missing niece, child in trouble...they knew I was in before I did."

"Come here and give me a kiss." I did, long, full. If I let it go a moment longer I would be in the water with her.

"Rest up, woman, I'm coming for you." Some promises you make hoping they will be true. Some you make dead sure you won't pull them off. We both knew which kind this was. We both needed the lie.

CHAPTER 25

When they took the blindfold off, Freedom was standing in a large room with comfortable chairs and a horseshoe shaped sectional. There were no windows. Pinpoints of light spun around the room from a mirror ball, splashing the purple walls. No bar, stage, booths or tables.

"Welcome home," Zero said. "Treat your new Daddy well and this shit will be epic. I'm telling you. You and me, we are gonna do some big shit up in here."

"Ok, Popi." Freedom tried to purr and make it sound sexy, but it sounded robotic and cold. Zero didn't notice. He was a fool.

"That's right Lil' Diamond, hell yes. That shit with Zacarías and Frankie was wicked."

"Frankie never saw it coming." Freedom was impressed with the El Salvadorian killer's skill. He was like a reverse surgeon; he ended life with an artist's flair.

Zero took Freedom down a hall lined with six doors. Behind each was a different girl, each named after a gemstone. Zero called it branding, called his string of ladies the Crown Jewels Collection. Freedom knew if she didn't hold her name close she would be lost. Lil' Diamond fucked men for money. Lil' Diamond flirted with Zero and his crew. Lil' Diamond let Zero fuck her in the little windowless room behind her door. In a closet, a small dresser and a short dowel with a few wire hangers held all her clothes and makeup.

Work began that night. Freedom had no clue where they were. Johns would enter and choose a girl from the collection sitting around the room.

"Ain't you cute as a button." He had greasy gray hair and beads of sweat on his upper lip. He paid Amethyst and took Lil' Diamond to her room. He wasn't mean or cruel. Didn't matter, she hated him for what he was doing to her. After two minutes he was done. He lay staring at the ceiling.

"I never do things like this."

"It's ok, baby." Lil' Diamond placated while Freedom stared at his pulsing jugular. One small slit and he would never be able to do this to any girl again.

"What are you thinking about?" he asked.

"How good I feel."

His name was Mike and he was a contractor. He said he had a loveless marriage. Three nights in a row he came to the whorehouse, asking for Lil' Diamond. Each time he pounded away for a few minutes, then talked about his sad life and sad wife and sad kids. When he said he had a daughter Lil' Diamond's age, Freedom wanted to slip a knife down his chest and puncture his heart. Or stick his lung and watch him drown in his own blood. Slow. Painful. Frightening. That was what this motherfucker deserved. If Jesus was watching, she prayed he was good with a knife.

When Amethyst saw how Zero treated Lil' Diamond, she got pissed. No little bitch was taking her spot as bottom girl. Try as hard as she might, Zero paid her no mind. He told her she was too old for him, but she would be great for guys looking for a MILF. He made her cashier, let her run the girls.

More like a business partner than a lover, only he kept all the money.

LeJohn continued to moon over Freedom. He was harmless. He snuck her in an MP3 player, a white iPod knockoff. It was loaded with gangsta rap.

"You don't like it?"

"No, I love it. I just wish you didn't have to go. Wish...you know, we could be together outside of here."

"I do too, baby, but you know Zero would kill me."

"Only if he caught you," she said playfully.

"You are crazy."

"Just a bit."

LeJohn had stopped fucking her once he found he had feelings for the girl. He said he would wait until she wanted to, no pressure. Not the others.

Freedom dreamt of Mad Hatters and rabbits and killing Zero and his crew, slowly. Even LeJohn wasn't spared in her dream world. She would replay the dreams or fantasize about killing them in the day. *One day I will flood this house with their blood*, Freedom thought.

"You my man," is what Lil' Diamond said.

CHAPTER 26

You have to be a real asshole to get searched crossing *into* Mexico.

Or a six-foot plus tall Viking with too many tats and not enough cash to be a rock star. They had the Tempest's rear seat out and were getting a cutting torch to attack the fenders when an RV full of drunks in hunting camo caught their attention. Like fucking locusts they moved on, leaving the Tempest in pieces.

Americans pride themselves on their ingenuity and work ethic—best in the world. Nope. Mexicans. They see a hole in the market, they fill that bitch. Three skinny kids in grease-stained coveralls appeared out of the shadows.

"Man, they fucked your ride up."

"No respect for the classics, right? Damn." The oldest was maybe twenty. He looked over the parts and my belongings, shook his head. "You ain't got no tools...you are fucked."

"You have tools?"

"Sure, what kinda mechanic don't have tools?"

"How much?"

"Two hundred, cash."

"Eighty." I gave him a hard guy face, but my heart wasn't in it. The fucker had to make his bills just like the rest of us wage monkeys.

"Ok, I like you," he lied. "One hundred and you get us a six-pack of cold cervezas."

"Done." We shook hands like it still meant something. It did to me. A fucked up sense of honor, doing what I say I will, hand shakes sealing a deal, ...all that old world bullshit would one day get me killed. There is a line in the The Wild Bunch, one of the few movies I could ever sit through:, "It matters who you give your word to." Or something like that. But that's bullshit. Morals don't shift to fit a situation. I have very few morals, so the ones I got I need to keep strong.

A six-pack and twenty minutes later the Tempest was good as new. They even washed her at no charge. Leaning in the shade with the boss mechanic, finishing our beer, he smiled and pointed at the rear body panel, the one made of carbon fiber that hid a thin compartment with my guns, cash and alternate IDs. "Your guy, he did good work. Here or Norte?"

"Norte."

"Solid. Those border boys never would find it."

"This a shakedown?" I was ready to drag his skinny ass into the shadows if he answered wrong.

"Chill, die young worrying like that. I was just admiring the workmanship." The calm camaraderie was gone. I drained my beer and hit the road.

At the Tecate cut off I parked behind a Pemex station and recovered the Ruger. It was raining lightly but still too warm for the vest, so I left it and the scattergun hidden. Rolling into Ensenada, I knew of two ways to get to Señor Sanchez: find his mansion some place up on gringo hill, or fuck with his cash stream and wait for him to show up. I went with door number two.

Wet Pussy, the neon sign said. It had a Fritz the Cat painting of a wet, big-titted kitty working a pole next to the entrance. Got to love a strip club that has no pretensions. Glendale, CA has The Gentleman's Club. Gives the impression of an empire-era smoking library, with high-backed faux leather club chairs. In fact, it was a shitty warehouse of a joint where men sat in booths while Eastern European girls rubbed their asses on guys' crotches until they busted a nut in their Jockeys. Wet Pussy is just what it sounds like—a stage with a pole, tables to drink at while making the deal, and seven red-doored rooms behind the dance floor.

A teenager with tiny breasts, pigtails and shaved pubic hair was dancing at the edge of the stage for a sweaty, middle-aged gringo. He was dropping dollars on the stage one at a time, slow, like it was big green. His full focus was on her childlike body.

I didn't hold back.

I hit him full force on the side of his head with the Ruger. It's a heavy piece, weighing close to three pounds fully loaded. It connected with his lust-flushed cheek with a meaty thud. He flew sideways, blood spraying from his torn ear. The baby dancer screamed. I put the boots to the guy's ribs and he puked tacos and blood. The bouncer was almost on me when I spun. Broke his nose with the revolver's barrel. He was a big man, but not built, fat. He didn't go down, so I cocked the Ruger. That massive hole stared death at him. He dropped to his knees and fought back tears.

One of the red doors opened. A drunken sailor stepped out with a young girl under each arm. When he saw the mayhem at my feet he released the girls and charged. He was military fit. Young. Wild. He almost made it to me before the stool I hurled busted across his chest. Give him props, he kept coming. I clubbed him with the Ruger and drove my knee up into his nuts. He gasped. I kicked his nuts again as he went down. I ran to the red doors, kicking them open. They were empty. It was early. They stank of sex sweat and pine-scented disinfectant.

With the pistol, I motioned the freaked-out whores to sit at the bar.

"What the fuck, dude? They liked—"

I kicked the sailor in the head. That shut him the fuck up. I zip-tied his wrists.

"I have a family, don't kill me, I can pay." Sweaty man was at the bargaining stage.

"You have a daughter?" I whispered in his ear.

"Yes, two."

I kicked him hard enough to hear a rib snap.

With the three men in ghetto cuffs, I pushed a table against the front door. The woman behind the bar looked near sixty. She'd seen all sorts of bad craziness, took this in stride. She poured me a tall tequila without needing to be asked. I drank it in one long pull.

"Call Señor Sanchez. Tell him Moses McGuire is here." She didn't play games, didn't act like she didn't know the man she worked for. She spoke rapid Spanish into a cell then handed it to me.

"Hello, this is Roberto Sanchez. My father is otherwise engaged. How may I help you?"

"Stanford?"

"Berkley, how did you know?"

"You don't sound like a big enough prick to be East Coast. Tell daddy he has ten minutes to get to the Wet Pussy before I start taking apart some tourists." I dropped the phone and crushed it under my heel.

"Uno mas?" the bartender asked.

"Why not." I made a circular motion including the naked and near-naked girls. The girls sat at the bar chirping away in Spanish. The oldest was maybe sixteen, wearing a paisley robe open, showing her naked body. Her hair was cropped short and brilliant blonde. Every once in a while she'd flash her big brown eyes my way—just enough flirt to see if that was what I wanted—uncross her arms and give me a full look at her breasts. If I was a pedophile, this would be a real playground.

"Bro, my hands are numb, what you say?"

Sailor boy started to cry when I stomped on his ankle. Heard a bone crack. Wanted to crush his head. The front door opening took my attention. The table I'd pushed against it gave me enough time to roll over the bar. Two men in black tact gear and ski masks came in low and ready. They swept the club with their MP5s.

I watched them in the mirror.

I put in my earplugs.

Waited.

They turned away from the bar.

I popped up.

Shot one took out a black clad knee. Shot two nailed his partner, who was spinning to shoot me. Took him in the left leg, just below the body armor. Boom, boom, and the room went quiet. I dropped down. Opened the Ruger's cylinder and replaced the two spent shells.

"That was my security team, I suspect," Sanchez said through the open door.

"Was. They're down but still armed. You might wanna tell them to take their fingers off the triggers."

"La guerra acabó," he shouted, and just that quick they slid the machine guns out of reach. "I'm coming in. Shoot me, the men out here will burn the place to the ground." It wasn't a threat, not his style, he was just laying out cause and effect. He looked slick as ever. Not a hair out of place. Sharp suit, carrying an alligator briefcase.

"Come, let the paramédicos do their work." I followed him across the club. He looked at the broken customers and shook his head but said nothing.

The office was rich, class. Modern, leather chairs and a glass and steel desk that cost more than my car. The door closed like a vault. Silence. There was a subtle hiss, calming, like distance surf. It cancelled what little sound escaped through the wall.

Sanchez led us to a small sitting area with matching leather couch and chair. The glass coffee table was a miniature of the desk. He popped the latches on the briefcase. I fought the need to draw down on him. He turned the case around. It was stuffed with packets of hundreds surrounding a bottle of 25-year-old Macallan. He placed two crystal tumblers between us, filling each.

"Drink, then talk." The single malt was pure peat smoke and sherry oak casks. Smooth. Warm. A liquid embrace from the prettiest girl in the room. "Good, no?"

"It's good. You have a plan that works out with you and me walking out alive?"

"Oh, Moses, Moses. Life is never that dire. Question? Why the tourists? They were no threat. Why?"

"Pissed me off. What's the money for?"

"I want to hire you. I should have from the start."

"You know Rollens is dead."

He pulled out his cell phone and clicked to a video. It was Rollens. She was screaming, contorted, almost inhuman. The machete was inside her. Sanchez turned it off. "I was sent that this morning. Message clear."

"She was working for you?"

"They thought she was."

I gulped the sipping whiskey. Sacrilege. Filled the glass and gulped a second down as well. Took out the Ruger and pointed it between Sanchez's eyes. He got very still. Good move. I breathed. I considered pulling the trigger.

Mikayla's voice whispered in my ear. *Kill him. No hesitation.*

"Freedom. Was. She. Real?"

"Who?" A bead of sweat rolled out of his perfect hairline.

"Freedom, Rollens's niece. Was she real?"

"Yes, as far as I know. An ICE officer with common interests sent Rollens to me. She was looking for a missing girl. You were the natural choice."

My finger started to tighten on the trigger. A second bead ran from his hair. His face was peaceful, all except for the slightest twitch in the outer corner of his left eye.

I let the moment hang.

It wasn't bullshit.

I was deciding how to play this. Pull the trigger? Fight my way out? Die in Mexico? Never see Sunshine again?

No happy ending, Mo, we die covered in our enemy's gore.

"Not this time," I answered Mikayla. Sanchez was starting to break.

"I... I chose you, Mr. McGuire. When my ICE contact told me about the cop and her missing niece, I put you up."

"Why?"

"Can you lower the gun?"

"No. Why?"

"I send putas Norte, LA. Only they don't make it to the customers. No one sees them. Desaparecer. I'm out a large sum of money. I have upset customers. Sex trade is drying up down here. Cartel bullshit scares people off I think. I can't afford this interruption in my cash flow."

"So Rollens and me, you staked us out like lambs, hoping to flush out whoever's snatching your whores? Only I fucked that up when I killed your stalkers."

"Yes, you killed two more of my good men. I don't hold this against you."

"Rollens died ugly because you weren't straight."

"It wasn't personal."

"It is always personal." I pulled the trigger. At four feet the flame caught his hair on fire. The slug dug a groove in his scalp, but didn't enter his skull. Blood flowed freely.

Pussy, Mikayla said.

I didn't answer her, she was right. But I was playing a long game.

"One day I will have you killed for that." With a silk handkerchief he cleaned the blood off his face. "No man disrespects me and lives."

"Bullshit. You tell your employees anything you need to, keep them in line. But you and I both know you got a good woman killed hard. When this is over, I will be coming."

"Bold talk. My men out there, I," he snapped his fingers, "and you are a bad memory."

I smiled, a cold, mirthless grin. "Whatever you say. We done?"

There were at least ten guns pointed at the office door when we opened it. So I guess it wasn't that soundproof. He came out first, waving his men off with a smile and a joke in Spanish I didn't understand. Sanchez had mopped up the blood and a black Stetson covered the singed patch of hair. As we passed the bar, only the bartender remained, the chicas scattered to the wind. The johns were both being wheeled out on gurneys. I had no elusions that this afternoon's adventures would change their view on fucking kids. It would take the grave to make that transformation.

Sanchez worked the room, slipped each of the local cops a small wedge, ensuring that the police report would leave me and Sanchez out of it.

A young man who could only be his son fronted me. He had long hair hanging loosely over his shoulders. An unconstructed suit, silk t-shirt. My bet was he spent a cool grand to look like he didn't care. "Stephan Sanchez." He stuck out his hand. I looked from it up to his eyes. "You are the famous McGuire."

"That's right, kid, mostly for killing men like you."

"You think you could kill me?"

"Sure. Killing's easy. You just have to have less invested in living than the other guy. That's the trick, care less. I give you that for free."

"Tough, got it. Huge balls, got it." He leaned in, whispering in my ear. "When this bullshit ends, if the old man is dead? You and me, we have no beef." He slapped my shoulder and was gone. Did he mean if I had to drop his pop he didn't want me coming after him? Or did he mean if I dropped his pop he would owe me a favor? Fuck it. This was one of those moments when I was glad I never knew my old man, and far as I knew, I had no son out there plotting my demise.

The bottle of single malt was under my arm, the briefcase with two hundred grand in my hand. The Ruger was back in my belt holster. Sanchez and I'd struck a deal. I would find Freedom.

If in doing so I found his missing women, I would tell him who had them.

If I happened to kill the sons of bitches, he had another briefcase full of cash for me.

I made it clear, when this was done one of us might have to kill the other.

"Once it is done," he said. We shook on the deal. Between us, that meant something.

Or I hoped it did.

CHAPTER 27

"Big man, you need something I have." The blonde teenager from the Wet Pussy was leaning on the Tempest. She had jeans and a Zapata t-shirt. She had inked *Yankee go home* across the front.

"Love the shirt."

"Fuck Yankee bullshit." She was hard. I liked her.

"What do you have I need?" She stood looking up at me. If she was five foot in her Converse I'd be amazed.

"You got cash?" She looked at the briefcase, making clear it wasn't a real question. "Come on." She climbed into the Tempest's passenger seat. Sixteen and giving all the orders. She took me deep into one of the rougher barrios, up against the mountains, had me park behind a garage.

"If you're setting me up, you are about to lose a lot of friends." The Ruger was back in my hand.

"You no want to fuck me, right?"

"Right."

"I no want to fuck you."

"Claro. So what do you want?"

"One hundred American."

"For?"

"I know where the girls are going." Her eyes shifted, looking to be sure we weren't being watched. "You know MS-13?"

"LA, Salvador, mean motherfuckers."

"They global, cabrón. Baja cartel? Bullshit. Mara Salvatrucha is global. You want your girl, you ask those sons of bitches." Then she told me I hadn't a chance in hell of surviving meeting them. Told me they caught her brother selling mota they hadn't sanctioned. Chopped him up. Mailed his ears and eyes to her mother. Her face was angry, fierce as any warrior. And she was fucking strangers for twenty bucks a toss.

I gave her a grand. I didn't waste her time with a lecture on all the things she could do with her life. It would have been bullshit. World is stacked against her. Most I had done was give her a couple of months without sweating the rent.

From the farmacía, I picked up a jar of Vicodin and one of Adderall, great speed they gave to kids with ADHD, perfect for what I had in mind. I packed the carbon fiber body panel full of cash and drugs and firearms. Crazy is what this was calling for. Only this time I was going to control the drugs, not the other way around. It was all about monitoring my intake.

Mikayla laughed at me. *You do what you need to do to get this shit done.*

I crunched two Vics and chased them with a beer to get her out of my head. I wanted to be mellow at the border crossing. Turned out I didn't need to worry. I breezed through Customs like I had diplomatic plates. Border guard even called me sir when he handed me back my passport, told me to have a good day. Kenny said his paper was good. It was better than good, it was goddamn golden.

The whiskey, beer and Vics went a long way toward taking the edge off the adrenaline Mexico left raging through my heart. For at least a moment, plowing up highway 5 with Shane MacGowan and The Pogues blaring, I didn't feel like taking anyone's head off. It wasn't peaceful—I was way too far down this death trail for peaceful—but it was...something less than rage, and I was willing to call that an improvement.

From a truck stop, I called Kenny while filling the ever-hungry tank. He passed me off to Peter. "Mo, fuck. No, really, fuck. These are big-time power brokers you are fucking with." He sounded almost clean and almost sober. "I went in from every legit channel. Pulitzer Prize fucking reporters won't touch it. The L-Fucking-A Weekly called it a wild, rambling rumor. This is after seeing the pix. Fuck, right? Fuck. AP, no. BBC, no. Al Jazeera? Maybe, but that may do us more harm than good. Right? Fuck. Blog? Who gives a fuck? Tweet until the cows come home and still fucked."

"Got it. Keep digging. It links to missing hookers." I told Peter all of the Sanchez conversation. Told him about Mara Salvatrucha's connection to missing girls, maybe.

"MS-fucking-13? They are cells in cells. Like chasing a thousand-headed snake."

"Slow down, Peter, please."

"OK, right, it's you, and you know shit from shit. MS-13 is spreading worldwide, why? A, they are the evilest motherfuckers on the block. B, they have no command structure. Every clique has its own boss. Wipe one out though, and the whole anthill of psychos comes down on your ass. They have strict alliances. You with me? We talking, Moses? Death fucking machines. Yes?"

"Yes. How do I find them? The one's got Freedom, killed Rollens?"

"Easy, yeah..." I could hear his smart wheels spinning like crazy. "Ok, not solid, but a plan?" I heard him talking in a rapid mumble to Kenny.

"Lay it out."

"Got it. Here, Kenny, tell him." I heard Peter fire a joint, take a long inhale and hold it while Kenny spoke.

"Peter's idea, we do a city grid of concentration of solicitation arrests. Last 48 hours. Compare and contrast to six months ago. Maybe we find out where the girls are, if they are in the state still. It's not a bad start point."

"Not fucking bad? Fucking brilliant." Peter coughed as he spoke.

"We'll refine as we work," Kenny said.

"Then do it." I hung up before he could ask if I wanted to talk to Sunshine. My speech was just slurred enough for her to guess how far I'd fallen off the wagon. I don't know why I cared. Wasn't like I'd said I wouldn't use anymore. Wasn't like I was working a program. I just took a vacation to get my head straight. Now I needed it cloudy.

Gregor's face didn't change when I dropped Sanchez's cash on his card table. "Two things. Take your family on a vacation. Hawaii, some place these bastards can't touch you. Second, if I don't come back for this cash, forget you knew my name."

"That it, Boss?"

"Yeah, I guess it is."

"Then bullshit. I'll send my family away. My cousin has a cabin off the grid. I roll with you."

"Not this time, pal. This is a one-way ride."

"Maybe yes, Maybe no."

"No, got it? No."

"He is going with you," Anya said. I hadn't seen her standing in the doorway. She held their baby in her arms. "Maybe you can stop him. I know I can't." She turned back into the house.

I sat on the back patio smoking while he packed up his family. Angel leaned against my leg. I stroked her side. Her eye was healing well. Her depth perception sucked, but she was alive. Nika moved up behind me, pressing herself against my back. She leaned over to take my cigarette. She inhaled then put the cig between my lips. Her eyes were coy.

"Come here." I had her sit sidesaddle on my lap.

"Yes, Moses?"

"Nika, you know I could never love anyone as much as I do you."

"But..."

"No but." I guided her head down so it rested on my shoulder. I could feel her breath warm on my skin. "What happened in Mexico."

"Shhh, we don't have to."

"Yes, we do. You and I both know that wasn't sex. For a long time I thought I had raped you."

"You didn't."

"Quiet. I have to finish. I did what I had to, to save your life. I get that now. I know how I must have looked to you: your battered, bloody, Viking savior. But what I am is a killer. A drunk. Pretty sure I'm clinically insane. And I'm a fraud. The reason I went to rescue you? It was because I thought it would make your sister want to fuck me." I could feel her tears soft on my neck.

"I don't care. I love you," she said in the quietest of whispers.

I held her tight. "I love you, Nika."

"Just not..."

"No." There was so much more to say. I just didn't have the words. So I held her and let her cry. Held her until her tears stopped. Until she punched my chest and sat up.

"You're a jerk, Moses." She was smiling.

"True."

"Took my cherry, least you can do is marry me. Get that panic out of your face, I'm kidding." She leaned forward and gave me a warm kiss on my cheek. "I get this can't work, but when I'm thirty and you are a hundred and twenty, then look out."

She was kidding, and she wasn't. It would take her what it took to see me clearly for what I was: her Uncle Moses.

CHAPTER 28

I have never seen Gregor cry, even when his arm was blown off. Heard the motherfucker scream in rage and pain, but never cry. His eyes were wet when he loaded his family into the Chrysler. Angel jumped in the back. As Gregor was buckling his boy in, Anya whispered to me. "You are a good man. Bring him back to me." She kissed my cheek.

After they left, Gregor opened his gun safe. He'd modified an AK style shotgun with a drum magazine. Held a hundred rounds. Folding stock. Shoulder strap. It hung under his black greatcoat. His CZ 75 had a custom extended magazine that held forty rounds. "Shooting one-handed? Easy. Reloading is the bitch."

"If you need to reload, we can stack your kills as a barricade." The corner of his mouth tilted up, almost to a smile.

He gave me a 1911 in a shoulder holster. Target trigger job. Throated mag well. The slide moved like oil on glass. Gregor had spent his downtime perfecting his gunsmithing skills. Ruger in my belt, .45 under my arm, and a Mossberg in the trunk. I felt as safe as a walking target could.

Gregor dug the Tempest. Didn't say so, but the way he moved his head to the beat of the rumble said it all.

"Where to, Boss?"

"The beginning. Pimp whose ear I took off seems good as any. He said he was protected. Could have been bullshit."

"Probably."

"But could be for real."

"One way to find out if he is protected? Bust his shit up and see who comes out of the brush."

"That's the plan."

It was back to East LA, only this time there wasn't a single woman selling favors in front of the graveyard. The track was gone. I parked behind a taco truck. I didn't bother asking Gregor what he wanted, ordered him an al pastor burrito with extra radishes. I had a carnitas, extra hot sauce. From the gas station I bought a six-pack of Pacífico and a pack of Marlboros. Two beers got the cook sitting with us on the hood of the Tempest.

"Man, I owned this Tempest, I'd paint it. Candy. You wanna sell it?"

"You wanna sell a lung?"

"No, I see your point." He fired a joint and passed it to me. Gregor said he needed a piss, but I knew he was scoping the area. Covering my ass.

"Your friend, he don't speak much?"

"Not much." I hit the joint hard, passed it back. "I used to pick up chicks here."

"And there it is." His eyes went cold. "Cop? Na, muscle, but whose?"

"What the fuck?" I started, but quit before I looked stupider. "Truth. I'm looking for a girl. Kidnapped. She was dragged into the life."

"Shit is hard all over. You the guy took off Van Nuys Paulie's ear? You the guy burned a tug joint down? You do all they say?" His hand slipped into his apron.

"Most of it."

"Here." He passed me the joint. "Might as well be stoned when you meet the devil." As the joint touched my lips, he pulled. A nasty black snubnosed almost made it clear before I placed two slugs from my .45 in the center of his chest. Double tap. His apron was spreading red as he hit the sidewalk. He would have to die alone.

From behind the gas station I heard the rapid popping of a 9mm. I did a full Starsky over the Tempest's hood and was cranking it before I was even seated. I stomped gas and lit the tires. A 180 burned rubber into the road. I was doing fifty-plus when I hit the gas station. At that speed it was hard to assess anything. A black SUV stood between me and where I assumed Gregor was. Muzzle flashes lit up a dumpster, followed by machine gun fire flashing through the smoked windows of the SUV.

Fuck it. The Tempest was roaring like the V8 from hell when it hit the gas pump, squashing it against the luxe SUV. Petrol showered over them as I reversed in a cloud of rubber smoke. I was twenty feet away when it went wrong for those assholes. Gregor stood up, let rip with the shotgun on full auto. One of the idiots returned fire. The flare from his barrel mixed with the liquid and gaseous petrol.

Flame blotted out the night, searing my pupils as they rushed to contract. Heat rolled over the Tempest. And just that fast, the fireball was gone. The SUV was on its side. A cinder man with no legs was dragging himself away from the heat. I put a .45 in the back of his skull. There were four other torched bodies. Each got a .45 in the brainpan. At least one was still alive when I shot him. Fuck them. Fuck them all.

Gregor's greatcoat was smoking, but other than missing some hair and his eyebrows he was intact. He watched me execute the burnt men without a blink. War has its own rules. You come for ours, we take yours. We ask no quarter, none is given.

In the gas station, I found the owner. He was hiding behind a Fritos display speaking rapid Spanish into a cell phone. He had MS-13 prison ink on his neck. One shot to his chest sent blood spraying over the crispy snack treats. I should have felt bad for killing him. Maybe I would later. Maybe not. I found the bloody cell.

"This is Moses McGuire."

"Who the fuck are you, dead pendejo?"

"You have a girl I want."

"Besa mi culo, puto."

"I'll leave her picture."

"One more concha, who cares?"

"Every day I don't have her, more of your soldiers die."

"They are not afraid to die!"

I tried to come up with a macho line, but I was tired of this bullshit. Many were going to die. Maybe me. Maybe Gregor. Pithy didn't seem like the way to play this.

I stomped the phone.

I stapled Freedom's picture to the dying man's forehead, used his blood to write my cell phone number on the floor.

I used club soda to wash the blood off my face and hands.

Gregor was in the Tempest, smoking a cigarette and drinking a beer.

"Think the message was clear enough?" I asked, crunching down two more Vics as I rolled onto Cesar Chavez Ave.

"Depends on the message."

"Give us the fucking girl." I used the Tempest's lighter to fire a Marlboro.

"Then no," he said, blowing smoke out the window. "They will not give her to us. You know that, Boss. This will either force them to mail you her head, or keep her safe just in case you are as crazy as the rumors say."

"Fuck. I'm playing chicken with a thirteen-year-old girl's life? That it?"

"Save this bullshit for women. You and me, we know she is dead. Or worse. We know this is revenge, not rescue."

"Yeah? Then why the fuck are you here? Really, why?"

"Boss, you need to kill these men, yes?"

"I don't know." I told the truth.

"I do." He told the deeper truth.

We drove across East LA. Something was bugging me, kept ticking at the back of my mind. Finally, I dialed Kenny.

"Any police chatter about a shooting, or fireball, on Cesar Chavez Ave. in the last half hour?"

"Hi, Moses, all social niceties gone? Fuck me and treat me like Moneypenny?"

"Sunshine, I thought you—"

"I know, baby."

"Who's Moneypenny?"

"Lord, you are lucky you can fuck, because there are rooms full of what you don't know." I should have been insulted. Wasn't.

Ten minutes later, Kenny could definitively report nothing was being reported. I told Sunshine the whole bloody BBQ. No way the cops weren't called.

"Get your tall ass back here. This shit is going sideways fast. Stay off the freeways. A clear route will hit the GPS on your phone. Kenny will keep it updated. Moses?"

"Yeah, darlin'?"

"If the cops catch you, I never get to kiss you again."

"Then let's make sure that doesn't happen."

ONE MORE BODY

Gregor took control of the cell phone, telling me when to turn. Crossing LA without seeing a cop would be a miracle. And at the moment I was feeling clean out of those tricky little bitches.

CHAPTER 29

"Right on South Burger." I shot him a look, but Gregor's eyes were glued to the phone. "Damn, left on Indian...no, Whittier. Cop's heading east. Pull into that parking lot." And so it went, checker-boarding our way west across LA. Me, I love following directions, always have. I certainly never hit my C.O. for sending us down a sniper alley in the Root. Paperwork confirms he hit his head on a low doorway. If they didn't need grunts ballsy enough to take lead he would have charged me. I was sixteen, pissed off and indestructible. Lost in memories of Beirut, I failed to notice the cop car pull out of an alley and flip on his cherry.

"What the fuck, Gregor?"

"Kenny, we have a problem," he said into the phone.

"I'm going jackrabbit."

"Kenny says he can block the cop's radio. Ten minutes, max, before the station bounces a distress call."

"Buckle up, baby boy." I was grinning wildly when I gave the V8 full gas. The Quadrajet kicked in with a high whine. I hit a red button on the dash and let the nitrous flow. It was good for over 400 hp. The torque pinned me back into the seat. I was doing 130 when I bounced across Cypress. Give the cop his due, the mother was hanging tough—barely, but still in the rearview. I locked the brakes at La Cienega, spun the wheel left and hit the gas. We fishtailed like mad but made the turn.

"Time?"

"Four minutes."

"Fuck." Near the top of La Cienega were the oil leases. Big, rusted grasshoppers dredging away. At 140 mph, the fence gave way like it was made of wet tissue. I locked the wheels, dust and dirt clods spraying around us. The passenger side was facing the oncoming cop. The dust trail slowed him some. When he saw Gregor's full auto shotgun he locked his wheels, stopped feet from the Tempest.

I materialized out of the dust, standing by his window. My .45 was aimed center mass. With my left index finger, I motioned down and he lowered the widow.

"How old are you?"

"Twenty-six."

"Ok, twenty-six. Do you want to die tonight?"

"No, sir, I don't. Will, but don't want to."

Gregor held up the cell phone. Time was up.

"Good news: I don't want to kill you. So let's play it very cool. Touch that Glock, it gets bloody." Leaning in, I ripped the mic off the radio. Next I tore out the keyboard.

"Step out. Slow. Easy." He did. I took his Glock and cell phone. "You'll need to step into the back seat." He complied. I handcuffed him to the D-ring.

"Twenty-six, you played this straight." I cleared the Glock and dropped the magazine. I tossed them in with him. "Don't touch that till we're gone."

"Yes, sir."

"Tell your Chief, what is his name?"

"Dobbs, Chief Dobbs."

"You tell Chief Dobbs that Moses McGuire is coming for his ass. No judge, no jury. If he's dirty, he pays the freight.

That goes for any blue boys who have strayed and are covering up for MS-13. Think they're scary?"

"Yes, sir."

"I torched six of their soldiers tonight." I leaned in, giving him the full benefit of what prison will do to a man's eyes. He looked away after a moment. "You just met real fucking scary. Tell your boss, next time I catch a blue boy I will be taking heads." I slammed the door, knowing there was no handle on the inside. A night in the hills was a hell of a lot better than what he deserved if he was dirty. But he didn't vibe dirty.

I circled the industrial area until Kenny said we were clean. He had the Tempest in and the roller door closed in about three seconds flat.

"You do any motherfucking thing quiet?" Kenny asked.

"Nope. I run, gun and let someone with a higher pay grade sort out the corpses."

"Neanderthal." He meant it as a putdown, but I knew what was coming could only be dealt with by a beast.

"Kenny, baby boy, get Mr. McGuire's car to Enrique. Bodywork, spray."

"I know what to do, Sunshine. All the hell over it."

I tossed him the keys. Sunshine was dressed in a black leather corset, her cleavage spilling out over the top. "This has to be the ever amazing Gregor." She took his hand and shook it warmly. "You must be tired." Gregor scanned the room. "It is safe, high-tech. Nothing moves within a mile that we don't know about."

"If you say so."

"We have a crow's nest, no bed up there."

"It'll do." He climbed the iron ladder, shotgun showing under his greatcoat.

In Sunshine's bedroom, I lifted her into the bed. She was looking uncomfortable. "Nervous doesn't suit you, darlin'. I shouldn't of brought this to your door."

"Yeah, big guy, that's it. You can be thick."

"So spell it out. You got another man? You ain't into white men?"

"Dense and getting denser every word. Shut up and listen."

"That an order?"

"Yes. You can take it, or roll on."

I looked at her, turned, made it to the door before turning back.

She started unlacing her corset. "Come here." It fell away from her body.

"Darlin', I got no idea what this is we got going on here," I told her. "Naming it don't change it or make it any stronger. Fact is, it won't last, but for now let's enjoy each other."

"Someone set the hook deep in you and yanked hard."

"Cass. She took me for a ride, confirmed for me that love is a whore's promise. Taught me not to trust my gut with girls."

"Girls? How old was she?"

"Twenty-two. But it wasn't like that."

"It is always like that. Baby, I'm fifty-four. I got some years on you."

"You look younger and finer than I deserve."

"Black don't crack. But I have the mileage, trust me. So before we go deeper into whatever this is or isn't, you need to know some shit."

"You fucked some men, I fucked some girls, can we leave it at that?"

"Bigger than that. Come here." I lay with my head on her breasts, listening to her heartbeat and her lungs fill up with air. I also listened to her words. "I was sixteen when I killed for the first time."

"I was sixteen when I joined the Marines, doesn't mean—"

"You will shut the fuck up or sleep alone."

I started to say something, thought better and kept my mouth shut. She smiled for an instant, then it faded.

"It was payback. The night I was conceived, three thugs went after my father. Beat him to death, crippled my mother. Doesn't make it right, just telling you the facts. When I was sixteen I executed those men one by one. I even convinced a rival to pay me thirty grand for taking them out. Afterward, I didn't feel guilt. I felt relief, almost happy. With the cash I could stop stripping. Killing one man is hard. Killing two is near impossible. But after three it just started to come naturally."

She was stoking my hair absentmindedly while she continued. "The LA mob heard of me. I thought they were going to kill me, instead they offered me a job silencing a talkative dealer. I popped him, I think in a carwash. No, a...oh hell, Moses, I lost count of how many men I killed. I was doing speed, staying up all night, looking for bigger and rougher hits. San Francisco, the deal was to take out some triad punks who had forgotten to pay to play in a mobbed-up town. Six armed guys. Thirty-six hours since my last sleep. I was half in the bag. I tossed a frag in the window. Then another. Hit the sidewalk. Glass and body parts rained down. I ran in with a M16, blasting. Killed a waiter and a lobster tank. The six I was after weren't even in the main dining room. Dead and dying civilians moaned. I felt numb. I looked down. A dead kid, and I was numb. Moses, I killed a kid."

"Finish it. I want to hear it all."

"I kicked into the back room. I killed five clean, the sixth nailed my back. I took him out as I fell. My driver got me out of SF, took me to a private doctor in Oakland. This was eleven years ago. I hadn't taken a life again until I did to save you."

"No guilt on that, they chose the move."

"Agreed. When I was rehabbing, I slowly started to feel things. It took years, but finally I saw that life was amazing and death was final. I was no longer numb. I cried for a month. Since then, I have learned to take pleasure where I find it. I don't look back and I don't count my tomorrows."

"I killed a woman in Beirut. Another in Mexico." I told her.

"I put a poodle in a nuker to get a mob guy's gumar to give up her man."

"Did you cook the pooch?"

"Didn't have to."

"Then you're clean on that one."

"Nope, big guy. I would have. Almost did. It stays on the count."

"I used to let baby girls friction fuck me in the lap dance room."

"I shot a man in the face while fucking him."

"I let a girl think she loved me so I could keep her by my side."

"I slit a man's throat in a tub surrounded by candles."

"I beat a priest with a barbwire-wrapped piece of two by four."

"You win." She kissed the top of my head. And someplace deep opened.

I lay silent for a long time. Not gathering courage, gathering strength. It was now, or I'd never say what came next. "My mother was a gin-head who loved Jesus and drinking and not much more. When I was six, her pastor was over. She passed out. I never told a soul this."

"You don't have to." She was stroking my hair again.

"He bent me over the dresser. There was blood in my Jockies after he was done. I hated myself for letting him take that from me. Take my power. Take control of my body. I hated him for making me helpless and weak. Luke, my older brother, once told me only way a man gets his power back is to win it, said it was a Viking thing. The pastor came back the next week. After mom passed out he took me into the bedroom for our secret time. He wasn't ready for what hit him. That barbed wire tore him the fuck up. No one heard his screams as I went after his legs. Blood was filling his shoes when he stumbled out. Never saw him again. I didn't feel numb, I felt like my Viking ancestors—victorious."

We lay there silent for a long time. When we made love, it was more a healing ritual than sex. I fell asleep still inside her. Even with all the bullshit raining on me, I slept peacefully.

CHAPTER 30

I was eating breakfast with the ever-expanding crew. Peter and Kenny were having a heated discussion about the death of print news.

"Ink is the only truly vetted news source."

"The papers are owned by same motherfuckers they should be investigating. Name one major paper owned by a person of color."

Blah, blah, blah.

Sunshine held my hand. When she thought I wasn't looking, she would look me over and smile.

Their shower was industrial. One line of showerheads, reminded me of prison. I was searing my flesh, hot as I could stand it. Mikayla appeared out of the steam. The heat couldn't touch her. She dressed all in black, shoulder holsters crisscrossing her torso.

Saw you last night. She was disappointed.

"Saw what?"

Saw you let the pig live.

"Twenty-six? I don't kill innocents."

He's not an innocent. Victim. She held up her fingers, counting. *Abuser. Collaborator. Hero. That is it. No others. He was police, protecting a pimp. He was a Collaborator.*

"Must feel good, being so certain. I don't kill innocents."

Even that woman in the Root? You think saving this young woman will clear that debt?

"No. That's life's job."

Get away from this woman Sunshine. She is turning you human. It will get you killed.

"Quitting is impossible. So is leaving her."

The psycho ghost with a battle-axe to grind dissolved into wisps of vapor. I'm sure she was still hiding in the shadows, with all my other ghosts.

When Kenny stepped out of the steam buck naked, I almost punched a hole in his head. He ducked and saved us both the embarrassment of explaining our naked tussle to Sunshine.

"Whoa, ease up man."

I answered him with a stare that finally made him cast down his eyes.

"Never step up on a man in the shower, unless you intend to stab him."

"Um, ok. Who were you taking to when I came in?"

"No one."

"Sounded like—"

"Nothing. Like nothing."

"Yeah, that's right. Now I remember it sounded like nothing."

I flipped the handle to as cold as I could stand. Held myself in place until I was dotted with gooseflesh. Having finished the ice water treatment, I started toweling off. Kenny stepped in beside me.

"Stand that close in Pelican Bay, you'll get a shank or a cock in your ass."

"Cool. I'll remember that if I'm ever stupid enough to get arrested." He stared hard as he could. I had to laugh.

"You're alright, kid." I pulled on my Levi's, started lacing up my Docs.

Kenny got dressed, watching me, puzzling out a problem. "I have never seen her like this, not even near."

"How?"

"She's... fuck, it's like she's almost happy."

"Seemed happy when we met."

"Counterfeit. She is flawless at making people believe she's happy when she smells money. A waft of green and she rolls out the party girl."

Standing, I caught a look at myself in the mirror. I looked like shit. Forty extra pounds of beer and carnitas, scars intertwined with tattoos. Caught Kenny looking at the scars across my back. "You ever kill a man, Kenny?"

"No, sir."

"Don't if you can help it. Barring that, don't let them shoot you. It hurts."

I was on my second cup of coffee and first painkiller when Ice-T's "Cop Killer" came blasting out of my pocket. Kenny and Peter were laughing at my confused face. When I finally got the phone out, the readout said Lowrie.

"Moses."

"Detective."

"You are fucked six ways to Sunday. They want you for kidnapping an officer. The APB said you are armed and extremely dangerous."

"They say anything about the six bangers I smoked in East LA last night? No, right?"

"Chief Dobbs has you on his shoot-on-sight list. He's spreading rumors you shot a cop in Reno."

"Just to watch him die?"

"This isn't funny, McGuire."

"No, it's not. Is this the part where you ask me to turn myself in, tell me you can protect me?"

"Son, that would be a bald-ass lie. If I was your father, I'd tell you to find a deep hole and start digging for China."

"But you're not my father."

"No, I'm an angry cop. Find the freaks who butchered Rollens and take them off the count. We clear on that?"

"You're saying I should kill them."

"Yes, son, that's exactly what I am saying. There are MS-13 soldiers being protected by LAPD. I don't know if the bangers did Rollens, but LAPD doctored her file. She's just another drunk driver now."

"How many bad cops you have?"

"Wrong question, son. How many good? That may be easier to count. Ninety percent of people are sheep, that's convicts, cops, whatever. It's the ten percent that lead you have to look out for. This deal here we have going, it makes Rampart look like a blip."

"Is he dirty, your Chief?"

"As sin, and he isn't my Chief. Dobbs tells us it's just politics. Said we had to make peace with MS-13, let them control the other gangs. We are outnumbered and outgunned, yes, but this crap makes us no better than the criminals we are paid to arrest."

"Make me a deal, Lowrie. If I disappear, make them bleed."

"Will do. Want to hear something corny?"

"No."

"Who cares what you want. I grew up in Hollywood, and all I ever wanted to be was a cop. I love this city, Moses, let's not let them have it."

"We'll burn her to the ground before we'll let them have her." I hung up, ate two more Vics. Sunshine took my hand in hers and held it. I could feel my pulse slow.

I passed what Lowrie said to me on to Peter and Kenny. Peter wanted Lowrie to go on the record. I knew he wouldn't. He was dying and had a pension to protect, for his wife.

"I came across this tidbit." Peter was digging through a pile of old school yellow legal pads. "Señor Sanchez? He has a son."

"I know, I told you I met him."

"Not him, another. District Attorney named Henry Rodriguez. Real law and order prick. Helped draft the Clean Streets Act, did homeless sweeps, criminalized poverty. Goes under his mom's name. He was born here, but the kicker is— drum roll—he's illegitimate. Still, Sanchez's kid."

"How the hell did you find that out?"

"Birth certificate. After Obama, every politician with any melanin posted theirs online. Along with banking records and donors lists. Did I say he was running for mayor?"

"No, left that out."

"Ok, Mo, listen." Peter was on a manic tear, but his research was solid as ever. "He needs at least four mil in a war chest to be competitive. Where does an East LA barrio-bred man get that much cash? Right? Daddy? Maybe. He said it was all small donors. Who has the kind of boots-on-the-ground organization to pull that off? Unions? Sure. But they're backing the incumbent. So? Moses?"

"Hell if I know, Peter."

"Me neither, but follow the money, right? Bob Woodward and Carl Bernstein. Follow the money."

"Let me know when you find out." Peter spun back to the workstation and was gone, lost on the information superhighway.

When Kenny returned the Tempest, even I wouldn't have recognized it. She was a pale, sun-faded blue and gray primer. The windows were dark enough to hide any occupants.

The dents in the front end were gone. Kenny popped the hood, showing off the tubular steel used to reinforce the front end. "Run this bitch into a brick wall and keep going."

"Nice work."

"Did it for Sunshine."

"I know."

"He's afraid if you get killed in a wreck," Sunshine rolled up to us, "he'll have to listen to my blubbering."

"You'd cry if I died?"

"Like a baby, baby. So you keep coming back and we never have to see that ugly picture."

I had to get out of there, and fast. Every moment I looked into her green eyes I fell deeper. One damn sure way to get dead was to have your head at home while your body was on the battlefield. When the Vikings first hit England they terrorized the Brits. It was a battle of two theologies. Christians said be kind and good, obedient and meek, and you will go to the land of milk and honey. The wild Norse believed that it all came down to how well you died. If you died in battle, the beautiful, fierce, winged Valkyrie would swoop down and take you to Valhalla, where you would drink ale, feast, fight and fuck. Vikings had a hold over England, what is now Russia, and most of what we now identify as the Western world because they didn't give a fuck about suffering, weren't afraid of dying, and only wanted victory and honor.

"Sunshine, we need to talk."

"Ok, baby. Why so stern?"

"In private."

"Bedroom is private." She grinned.

"Your office." My stomach soured. Bile entered my mouth. I choked it back down. I closed the door and sat in a club chair.

"This the motherfucking time you tell me it's over? Now?"

"Cut me some slack here. We had fun, but love? Not on my plate."

"I didn't say—"

"I was high on Vics, adrenaline and fear. Said some shit. It got real, but that was the drugs talking. Wanna know why I fuck strippers? No psychology, I do it because they look good and it feels good."

"Fuck you, Moses. Fuck. You."

I walked past her and out of the office. She followed.

"This that corny scene where you push me away so I won't get hurt when you die? That this? Well, fuck you. I am not in love, you arrogant bastard." She rolled to the gym.

It wasn't long before I heard weights slamming up and down. Kenny walked over, looked at the closed gym door then at me. "Why today? We are all stressed, exhausted, but now..."

"Kenny, what I need is to find out where these girls are. Only plan I have now, keep blowing their shit up until their boss meets me, then I tell them give me the girl and I'll be a ghost."

"Dumbass plan."

"Then find out what has happened to the streetwalkers in this town. If they are buried in the desert, tell me under what rock. Find them."

CHAPTER 31

I burned rubber down the street. Gregor said nothing until we hit the 405.

"That was a weak move, Boss."

"Thanks, Doctor Phil. I really need to hear your take on my bullshit life." I crunched a Vic.

Gregor watched me grimly for a few more miles. "I think you are afraid you will fall in love and she will leave you."

"I like your stoic mute act better."

He looked at me, pissed, not hurt.

Fuck them all. I pulled off in Santa Monica, found a liquor store and bought some smokes and a pint of Johnnie Walker Black. Leaning on the trunk of the Tempest, I fumbled with my iPod. The Pogues kicked into *Run Sodomy & the Lash*, the Celtic punk making me smile even on a day like this.

Looking up, I saw I was parked under a billboard. Staring down at me was a handsome, clean-cut Latino. His shirtsleeves were rolled up and he was shaking a cop's hand. It was a coded message; I am the law and order candidate. He was a Democrat, and needed the base as well. Ad copy was placed artistically around him. It was slick. It read:

When was the last time you saw a hooker on the street?

When was the last time you saw a drunk urinate in public above Main Street?

Have you noticed the closing of dozens of medical marijuana pharmacies?

District Attorney Henry Rodriguez has personally made our downtown a safe place to eat and shop.

In the corner was a small piece of text:

Brought to you by fans of a clean city.

"We smoking, Boss?" Leaned next to me.

"Looks that way." Gregor had given up smoking and now only did it when I did. I passed him the pack and he shook one out.

"Menthol? I hate menthol."

"Me too. Figure if I live, I'll be happy to quit."

Now he was staring at the sign. "Did you see Soylent Green, Boss?"

"No."

"Too bad."

First we hit Capone's. The club was near empty. Three unattractive girls were working the stage, jiggling all over the place for the one customer. We never sat. I dropped a twenty at each girl's feet.

Got off the 5 at Fletcher. I was back at The Pink Pearl— what a dumb fucking name for a strip club. Years back, when it was Club Xstasy, I met Gregor there, broke his nose. Then, the joint was run by a man I thought of as a father figure. At least until he sold me out. I swore if I saw him again I would kill. Truth was, I would.

"It vibes wrong."

"If you say so, Boss."

I drove past the club and dropped Gregor a few blocks away. He would circle around, be sure we weren't being set up. I parked out front, slipping the keys under the dash where Gregor knew to find them.

The scotch and pain pills were smoothing off the rough edges when I entered the club. I waited for my eyes to adjust. Cherry Red was leaning on the pool table texting away, wearing cut offs and a crop-top. Neither hid much of her compact, hard body. She was alone.

"Here comes a thousand pounds of trouble stuffed into an extra-large sized man," she said, dropping her phone into her purse.

"Where is everyone?"

"Bartender's out back getting stoned. Two girls called in sick. You get me." She spread her arms out wide. "You like?"

"Very nice. But you can dial it way back, baby girl, that's not why I'm here."

"Wanna bet?" Grinning she walked up to me. Lacing her fingers into my belt loops she craned her head back. "You are one tall motherfucker."

"So I've been told."

"You got any of that candy?"

I dug in my pocket and came up with the bottle of Vicodin. Gave her one and ate one myself. I was feeling no pain, or much of anything else.

She tugged at my belt loops. "Take me into the VIP room."

"Baby girl, nothing I would rather do, but I need some answers."

Her eyes darted around quickly, then full beamed up at me. "Look, the manager videos us. He sees me shooting the shit with you again, I get fired. So, take me in the VIP room. It's forty a song. I'll tell you whatever you want, and you get a lap dance."

"Can't beat that," I said, wishing for another way. Play it as it comes. Fact was, she was the only stripper I knew. Her intel had been solid. She had no reason to lie.

Cherry Red took my hand, walked me through thick black curtains. "Sit."

"How old are you?"

"Twenty-seven, and no, I don't have those daddy issues you were secretly hoping for. But, you interest me. Now sit."

A leather club chair was on a platform, surrounded by mirrors.

She unzipped her shorts and let them fall at her feet. Her G-string covered almost nothing at all. She stretched up as she took her shirt, and then her bra, off. My mouth went dry.

"Yeah, you look good."

"I know."

She hit a remote on the wall and thumping music started to play. She leaned over, letting her small breasts slip across my face. A nipple grazed my lips. I fought the slow, steady march of blood south, unsuccessfully. Her lips brushed across my ear. She whispered, "You had some questions?"

I was struggling to sound neutral. "Have any girls disappeared from here lately?"

"Shelly and Lauren, both missed several shifts." More warm breath in my ear. More blood leaving my brain. Between the seduction and the painkillers, this was seeming like a not half-bad idea.

"Were either of them doing more than dancing?"

"Both." She rubbed my building erection with her thigh. The song ended. She stood up. "Want another?"

I nodded and handed her two hundred dollars. She smiled and pressed play. Prince and the Revolution filled the room. Cherry Red dropped her G-string and sat on my lap. Through my jeans, she started to rock her vulva against my stiffening penis.

"Baby girl, you are going to get me in trouble."

"With who? Just you and me in here. Now, what else?"

I fought to concentrate. "Were they freelancers or did they have a pimp?"

"Billy, the bartender. He split the money with them."

"Where is he?"

She unzipped my jeans and slid her hand in. "I'll take you to him. That feels good, right?" She was gripping me in pulsating tugs.

"Yes, we have to..." Stop didn't come out. She pulled my penis free and was guiding it against her wet and swollen lips. As she pushed slowly down and I entered her, all logic and honor left me.

Cherry Red was in mid thrust and I was starting to moan when the curtain flew open. The two men in black tactical gear didn't hide the MS-13 facial tattoos. They each held cut-down street-sweepers aimed at us. I had no play. One fast move and the girl would surely be dead.

"She's not a part of this," I said. They shrugged at each other.

"I don't think they speak English." I had my hands on her hips and was lifting her off me when she leaned forward. "Sorry," she whispered into my ear. Then she was up. She gathered her clothes and walked past the gunmen. At the curtain she paused, looked back at me, then was gone.

"Armas," a gangster said, jabbing the barrel of his shotgun at me. "Todo."

ONE MORE BODY

I stood up, very slowly. With my index finger and thumb I took the Ruger from the holster by my spine. I tossed it to them. From my boot, I took a lock blade and tossed it. I laced my fingers, put them behind my head and turned around.

CHAPTER 32

"You are a dumb son of a bitch, and a huge pain in my ass." His accent was slight, maybe LA born.

I'd ridden across town in the trunk of a car. A hood covered my head, arms tied behind my back. I knew we took at least one freeway. We crossed several railroad tracks in a row.

I was blinking from the sudden flood of light that hit me after the hood was removed. We were in the back room of a small warehouse. A roll-up door served as the back wall. Through a long window I could see that row after row of sewing machines filled the space behind us. Women were hunched over working on brightly colored sundresses. The clacking and buzzing was loud even through the closed door.

"What should I do with you?" The overhead light was haloing the speaker's shiny black hair. He was taller than the others—not saying much—and wore a suit. His face tats reminded me of a skeleton. "This man," he pointed to my left, "thought he could steal my money."

"No, Jefe, no." The man was tied with his arms behind his back, pinned between two beefy tatted up MS-13 soldiers.

"This man wants to be me." The leader held up his tie, then looked at the bound man in a sweat-stained t-shirt. "I think I'll help him."

"No, Jefe. No. No. No."

A knife was in the boss's hand before I saw it move. With a slash, he opened the man's neck. Reaching into the wound, he pulled the man's tongue through it. It hung down like a grotesque, bloody tie. When the soldiers holding him in place released him, the man fell to the floor. His screaming was a guttural, nonhuman sound. He writhed and kicked and moaned, and after three minutes he started to gurgle, then died. The whole time, no one said a word.

The boss turned from the dead lump on the floor to me. He smiled, the unpleasantness behind us. "I am Zacarías Araya. You are Moses McGuire, the famous killer of men who trade in women. I trade in women...awkward." He tilted his head playfully. "This moment should be played out on a field. Both of us strapped and ready. Close-up eyes. Close-up hands. Leone, right?"

"I have no idea what you are talking about."

"Leone, *The Good the Bad and the Ugly*. Did it bother you that Good and Bad were Americans and Ugly was Latino? Bothered me. Instead, we meet in the back of a sweatshop and I have my men chop your head off and mail it to your Armenian friend's son in Castaic."

I leapt at him, made it about six inches before the two men threw me to the floor. Zacarías spoke to them and they dragged me up onto my feet.

"And now it gets good or ugly, depending on your perspective."

The men pushed me down onto a metal chair. They dropped a car car tire over my head, resting on my shoulders, and splashed gasoline across it.

Zacarías lit a gold lighter. "My name, Zacarías, it means he who God remembers. Do you think God will remember you?"

"I don't think the son of a bitch ever noticed I was here."

The hand with the lighter went up.

The sliding wall exploded in as the Tempest careened through it. Gregor crushed one man against the wall that separated us and the sewing room floor. Instantly, Gregor was out and blazing. The MS-13 soldiers were too stunned to react quickly. The man to my left took a load of shot to the head. A few stray BBs peppered my face. I could feel the bleeding. So what? Bending I shrugged the tire off my neck and was up and running. As a gangster aimed at Gregor's back, I rammed him with my head. He stumbled and I drove my forehead up into his nose. He was trying to get his pistol up when I took a chunk of his cheek into my teeth. I ripped. He screamed. I kneed him in the balls and he went down. I stomped his head. He stopped moving. I stomped again.

The room was silent. All the seamstresses had fled. Six MS-13 soldiers lay dead.

"Where is Zacarías?" I was looking around.

"Who?" Gregor asked as he sliced through my binds.

"Only one in a suit. Tatted up face." I found my Ruger, it was shoved into a dead man's belt.

"A couple of men slipped out while you were eating that man's face."

"They know about Castaic, your family."

Gregor dove into the Tempest. The wheels were spinning when I crawled in the passenger window. He was in his own personal zone, driving with near inhuman precision through the torn up streets of downtown LA. I called Kenny and gave him the address of the sweatshop. Asked him to do a property owner search. "Also, get everything you can on Zacarías Araya. He's MS-13. I think he runs the downtown clique." We bounced over a railroad track and my head slammed into the roof. '*Click it or ticket*,' I remembered Rollens telling me. Then I remembered how she died. These animals knew where Gregor's family was.

It was nearing quitting time, that magic couple of hours when LA freeways go into lockdown. Castaic is fifty miles north of LA. An hour drive, best of times. Could be three hours in traffic.

We were plowing past Devil's Kitchen Pizza when I saw it. "Stop." Gregor locked the brakes. "Hide the car and get back here fast."

A group of upper-class bikers were hanging, drinking beer and laughing. A tall guy with a soul patch dyed blue was leaning on his KTM Duke 690. I got up in his face and whispered a cold hiss. "You are going to rent me your bike. Here is ten K. Lives on the line. Call the cops, I will come for you and your friends. Play it straight, you get the bike back and the knowledge that you saved a family's life." He looked at the wad of cash and laughed, handed me a helmet. Too small, so I tossed it back to him.

Around the corner, I found Gregor. He climbed on the back without a word, wrapped his arms around me. I popped the clutch and raised the front wheel.

Splitting lanes is crazy on the best of days. One idiot decides to change lanes without signaling and you're road kill. Without a helmet, knowing the cops have a shoot-on-sight order, as do half the bangers in town? That is certifiable. Clocked over 100 mph past slow-rolling traffic, scanning for the openings. Thirty-five brutal minutes later we cleared Los Angeles County, roaring up Highway 5.

Ten miles later we were flying down an empty country road, sun sparkling off Lake Hughes. I was in race mode, laying it over on every curve, using torque to pull the bike back to vertical. Gregor nudged me and I turned off. We bounced over the cattle guard, the gravel slipping and sliding under the Duke's street tires. I backed the throttle down, gently. One jerky move and we would be eating gravel for dinner.

The house was more hunting cabin than home. A wide deck made of bleached timber surrounded it. Gregor's Chrysler was the only vehicle in sight. Gregor was off the back and running before I had the stand down. The plank stairs bowed slightly as he pounded up them. Ripping the door open, he disappeared into the shadows. It was cold at this elevation and had started to drizzle. I had the Ruger out and was sweeping the yard, scanning for anyone in the tree line. A couple of squirrels chittered in a bush. A jay flew over, cawing. Gregor stepped out of the house, pale. He shook his head.

"We don't know what we don't know."

"I know they aren't here. That I know." He looked ready to take my head off so I didn't give him any more of my useless wisdom.

I dropped and aimed when I heard the branches break.

More branches cracked.

Gregor swung his 9mm up.

Crashing out through the undergrowth came a one-eyed Bullmastiff.

"Angel? Angel?" Nika was calling from the brush. "There you are, useless dog." Nika's smile fell when she saw us with guns drawn.

"Where is Anya, my son?"

"Not far, I ran ahead. Angel...who is coming?"

"Some very bad men," I said. "Killers who missed us so they are coming after what we love. Grab what you need, we can't stay."

Angel hit me at full tilt, knocking me on my butt. It's hard to be a badass with her pinning me down, licking and slobbering all over my face.

Gregor only relaxed when his woman and child appeared. His mother was carrying a bundle of pinecones. Anya kissed her husband and handed him their son. She didn't look at me. I knew she blamed me for whatever was coming down. I did too. Not that blame helped at this moment.

Ten minutes later we headed back down the gravel driveway. I took lead on the Duke. Gregor gave me a minute head start and I was gone. Laying it low. Even with all this bullshit, I was enjoying the pure joy of being back on a motorcycle. At fifty the light rain felt like needles. I didn't care. I had, for this moment, freedom from my mind and all the dark places it liked to roam. Dragging a knee around a corner, if you think of anything but that moment you are dead. It was as close as I came to meditation.

Rising up out of a dip in a straightaway, I saw a black Escalade. More MS-13 soldiers. Three hundred feet separated us when a man leaned out the passenger window and let rip with an AK. Lots of flame and smoke, but no bullets came even close.

Pulling the Ruger with my left hand, I fired two wild shots. I am many things, but ambidextrous ain't one of them. So I did what any sane man would; I aimed the bike dead center at the SUV and cranked the throttle wide open. Standing on the pegs, I started to scream out my rage. I could see the tattoos on the driver, his eyes wide.

I dove off the bike as it hit the grill and flipped toward the windshield. I grazed the SUV's hood then tumbled into the gravel on the side of the road. I was rolling and sliding. I knew skin and flesh was shredding. Something behind me crashed once, then twice. Metal tore and ripped. I slid to a stop. I didn't dare move or look around, afraid of what I might find if I did. Tires crunched on gravel. A car door opened. A shadow fell over me.

"You going to make it?"

"I really doubt it."

"Too bad." Gregor reached down and helped me up. Every muscle hurt. My Levis were ripped to hell. I was scraped and bleeding from my hands, knees, face, elbows.

"Boss, that was the stupidest thing I ever saw a man do."

"Agreed. Where are they?" Looking around, the SUV had vanished. A section of guardrail was ripped apart. Twenty feet past it was a steep drop into the icy water. An oily rainbow ring was all that was left of the Escalade.

"You need a hospital, Boss?" I was stretched out in the back seat, my head on Nika's lap. Angel lay on the floor, watching me nervously.

"Need one, won't get one. Too many question and cops waiting to kill us."

CHAPTER 33

I was lying facedown on Sunshine's sofa, buck naked, while Anya picked rocks out of my backside. Nika stood beside her holding a stainless steel bowl filled with warm water, soap and a washcloth.

"Quit squirming.   Your namesake is less a baby, rebenok."

"He is no child."

"All men are children."

"Look how much pain he took to save us."

"Little sister, he took pain because that is what Moses does."

"No, he is heroic, and you reduce it to pathology."

Sunshine rolled in, looked at us and started to laugh. "You must think you died and went heaven, surrounded by beautiful women."

"Oh yeah, heaven. I'm sorry about—"

"Being an asshole? Making me feel like a fool for loving you? Yeah, I said love. Fuck your rules. This is what it is. Deal."

"When I was staring down that truck, you know what I thought I'd miss most?"

"Pussy?"

"Yes, but more specifically yours, and everything else. I wanted to get back here." Nika was watching us from the corner of her eye. When Sunshine kissed me I felt tears on my cheek. Hers or mine? Maybe both. I had spent a lifetime trying to get home to this moment, and the last day doing everything I could to avoid it.

"We're done, leave them." Anya led Nika from the room, closing the door softly.

Sunshine kissed me deeply. I sat on the end of the sofa, forgetting the pain. Sunshine kissed my chest. She licked my nipple, sliding her hand under the towel covering my lap. I enlarged at her touch.

"Stand up." I did without question. She gripped my erection and was about to take me into her mouth when her eyes flared angry. "You monumental asshole." She rolled back away from me.

"What?"

"They shot my back, not my goddamn nose. Who did you fuck?"

"No one, Sunshine..." And then I remembered Cherry Red. It wasn't sex. Or it was, but I was trying to get free of Sunshine. "Fuck. It was a stripper. Lap dance went too far."

"None of this is helping you."

"I didn't even come."

"Men are all assholes." She rolled out, leaving me standing naked with no clue what to say to fix it. I sat down, head in my hands. I felt numb. I was as close as I would ever get to real love and I fucking blew it.

The door opened and Kenny came in with a fresh set of clothes. "That detective has been calling." He handed me my cell phone. "You remember what I said would happen if you hurt her."

"No, but it can't be worse than what's in my head right now, so go for it, kid."

"I'm eighteen."

"Yeah, a kid. Kill me or walk on."

"Here's a flash, Moses. We have a family that MS-13 wants dead. Somewhere is a girl named Freedom being raped or worse. We fail? Peter, me, all of us go down, or underground, for the rest of our lives. And you choose this moment to fuck with Sunshine? Fuck you, old man." He stood there breathing. Talked out. Finally he simply walked out.

After getting dressed very carefully, I dug a number out of my wallet and called Deloris, the Internal Affairs cop. I told him we needed to meet. I took a cab to where we'd left the Tempest and twenty minutes later I was sitting in the bleachers watching a swim meet at the Rose Bowl pools.

"Nice," Deloris said, sitting down. "Exits every direction and all these kids to ensure we don't go O.K. Corral on you."

"You left Carbone out, so either you think he's dirty, or you are."

"Or it was his day off."

"I.A. doesn't get days off. A man named Zacarías Araya tried to have me die real slow and ugly."

"He doesn't fail often."

"I got lucky. It was his boys with the rocket launcher. His boys took out Titan's condos."

"Damn it." He nodded, but didn't look surprised. "This motherfucker is out of control." He took out a cigarette. A swimmer's mom shook her head and nodded at a no smoking sign. Deloris looked ready to bite her face off. Instead, he nodded and put the cig back in the pack.

"Your Chief is dirty."

"So the rumor goes. Without proof, we got worse than nothing. Without proof, I have a powerful enemy that I can't contain."

"You threatened to put me in a shallow grave."

"No one would miss you. Him, they would."

"Think I can scare him into walking away?"

"Not in a million years. You got anything else? Anything that might help me?"

I gave him Peter's cell number. Told him Peter was close to having the whole story ready for press. Told him the walls were coming down, time was coming to choose a side or get flushed with the rest.

"So you say." He walked away, never looking back.

No one followed me out of the Rose Bowl parking lot.

In Altadena, I pulled into a liquor store, bought a pack of Camels—fuck menthols—and a bottle of Johnnie Walker Black. They didn't stock any single malts, so this would have to do. I had a long drink, smoked a butt.

In the hills above Altadena, I rolled in the dirt and brush. I drank and poured liberal amounts of whiskey into my hair. Between the scabs and road rash and mud and twigs, I knew I'd fit in perfectly where I was headed.

I parked below the 4th Street Bridge. I hid my cash, guns and I.D. in the body panel. I relaxed my bladder and let warm urine run down my leg. The smell of piss is like an invisibility spell; people turn away before even registering you are human. That worked fine for me.

Down on the nickel, 5th Street below Broadway, I lay flat on my back. A shambling sea of humanity roiled around me. Nobody stopped to ask if I was ok. I wasn't. I had eaten a couple too many Vics for effect and the world felt shaky.

"On your feet, Lurch." His face was shadowed by a shiny bill. His partner was slipping on rubber gloves. "No sleeping on the sidewalk after dark."

"It's after dark?" I'd been staring at a streetlamp and lost time.

The club hurt when it struck my shoulder. It wasn't full force, just checking to see if I would get violent.

"On your feet, or do I call backup and haul your giant ass in?"

"What?" He was talking under water.

"Daddy, come on now." And she was there, arm under mine, lifting me up. She was strong, built like a fireplug. Military short hair and faded desert fatigues. She was definitely ex-military, and hell-bent on remaining all she could be.

"He really your old man, Cam?" the younger cop asked.

"Close enough. They served together."

I was on my feet, listing but staying upright and generally walking a straight line. The cops parted and let her lead me deeper into skid row.

She took me to a small encampment down by the river. The rain turned it into a torrent this near the channels. Six vets in camos ranging from sane-ish to stone cold, batshit crazy sat around a fire watching the embers.

One, all fucking five foot six of him, jumped up and fronted me. His hair was the color of a penny. "Where the fuck did you serve?"

"I don't know, but there was a lot of goddamn sand," I said. A couple of the older guys laughed at that.

"Two kinds of vets." The guy speaking had long, silver hair and kept his eyes on the water. "Those with crotch rot from the jungle and thems with sand up their asses. Sandies seem meaner. But that could be age. Cam, bring this tore up bastard down where I can see him." The silver-haired vet was named Kilroy. His face was latticed with scars and wrinkles. Cam put a flashlight and large magnifying glass in Kilroy's hands. He searched with cataract-covered eyes to make sense of my busted up mug. Behind us the fire crackled, before us the waters rumbled. No one said shit while he investigated. I was getting a clear picture that if he didn't like what he did, or didn't, see I was going for a final swim.

"The Root?" Kilroy asked when he leaned back.

"Yeah."

"You there when the barracks when down?"

"I don't want to talk about it. Long time ago. Fuck it, right?"

"Fido!" A young man on the edges howled.

"So, do I pass? Am I head-fucked enough to enjoy your fire and personal madness?"

"You crazy enough. Cam!" She knelt at his side. "This man, he is going to get a lot of people killed. Smell it."

"Dude, that's piss."

"Shut up. He smells of death, coming and going."

"What do I do?" Cam asked, holding the older man's hand.

"You choose. But hear him out."

Beers were passed around. I sat with Cam and Kilroy, told them every thing I knew about MS-13 talking over downtown. About hookers disappearing. Politicians and a Police Chief touting the cleaning up of the streets. Told them about everything but my crew. I left them out.

"Either of you hear of Zacarías Araya?"

"King Araya," Kilroy said. "Nothing from a dime to a semi load moves down here he don't get a bite of. Old school Nam warlord shit. Some of his men are Uncle Sam trained. Heard they wear fingers around their necks. Don't fuck with him."

"Already did. Killed his lieutenant."

"See, Cam? See? Death floats all over this man. You see that spooky bitch at his shoulder, in the bloody trench with the razor? Who the fuck is she?"

Cam didn't see anything beside me. I don't know if I felt better or worse having Kilroy see Mikayla.

All the lost boys, spare one, curled up for the night. They always left one on sentry. Their camp was surrounded by wires, cans with stones in them hanging down. Early warning system.

I was relatively sober and ghost free when Cam and I sat down near the rushing water.

"Ask," she said.

"Ask?"

"Yeah, am I a dyke? Have I seen combat? What's my story?"

"Truth is Cam, dyke, straight or bi? Don't mean shit where we're going. If you haven't taken a life, I'd like to know. Could make a hell of a difference in how things play out."

"Was in Fallujah, intel guidance support. Three men tried to rape me. They didn't survive."

"How'd it shake out."?

"They got buried with full honors and I got kicked to the curb. It fucked my head. Helping this crew keeps me from..."

"Hating yourself?"

"No. Hating you and your gender."

I slept for an hour and kept dreaming about El Rancho and the plump Mexican woman who said I could fuck her any way I wanted. In the heart of Araya's kingdom. Had to be sanctioned. I went from dreaming to thinking in my dream to sitting up awake.

"Son of a bitch."

"What?" I had woken Cam.

"I need to get to a club called El Rancho without being seen."

"Now?"

"Now."

"Ok."

215

With a flashlight to guide us, Cam opened a rusted door and led me into a steel room built into the wall. Tunnels ran off under the city in several directions. Cam knew a loose collection of abandoned subway tracks, sewers and passways between buildings. The map lived in her head and she never missed a turn.

"Every city has its veins. They build up and leave lines below." Her voice echoed off the huge curved access pipe we moved through. "In Vegas, hundreds of people live in the tunnels, storm drains. Some call them mole people. Lot of vets. Lot of broken heroes just searching for a roof and solitude."

"How many in your crew?"

"Kilroy's Boys, that's what they call themselves. Depending on who's locked down or on a run, we bounce between five and twelve. Here we are."

She led me up a ladder. From a storm grate, we stared out at El Rancho. It was a small joint, could seat maybe seventy-five, hundred max if the Fire Marshal looked the other way. Behind it was a parking lot with roughly four times that many cars.

"Anyone leave their car down here for safekeeping?"

"No one."

"Then where are the drivers?"

"Give me some time, but my guess is the shuttered four-story between us and the river." It was decay personified, faded paint covered by fifty years of smog and grime, all the windows boarded over. A tall iron sign had once graced the roof, many letters now missing, it read: MENS F CLOT. That made me smile. Don't know why, but it did. The back of the building dropped into the fast moving channels of the LA River.

The sun was coming up when Cam dropped me at a grate a few blocks from the Tempest. She had her mission. I had mine. We had twelve hours to spin the game our direction. Or die. That was always an option.

I like her. Mikayla drifted into the front seat.

"Doesn't surprise me."

Because we are both life takers?

"That, and you're both willing to go where it goes without apology.

I made it across LA without having to kill anyone, which was a blessing. Thirty minutes of Mikayla's revved up death ramble was not.

"So, my dead friend, your plan is we go into a building that may or may not be holding Freedom—hell, it may or may not be a shooting gallery, or the hub of MS-13's dope operation—but we go in there blazing and die proving what?"

She is there. We get her and kill the bastards who took her.

"We're both clear, that is not a plan. It's an ambush, not a plan."

Ambush got Nika out.

"We got lucky. Now go wherever it is you go when you go. I need to think."

She went nowhere. Just stared out the window.

CHAPTER 34

Freedom knew exactly how long she had been held in the room with no windows. Long enough to sharpen the tip of a wire hanger into an inch-long, razor-sharp blade. With a pair of metal fingernail clippers and file combo, she fashioned a second blade farther down the wire. The remaining wire folded into a grip. Holding the wire between the two blades, her weapon could sever tendons. Stab. Grab. Pull. She wished she could pick her first kill. She wished she could have picked her first lover. Life chose. She reacted.

On the MP3 player LeJohn had given her was Nicki Minaj. Mistake. Freedom used to hear her easy, cute sexuality. Now it was clear when she said, *All these bitches are my sons ... You ain't my son, you my motherfucking step son,* it meant Nicki owned them. She would decide. She also sang a song to her alter ego.

Fuck.

They should have killed me, Freedom thought.

Mike, that fat fuck contractor, continued to stop by every night after work. He would pump and sweat onto and into Freedom.

"I hate him, LeJohn, his old, wrinkly, white skin."

"I know, baby, just 'til we can get free. Then no more. Then you choose."

218

"I'll hold on. But he gets rough, scares me."

"Baby, we always on the other side of the door." He snaps a switchblade out, stabbing the air. "Scream and I will cut his pale ass." That earned him a kiss. Earned him a quick, gentle fuck. Quiet, so the others didn't hear.

At first she would go away. Now she looked him in the face. Watched his carotid artery pulse. When he came, his eyes dilated. That would be the perfect moment to strike. Just as a man squirts he is at his least focused.

Fifty million years ago she wanted to be a doctor. Evolution was real and fast. She didn't feel like a monster anymore, more like a lioness planning her kill.

Next night, after the contractor left, taking his stink of tar and sawdust with him, LeJohn found Freedom coving up a bruise on her throat.

"He do this?"

"Who else? Nothing. There, see? All gone." She covered bruise she had given herself with more makeup.

"Bitches front and motherfucking center." Zero was home, always the same. He would have the girls circle around him and look at each. Pull lips down, send some to brush their teeth. He would stick his fingers into another, sniff. If he approved he'd lick it, if not he'd send the skank to take a bath. He crooked his index finger at Freedom and led her back into his room. It was lush. A circular bed, satin sheets. A wet bar.

"Champaign, Lil'Diamond?"

"Please, Popi. You look exhausted, come here."

Zero sat, his back to her, as she worked his shoulder muscles. Bury her spike into the base of his neck? Sever the central nervous system and he was lights out. If she missed, he would kill her for sure.

"Zero, you my man. I have to tell you when a rustler is looking at your herd."

"That cowboy talk makin' me hard."

"I'm wet, baby. But keep an eye on LeJohn." She dropped it before he acted. Played it off as if she had read it all wrong. She was playing a long game. Sowing seeds she would wait to let grow strong.

Zero always fucked her from behind, so he could watch himself in the mirror. He was large. It hurt. Even with lots of spray lube, it still hurt. She bit a pillow to keep from screaming while he pumped into her.

She had an aerosol can just like it beside her bed. Next to a Bic lighter.

This right now hurt.

Soon, they would all hurt.

They really should have killed her when they had the chance.

CHAPTER 35

It was time to hit them. Too many people knew we were sniffing around. These psychos might cut bait and run, might clog the LA River with little girls' bodies.

Sunshine's building had a cult compound feel. Gregor's mother was working a big stew pot in the kitchen, while he taught Anya how to load magazines. Peter and Kenny were laying out maps, connecting pinpointed areas with string. Nika had her eyes on Kenny, helping.

Angel's was the only greeting I got, a big, sloppy kiss across my dirty, stinky face. Then I got it. They all thought I'd taken a headfirst-dive off the wagon. And, yes, I had, but not like they thought. Fuck them.

I showered and shaved. Hell, I even buzzed my hair. Put on a clean Shane MacGowan and The Popes t-shirt. I was as presentable as I'd ever be. I found Sunshine in her armory. She was meticulously cleaning and reassembling a .50 BMG sniper's rifle.

"Sunshine?"

"Don't." She pulled her hand away from my touch. "Big man, I know what you are, knew it the minute I saw you. I just didn't know how deep under my skin you would get."

"I love you, Sunshine."

"Easy words when it doesn't look like you'll see another daybreak. You still alive tomorrow, you make a run at me, then we'll see."

"That is real far from a no, babe."

"Just as far from a yes. Now I got to get this put back right or I might put a hole in you instead of my target."

Based on Cam's and my findings, Kenny had it down to a couple of buildings. One was owned by Homies Working It Out, Inc.

"And that is owned by a shadow corp of a shadow corp. Two double blinds and a partridge in a pear tree." Peter was rolling high. "All owned by...ta da! Our very own wannabe mayor, District Attorney Henry Rodriguez. Hell of a way to keep the streets clean. Did you ever see *Soylent Green?*"

"No, why does—"

"'Soylent Green is people?' Never mind. Did you link Chief Dobbs to any of it?"

"I spoke to an I.A. cop. No doubt about it, the Chief is dirty."

"He told you that?"

"No, but he didn't bat a fucking lash when I said it. This is common fucking knowledge."

"And without a source we got nothing. Moses, I'm going in there, El Rancho, this afternoon."

"Tried to talk him out of it," Kenny called across the room.

"We need eyes on the joint, be sure which building, and I'm the only one here that will pass for straight."

"No. Fuck no, Peter."

"You don't get to say no."

"Just did. No. These freaks will rip your lungs out and make you eat them. No."

"Moses, you are neither king nor captain of this anarchistic pirate ship. I'm going in at noon."

"Kenny?"

"He's right, Moses, we need the intel."

I walked away before I bitch slapped the pair of them.

"Fuck tha Police" jangled from my pocket. Detective Lowrie.

"This is a strange one, McGuire. That I.A. guy?"

"Deloris?"

"No, the young one, Carbone. He wants me to set up a meet with you, him and District Attorney Henry Rodriguez."

"No shit. Why me?"

"They seem to think you are about to do a very stupid thing."

"What did you tell them?"

"I said that sounded like you. They want me to tell you they can wipe your record clean."

"That must be the going price for my soul. Fuck three strikes, what do you think?"

"I think they have the juice to do it. I also think it's a hit, McGuire. The D.A.'s the only cheese big enough to get you into the open."

"I think you're right. Tell them two hours—Mt. Fiji, behind Occidental. Bring the papers and six hundred grand. I'll have my lawyer check them. If it's clean, I'll join them. Anyone else shows, I'm in the wind. Call back with their answer." He called back in ten minutes and said they needed more time to get that much cash. "Tell them they have 'til six. Cash by close of business."

"You want backup?"

I told him I had no intention of making the meet, just wanted them kept busy. I told him about the building in downtown. Plan was we hit it at midnight. He had ten cruisers that would box off the parking lot and street door. He'd call SWAT at first gunfire. The whole thing was shaky as hell. He was counting on dispatchers and a SWAT team from a department proven to be rife with rats.

"Kenny, I need two burners!"

He tossed me the phones from a stack without looking to see me catch them. Nika was helping him cross reference maps on several screens. If so many lives weren't on the line it would have been a cute scene—two kids doing a science project.

I closed the door to Sunshine's bedroom. This was a private call. "Sanders, I'm about to make you an even more decorated agent." Sanders was FBI, worked out of NoCal. He swept up after a battle Gregor and I started up there. He played it straight, got a new job and pay grade hike for his trouble. We walked away clean.

"Fucking McGuire. Any chance in hell we could avoid a blood bath? We have a team looking into Henry Rodriguez, Chief Dobbs and possible connections to gang leaders."

"Same team looking into Kennedy's assassination?"

"Unfair. We have to build a case, make it stick."

"I don't. You want in?"

"I'll scramble my crew." I trusted his ambition and true desire to do the right thing would motivate him to follow through. I told him to be in LA by nightfall and hung up.

My next call was to the man who actually ran the LA mob, the man even The Pope was afraid of.

"This is Leo. My secretary said you were calling about a man named McGuire. You must have a wrong number, never heard of him."

"Too bad," I said. "He wanted you to know open season on scarface doves begins at midnight. SPCA will be busy working downtown. A straggler hunt could be productive."

"I do love a good dove hunt." He passed me a string of nonsense words and hung up. Using an old prison code we'd adapted, dropping the first letter and using the second to get a number, I had a clean line and a time.

Our second call was also coded. Nothing said would send us to jail. I needed his help, he was tired of MS-13 fucking up his business. It was going to be a night of bold, big moves. Leo was in. He would hit MS-13 cliques in Hollywood and NoHo, cutting out their backup. I didn't need to worry about his dependability, or his discretion. In the modern world of Cosa Nostra you never knew who was selling whom out. But, like me, Leo was old school.

"You really going to meet with D.A. Rodriquez?" I was digging around the armory when Sunshine rolled in.

"Only way to keep them off the scent for tonight." It wasn't a lie. It wasn't the truth.

"You know, if he kills you his problems go away."

"I know he thinks that."

"Do you want to die?"

"No, not anymore. I may not have a choice."

"Fair enough. What are you rooting around in my gear for?" I told her about Cam and her burnouts. I was looking for M16s and vests, a chunk of C4 and some det cord. "Oh, is that all?" She made an exaggerated show of it, but found what I was looking for.

CHAPTER 36

At noon, Peter was in the men's room of the El Rancho strip club. A huge-breasted dancer found him some coke. For an extra twenty she let him snort it off her tits. He was an eight ball to the good, or bad depending on how you see it, when he started getting randy.

"You wanna get fucked? I let you do it up my ass in the stall."

"No. Great thought, stellar, but—"

"I blow you while I shove my finger up your ass?"

"Still stellar, but I'm—"

"Into that strap-on-I-fuck-you shit? Cause I don't do kinky."

"No, no, no. I want, um, need..." He took another deep snort. "I'm a bit addicted to black girls, double underline on 'girls.' Pure chocolate, see me?"

"Oh, yeah baby, I thought you was maybe a freak. Come on, I'll hook you up."

Kenny sat at his desk, Nika leaning over his shoulder. They focused on a small moving blip on one of his screens. "He's moving. Downstairs." Kenny tracked every step Peter took. He overlaid the strip club's blueprint across the tracking signal. He and Nika smiled when Peter stopped in the restroom. It was a life-sized video game. And then it wasn't. Peter's blip went down a flight of stairs, stairs not on any map. And then it stopped moving.

"Phones, electronics, iPods in that basket, weapons in the blue box." At the bottom of the makeshift stairs Peter faced a chain-link gate with a small opening in it to deposit your goods. A tall man with an AK swept Peter, back and forth, ready. A girl with MS-13 tattooed on her neck took Peter's electronics and sealed them in a manila envelope. She taped his driver's license to the front and put it in a pile with many others. His wallet was nearly empty.

"You guys take Amex? No?"

The girl pointed to an ATM. Peter pulled $280 using a card Kenny gave him. With only cash in his pockets, he was allowed past the gate. A second MS-13 soldier patted him down. The whole thing took three minutes, tops. The TSA had a lot to learn from these boys.

"Hit on the ATM," Nika said. "He took two eighty."

"He's traveling east then. Damn it. Damn it. I hate not knowing exactly where he is." It wasn't like knowing would do any good. There was no extraction team waiting for Kenny's signal to swoop in and save Peter. If it went bad he would die ugly, not a damn thing anyone could do about that fact.

Peter was motioned down a long tunnel, parts freshly dug, other parts old and made of brick. Halfway down he was met by a bald, prison-buff pimp in a too-tight suit.

"I'm Zero. Word is you like your chocolate fresh."

"Are we beyond prying ears?"

"Yes, just you and me."

"Can we cut the euphemisms?"

"Euphemism?"

"I like young, black pussy. At the gate they said you had someone who would meet my needs."

"That euphemism, hell we got 'em all. You like schoolgirl, pigtail bullshit?"

"Yes."

"I got your bitch." Zero pulled out a walkie-talkie. "Get Lil' Diamond ready. Uniform. No, bitch, not prison, school."

"Help." Peter shrugged.

"She ain't cheap. Only been fucked maybe once. Basically paying for a virgin." At the end of the tunnel was another gate. MS-13 soldiers stood on the other side. They gave Peter and Zero a once-over and then opened up. Two more soldiers sat in elevated chairs, like lifeguards at the pool. Anyone trying to attack from the tunnel would be cut to pieces. The tunnel narrowed down to a two-man width.

"Saturday nights this must be a traffic jam." No one answered Peter.

Up more steps, then into an open room that had once been a production floor. Now it was operations central. They had tables laid out with poster board above them, pictures taped to the boards. The tables were grouped by type: young Latinas, Japanese mama sans, pretty boys, hard boys, tattooed girls, clean-cut cheerleaders. They had a table for every kink.

"This is the Big Lots, the Costco, of the sex trade, no? Well done, all," Peter said, feeling sick.

"Pretty slick shit for sure," Zero said.

"It is something." To Peter it looked more like the sickest job fair ever—a supermarket of pain.

"Follow. If she ain't right we have lots of others."

The sign over the table where Andre sat read *Zero's Crown Jewlz*. The table was covered with glossy shots of their stable.

Zero's sausage of an index finger landed on Freedom's picture. Peter's heart raced. It was her. After all this, she was real. Tarted-up and giving I-want-you-to-fuck-me eyes, she was still the girl Moses had shown him. Bile came up the back of his throat. He was trembling. He understood Moses's desire to kill. He stuffed it down, used the energy to add enthusiasm to his words. Junkies know how to lie, if nothing else.

"Ohhhh, yes, yes. She will do." He licked his upper lip, remembering to pull back, ease up a hair. "How old?"

"Thirteen. And clean."

"Yes."

"Three hundred. Now."

"That's, well, that is…"

"Expensive, I know, but for that you can do whatever. Come in her mouth, on her tits. Fuck her ass. Soundproof room. No one bother you."

Peter concentrated on counting out the cash, unsure of what might come out if he spoke.

An industrial elevator was open to the room. It creaked and groaned as it climbed to the third floor. Peter was feeling dizzy. Needed a bump. Needed a drink. Needed the safety of his laptop.

Two angry-looking black men guarded the door. Zero nodded and they stepped aside. Once inside, they were on Zero's turf. He grabbed Peter by the shirtfront and slapped him hard. Peter gasped, stepping back. Zero slapped him again.

"Look, bitch, this here, all this? It's mine. You treat it with respect you get to live."

"I didn't, I wouldn't."

"You wanna fuck baby pussy? Fine, whatever. You damage my goods, I will throw you down that elevator shaft." Then he cracked an easy smile. "Ha! Fuck you, white boy, just fucking around. Want a drink?"

"Yes. Please."

"Please, that's nice. I'm just fucking with you. What was your name?"

"Peter."

"Peter Peter, pecker eater?"

"What? No. Brixton, Peter Brixton."

"You're all right, Peter Brixton, for a bitch." He handed Peter a Dixie cup with a healthy shot of Chivas.

Peter slugged it down.

"Five bucks. No, I'm shitting you. Look at your face. Go get fucked, have fun. Room six."

Freedom had on her school uniform. Now she heard men talking in the living room. Her punch knife was between the cot and the mattress. Waiting. Calling. She wasn't surprised by how nervous the john looked when he entered. They had all the control, and still the bashful pricks wanted her to make them feel good about that. Fucking twisted.

"Hey, handsome, you have a name?" She looked into his eyes soulfully.

"Peter, and you don't need to do that."

"What, baby?"

"Flirt. I came to tell you, to say... shit."

"You just want to get to the business, cool. You want me to blow you first?"

"No." Peter put his hands on her shoulders and gently held her back. "I'm a reporter. Moses sent me to find you."

"Who?"

"Oh, you wouldn't...Moses. Your Aunt Rollens hired him to find you and bring you home safe."

"Look, baby, you want to role-play, cool. Are you my uncle the reporter? Did I run away? Have I been bad?"

"No, this is real."

Freedom was starting to worry this man might be crazy, dangerous crazy.

Peter sat on the bed and fought to slow his racing mind. It had never occurred to him that he might have to convince her of the truth. "Ok, ok, wait...here. Whatever else is true or not, tonight at midnight Moses McGuire will be coming for you. He will, I repeat, he *will* kill anybody who tries to stop him."

"What does he want with me?" She sat next to him, slipping her hand under the mattress, feeling her punch knife.

"Freedom, he wants you to be, um, free. After that it is up to you."

"How you know my name?" she whispered. She knew Zero or one of his boys would be listening. She started to moan a fake orgasm. The sound was real, but her face was devoid of any emotion as she stared coldly at Peter.

It spooked Peter, made him question every girl he had ever paid to fuck. There hadn't been many, but enough to make him want to puke. He looked away. As an afterthought, he took out a tightly rolled picture he'd hidden in his pant cuff. He gave it to her. Her moan stopped mid 'yessss.' It was a copy of her cheerleading picture. Beside it was a picture of Rollens.

"That's Mrs. Mayers. She ain't my aunt, she was my social worker. This is for real?"

"Yes. Midnight you lock the door, push the bed against it. We will come for you. Promise."

After Peter left, Freedom lay on her bed. Mrs. Mayers had tried to make her life better. And they had the picture of Freedom from her file. But who the fuck was going to risk their life for her? Her own kin didn't give a shit if she lived or died. She chided herself for cursing, even in her head. She was better than that. No she wasn't, Lil' Diamond told her, you a fifty-dollar pump. A skeezy ho.

No. That wasn't her. If she gave in, then Zero and his boys won. No. She was strong. She was not falling. She ran her thumb over the point of her makeshift weapon. It bled a little. She sucked it until it stopped.

Fact was, she believed the reporter and his friends would try and save her. They would fail, but the chaos they caused could give Freedom her chance. At midnight she would start killing Zero's crew and anyone else who blocked her path. It was kill now or become Lil' Diamond forever. If she died trying to escape, at least she died trying to live up to her name. Freedom was the only thing her mother gave her worth a damn. Now she would own it.

By two o'clock Peter was back at Sunshine's and had paced off the tunnel.

"One hundred thirty-six feet," Nika called to Kenny after she measured it with a laser tape. Kenny was pounding keys and swiping his mouse.

"Motherfucker, we got you now," Kenny said.

"It is Henry Rodriguez's building?" I asked.

"It's his alright. A ghost of a ghost company he owns. May not prove it in court, but this is his building."

"I have to roll. Tell Sunshine—"

"Tell her what?" Kenny was still pissed.

"Right." I loaded the duffle bag full of felony arrests into the trunk of the Tempest. Gregor tossed his baby in the air and the boy giggled. He kissed Anya long enough to let her know death was the only thing to keep him from her.

CHAPTER 37

Gregor had me drop him at La Placita, an ancient Catholic church off Olvera Street. He would make peace with his God, make confession, clear the slate so if he died he would be reunited with his ancestors and his family when they ultimately passed. I envied his sureness. His faith. I doubted a few words and an act of contrition would wipe the slate clean between me and the big thug upstairs.

I hit the windshield wipers once to clear the drizzle. The clouds were blowing in fast and dark. Out over east LA lightning flashed down. I counted to five before the thunderclap hit. The storm was coming.

As I approached the vet encampment, I made sure to rattle the trip line. These boys were spooked enough as it was, they didn't need me sneaking up on them.

"I smell death. That you, McGuire?"

"Yeah, Kilroy, it's me."

"I see you brung lady death with you." Man was mostly blind, but he could clearly see Mikayla.

"Can't seem to shake her."

"Don't seem to try real hard."

It took less convincing than I thought it would to get the vets to join us. Cam told them about the building full of sex slaves, here in the town they fought to keep free. She offered them honor over the life they'd all slipped into.

"What're the odds we make it home on this one?" Vet asking was ripped, shirt off displaying a tattoo of the Mexican flag crossing Old Glory on his back.

"Slim."

"I'm good with that. Fuck it, ese, let's do this."

Seven men lined up to be armed.

Seven brave, brain-fucked soldiers.

"Thank you, sir, we will make you proud," Penny said.

"Beat the odds, kid, make it home." I meant it.

Along with the armored vests, I gave Cam a burner. It had one number programmed in it; mine. She'd already scoped a route under the building. The C4 was to blow the basement floor. "You know anything about demolitions?" I asked.

"Not a thing. Bugs does though."

Bugs was always talking to dead enemies in Farsi. I didn't know if he was called Bugs because of the tattoo of Bugs Bunny on his chest or because of the scabs on his arms from picking at the bugs he thought were just under his skin.

"I feel much better," I said.

"Good. You should."

I was getting ready to head out when Kilroy called me to him. He said he needed me to walk him down to river's edge for a piss.

"Hold my arm. I don't want to drown just to relieve my bladder." I held his arm. He unzipped. It was a long time before any urine came out, then it slowly built up steam to a healthy flow. It was more of a personal moment than I'd have thought. The rain was soft. Mikayla stood apart from us, looking into the building shadows.

When he was finished, I turned to lead him back but he stopped. "I need to tell you something. I think it may be important."

"Ok. May be?"

"Only important if you hear it."

"I'm listening." But I wasn't. I was already moving on in my head.

"She, the dead lady, is wrong. You want to go in guns blazing. You want to kill all but the victims. Victims. Villains. Heroes. Collaborators. All that? It is bullshit. It is more complex. We are all, all of those, and none. Moses?"

"Yeah, Kilroy."

"Pay fucking attention. You can be forgiven. They can be forgiven. No one is beyond redemption. No one."

"Not real sure about that, Kilroy. Some shit you can't take back."

"Didn't say you could, brother, but you can heal. You can do good. You can return balance to the world. Fuck it, you aren't listening. I know, blind man hippy bullshit, right? But what if I'm correct? Check this. There was a junkie. He sold dope. He pimped. He went to jail. He found a better way. He became Malcolm X and he changed the world. Redemption? I don't know, but if you give up on the concept...fuck, brother. Fuck it. I'm tired. I talk too much. Get me back to the fire, I'm cold."

I had nothing to say. Mikayla was calling the old man a pussy. She was wrong. Maybe both of them were wrong. Didn't matter at this point. The last thing I needed was a headful of this shit. I needed a clean mission. Go in, kill all that I came across until Freedom was free. Philosophy was a luxury given to blind men too old to fight. Poet warrior? Intellectual soldier? Those weren't me. Kill 'em all and let God sort it out was my only way through. Protect my people. Kill theirs. The end.

I stood with my back to the mad platoon.

Cam joined me, staring into the fast moving water. "You ready?"

"I better be."

"Don't let the old man get in your head. Word is he was lead gunner with a company that zipped a village in Laos. It fucked him up. He's also wise. Fido, right?" She let out a small laugh. She was nervous and talking to keep from thinking.

"Fido?"

"Fuck it, drive on."

It was time to move. Time to get Gregor and go to work.

The plan was simple. Cam and her crew were going in from the basement. Lowrie and the cops would use the sound of gunfire as probable cause to go in the front. Gregor and I would find a way in and work our way to the third floor. Sunshine and Kenny would find a roost offering sniper support.

Simple.

No fucking way it could go sideways.

CHAPTER 38

When they kick at your front door, how you gonna come?
With your hands on your head, or on the trigger of your
gun?

It was Clash time. I had "The Guns of Brixton" cranked to the point two clicks past distortion. I couldn't hear the rain pounding on the sheet metal of the Tempest. The Adderall and music had my heart thundering and racing to the beat of Topper Headon's drums and Paul Simonon's bass. Easy to forget with Mick Jones's sweet charm and Joe Strummer's bad-ass bravado that, without Headon and Simonon, it was senseless noise. Rhythm. The Clash are anger drawn in melody and defined by rhythm.

This is the kind of bullshit you think about when you don't want to think about the job at hand. I turned off the iPod and tossed it in the glove box. Gregor lowered his binoculars and told me it was time to move.

Getting in was easy. Around the four-story warehouse was a tall cyclone fence topped with barbed wire. A gate opened to give cars and delivery trucks access to the side loading dock. Gregor and I walked in hugging the rear of a white van. The rain was pouring, hiding sound and obscuring sight. At a dumpster we pealed off into the shadows.

Easy is what you look for, yet easy is almost never a good thing. It hides unseen dangers. The white van disgorged three men in tac gear. They climbed the stairs to the loading dock and disappeared into the building. We waited thirty seconds. Nothing in the back area was moving. Just the rain and us. I cupped my hands and lit two cigarettes. We smoked and thought. There was no turning back.

"Let's go," I said, dropping my butt to sizzle in the mud.

"Why not."

And so we crossed the yard and up the steps. Before we could clear the steps, four MS-13 soldiers popped up from behind crates. They had AKs and wild eyes. They yelled at us in Spanish, the gist of which was raise your hands or we splatter the pavement with you. A third man stepped out, laughing and clearly drunk. When he saw the situation he got suddenly angry. Whipping out a revolver, he pointed it at us. He swayed a bit. He aimed at Gregor's head, snapped back the hammer.

Time froze.

Then the night broke loose in flashes of fire, blood and ruined bone. A hole burst out of the drunken man's chest. He fell facedown in the muddy water. We didn't hear the sniper's shot. The other soldiers looked up quickly, searching for the shooter.

Mistake.

Gregor had his auto shotgun up and blazing. I let rip with my 1911. Two seconds and four lifeless bodies were in the mud.

We ran up the stairs and into a room piled with linens, cases of whiskey, disinfectant douches and insect spray. The old man taking inventory shouldn't have gone for the gun in his belt. I was at a dead run and hit the side of his face with all the force muscle and momentum could deliver. Something in his skull snapped and he was doing the ragdoll tumble.

Thumping hip hop from upstairs and thunder from the storm covered the noise of the skirmish. Stealth was our best move. Soaking, blood-splattered, and swinging serious firepower, stealth meant sticking to the shadows and hoping for the impossible.

On the second floor, we were moving down a narrow hallway when a door opened. A middle-aged man came out, a young—very fucking young—girl under one arm, a boy under the other. They were maybe eleven, Vietnamese, and terrified.

My first shot shattered the john's left cheek. He was stumbling back when I shot him in the chest. I was firing fast. He fell onto the bed where he had just fucked these children. His blood bloomed red across the sheets.

Stealth was over. Gregor grabbed me and we ran. The gunshots brought opening doors. Opening doors brought dead bodies that we sent flying back. Two badasses in Ray-Bans rolled into the hall military style. Trained. Gregor emptied his shotgun into them before they could take aim. Gregor let the long gun hang on its sling and pulled his CZ 75. One move. Smooth.

A Vietnamese woman came out behind us, running with a carving knife. Screaming at us. We weren't her heroes. I shot her just above her left breast and she dropped. She was screaming but not getting up.

Fido.

At the end of the hall an older Vietnamese man stepped out, pistol to a pretty little girl's head. Gregor didn't hesitate, double tapping the man's head. The pimp was falling before his brain could register he was dead. The girl screamed. She was blood-stained and freaked. No time to comfort her. Move or die.

We hit the second set of stairs. Machine gun fire ripped the jamb, driving us back.

The alarm on my phone went off. Midnight.

Deep under the building, an explosion rocked the structure.

Cam and her crew were blown back down the tunnel. Bugs misjudged the amount of C4. Cam searched the debris for survivors. Under a slab of cement lay Bugs, his body crushed, blood running from his mouth and nose. He had a funny smile on his face. He was DOA.

Fido.

Penny was first up through the hole. The basement room was in tatters, cash swirling in the air. They had unknowingly come up in MS-13's count room.

"All targets down." Penny looked around the room. "And, it is motherfucking raining money."

Freedom felt the explosion as she climbed onto Mike the contractor's lap. She kissed him. Then used her sharpened hanger to punch a hole in his larynx. Slicing back she took out his carotid artery. Blood sprayed across her face. He was gurgling, holding his neck. She leapt off him and rolled onto the floor. She let out a painful scream, bringing LeJohn through the door. Freedom struck. She severed his left Achilles tendon with a puncture and a pull. The boy screamed as he fell and Freedom was on him. She had his switchblade in her hand and open before he realized she wasn't trying to help him. His eyes pleaded. She slid the knife between his ribs and into his heart.

Outside the building police sirens wailed. Lowrie radioed for back up. SWAT was twenty minutes out, best case. Andersen, the young officer Moses had dubbed Twenty-six, hit the gas.

"Ready for this, son?" Lowrie asked.

"No, sir." He led a small phalanx of cop cars roaring toward the MS-13 warehouse.

Gregor reloaded his auto-shotgun. He crossed himself and ran onto the landing, flooding a steady stream of buckshot up the stairs. "Clear!"

I followed him. On the third floor a teenage boy lay bleeding out. I felt sorry.

Mistake.

The kid fired at me with a 9mm. My hip burned and I stumbled back. The kid's second shot hit where my head had been. He didn't have the strength to shoot again. I didn't have the will to kill him. Time would most likely do that.

Lion was an unrepentantly violent man. Freedom remembered the punching she took after he raped her. She was glad he fought back. She slashed his arms. Stabbed his thigh, slicing the femoral artery.

"Bitch, you going to die."

"No, you are going to die." He was holding his leg trying to stop the blood when she took out his throat.

Freedom was covered in the blood of her captors. She was looking for more. Kill them all and no one would ever hurt her again. Amethyst came out of a back room. Seeing the blood-saturated walls and carpet she started screaming.

"Shut up." Freedom was red with blood. It dripped from her pigtails. Amethyst shut up and backed out of the room.

An RPG hit the first police car while they were still in motion. The policemen inside were blown to pieces. Lowrie leapt from his car, racked and fired his gauge at the warehouse door as fast as he could pump. A slug took him in the gut.

He went down. Twenty-six dragged him behind an undercover car. They were outgunned.

"Funny place to die."

"How's that, sir?"

"As a rookie, this was my beat. Found a woman's body in dumpster." He coughed up some blood. "Hooker. No one cared. I did." More coughing. More blood. "Help me up and let's get these bastards."

From the front door, a man knelt and aimed an RPG at the car Lowrie was behind. Before he could launch, a massive hole exploded in his chest. Two men died at his side. No one saw where the sniper was shooting from. Another man grabbed the RPG and ran back into the warehouse. Sunshine punched two large holes through the concrete. Her third shot nailed the man with the RPG. Through the jagged break in the wall she saw him go down, firing the rocket. Inside the room, pimps and johns alike were hit by shrapnel.

The police fired but didn't enter. Containment. Let SWAT breach this bloodbath.

An armored chopper flew in hot. Banking, it came back to hover over the front of the building. "This is the FBI," a loudspeaker boomed with Sanders's voice. "Come out with your hands in the air and you will not be hurt. There are two ways out, walking with hands on heads or carried in a body bag."

By the time Gregor and I hit the third floor landing it was total mayhem. Soldiers were running the other way. My hip was failing so I used the wall to hold myself up. Gregor was kicking open doors. At #14, the room Peter told us was Freedom's, he paused, waiting for me to catch up. I dropped down, aiming up at the closed door. He kicked it in.

We both froze.

A blood-soaked girl held a switchblade to a bald man's throat. "Move and he dies."

"Your choice, girl. I'm Moses, and it's your move."

I wasn't ready for her next action. She sliced the knife across the man's throat. He fell, gurgling. She stood, a tremble starting to build into a full body shake. She was red and slick from head to toe. Somewhere in a back room girls were crying. I took a step toward her. In a flash the knife was pointed at my gut.

"Baby girl, I killed a lot of people to get you home. Let's not end it like this."

"How? Fuck, you could be—"

"I'm not. I'm here for you. Your guardian angel." She looked me over. I must have been a sad picture. "I ain't much, but sometimes you have to go with what you got. Now let me get you home."

"I, I don't have a home."

"I'll find you one. My word to you. Wait, here." I took the Saint Jude medal off my neck. "A powerfully good man gave this to protect me. I think you need it now." I stepped forward, medal extended. Something she saw in my eyes convinced her. The knife clattered to the slick flood. I placed the necklace over her head and hugged her to my chest. "This all stops now." It was a half lie. Some of the pain never left, but I could stop further damage. "My word."

Holding her, I leaned against the wall for support. "This here is Gregor. Best man I know. Do what he says and we'll get you out of here."

"You?" She looked panicked.

"I have to end this bullshit so they never come after you again." I kissed her blood-smeared forehead. "Get her clear. Take her out the basement," I said, pulling myself up. The Vics were doing their job and holding the pain off.

"You?" she asked again.

"Penthouse." Freedom looked at Gregor, still not sure. "Girl, Gregor will die to get you out of here. You stay, and they will want to know about the bodies in there. Now go." The firmness in my voice did the trick, or maybe she was just out of options. She followed Gregor to the stairway, disappearing down into the chaos. From below I could hear automatic fire. Cam and her crew, I hoped.

Starting up the stairs, I used a fallen AR15 as a cane. From the pocket of my leather I took a flash-bang grenade. I tossed it up onto the fourth floor. After the boom and white light, I swung in. It was a large, open floor. I killed three soldiers before they knew what hit them. Flame fired at me. Blood sprayed from my leg. Only luck kept it from snapping the bone. I dropped the empty .45 and fired the Ruger through the file cabinet the shooter was hiding behind. Blood painted the wall beyond it.

Two men scrambled up a small ladder toward the roof.

I fired my last three shots double action, not taking time to aim.

One died when I blew him off the ladder. The second, guy in a suit, disappeared up onto the roof.

Dropping in a speedloader, I snapped the cylinder shut and went up the ladder. I led with the Ruger as I climbed onto the roof. Rain lashed hard and cruel. Zacarías Araya sat by a fallen, rusted TV antenna. He was holding his gut and bleeding.

"You...you fucking gringo. One bitch? All this for her?"

"Something like that."

"Moses, God's messenger. Do you think God will remember me?"

"I don't know." I pulled myself to a sitting position. Below, the chopper was swirling the rain around. I could see SWAT had arrived and was storming the building from all sides.

"I will be a king in jail. Mara Salvatrucha takes care of its princes. And you, you will be dead. Of this, I will make sure."

"Fuck you." I raised the revolver. "Say hi to God."

I pulled the trigger.

I wanted to rest, just a moment. I had earned some peace. On my back, I stared up at the falling rain.

I closed my eyes.

CHAPTER 39

I woke in a hospital bed. A tall nurse was shaving me. He had a gentle, Australian accent. "Hello, mate. Wasn't sure you would make it."

"Where?"

"Home," Sunshine said from behind the bed. Rolling out, she took my hand. "You been out for three days."

"Freedom?" My voice was raw, hurt to speak.

"She made it. Ballsy girl."

"Gregor?"

"Un-killable." Then she told me Lowrie had died on the scene, gun in his hand. He held out until the FBI and SWAT rolled in. "Way that kid Twenty-six told it to Peter, Lowrie's last words were, 'Kid, save my city. She's worth it.' The kid was the first cop to talk to Agent Sanders and agree to turn state's evidence against the Chief."

"If I remember right, you saved my life out there." I took her hand and stroked it.

"I did, and you owe me."

"What do I owe you?"

"Everything."

Over the next day I was clued in on all that had gone down while we were on our bloody trail.

Peter handed all his research to the FBI in exchange for being imbedded during the cleanup, arrests and interviews. Chief Dobbs was never arrested. He ate his barrel rather than suffer that humiliation. With him died the link to D.A. Rodriguez. Rodriguez might skate, but his run for mayor was done—the ugliest scandal in the rich history of LAPD scandals went down on his watch. They couldn't prove he had direct links, but he would be asked to step down for health or personal reasons.

Kilroy's crew lost three. Bugs was blown up, Penny was gunned down leaving the counting room, and a kid named Jimmy B. got gutted with a machete.

Cam left her dead. The wounded limped out and down the tunnels. Gregor helped her carry out over a million dollars in black plastic garbage bags. Cam said the money could buy a house for the vets. Maybe it will. Maybe she and Kilroy will go to Vegas and put it all on red. Whatever. It all came down to fido.

"Considering they're three clicks past crazy, they were lucky to only lose three. We patched up the wounded here. Your friend Kilroy is a stone trip," Sunshine said.

"He is that. Wait...us? Kenny?"

"We lost three."

I wanted to puke. "Who?" I asked, but I didn't want to know.

"Moses McGuire, Sunshine O'Shay and Freedom Jones. They all died that night."

Sunshine told me they found our bodies in the wreckage. Kenny had received the ashes. That third strike, the bitch hanging over my head, the weight no man should shoulder, died in a firefight in a warehouse along with my name.

247

"We can't come back to Los Angeles again, big man."

"That's ok. I love this city, but she's never brought me all that much good luck." It was time to get lost someplace warm.

Sunshine tossed a passport on my lap. It had my picture, but the name was Joseph MacGowan. She dropped Freedom's passport on top of mine. It listed her name as Freedom MacGowan; it came with a clean birth certificate. The last to fall was Sunshine's. Her name was Serenity MacGowan.

"Will you marry me, Mr. MacGowan?"

"Looks like I already did."

"Don't be an asshole."

"Sorry. Yes. Yes, I would be proud to marry you. Fact is, nothing I'd rather do." I leaned in to her and gave her the kiss that sealed any deal we ever had.

When I was able to get out of bed, I had Peter call I.A. Detective Carbone. He set up a meet with D.A. Rodriguez. Peter had evidence to sell, said he could prove a link between the D.A. and the building's ownership. It was bullshit. Peter could show it, but would never prove the fact in court.

I also had Peter call his partner, Deloris, to let him know when it was going down. Let him clean up his own mess.

They met under a eucalyptus tree behind Occidental College. When Peter arrived, Detective Carbone was leaning against a Town Car. He patted Peter down. The young detective was too sure of himself, didn't hear his partner move up behind him.

"Why don't we sit this one out?" Deloris said, shoving his pistol into Carbone's ribs.

"Vanish," he told Peter, who was gone in seconds.

Deloris walked his ex-partner into the trees, where his car was waiting. He gave Carbone ten hours to do the honorable thing. Kill himself or turn state's evidence.

When I climbed into the Town Car, Henry Rodriguez looked arrogant. This was his world. "Who the fuck are you?"

"Just a man finishing a job he started for your father." The .22 magnum subsonic made a sound like a twig breaking when I shot him. Two in the head. I took pictures of the body with my cell and ghosted into the night. The paper would find a bag of cash in the car's trunk. They would call it gang retaliation for money he took from MS-13. Close to true.

Mr. Sanchez was happy to see me. I was using a cane; my hip would remain fucked for a long time. I walked like a useless old man. Sanchez's men pat searched me, found the .44 and the buck knife.

Alone in Sanchez's lavish office, he motioned me to sit. He poured us a Macallan fifty-year-old this time, hundred and fifty dollars a shot booze. I must have been a very good boy. "To you, sir." He raised his crystal tumbler. I have never had a fifty-year-old Macallan. I should have loved it, but it left a bad taste in my mouth. Maybe I would stick to mescal from here on.

"You have done what no other could."

"You sent me to find out who was stealing your girls. I did."

"You took down those MS-13 putas and half of the LAPD. You are quite a man, McGuire. Another drink?"

"No."

"How would you like to become my head of security? I can make you a rich man."

"Thing is, Sanchez, there is more to the deal and how it went down."

"Regale me with the gory details." He leaned back in his chair and lit a cigar.

"MS-13, they were soldiers. You sent me for the head of the man stealing your girls. Here it is." I dropped a folder on his desk. In it was an 8x10 shot of the very dead D.A. Rodriguez.

Sanchez went still. The corner of his left eye twitched.

"This is my son."

"Yes, it is."

"My son. You killed my son?"

"This whole deal was his. His way to clean up the streets and raise cash for a run at the Mayor's office."

"A lie. He could have come to me for the money."

"Your name would be poison. Feds were on to him. He never would have pulled it off. I just ratcheted up the timetable."

"Did you, yourself, kill him?"

"As agreed."

"Hijo de puta!" He bounced his cigar off my chest. I let it lie, burning a hole in his cashmere carpet. "I'm going to kill you, cabrón. Not now. Our truce will hold until you leave my office. Then?"

"I'm through looking over my shoulder."

"So what will you do?"

"Break the truce." I raised the cane and pulled the hidden trigger. The blast of the .410 took him between his eyes. The blow toppled his chair.

His security men rushed in. Two threw me to the floor. A third fought hopelessly to save the dead old man.

They dragged me into the main courtyard. Without a cane or help there was no hope of standing. I curled fetal while they took their kicks. They were halfhearted at best. Not much macho in kicking a crippled old man. They might have killed me out of a lack of anything better to do if Stephan Sanchez hadn't called them off. Out with the old Jefe, meet the new Jefe.

"Get our guest into my office."

Stephan said he would make good on his promise to leave me be if the old man was dead. He asked me how he could repay me. I had some ideas.

Entrepreneur that he was, Stephan had been fighting to take the family legit. He was going to open an entertainment complex: one-stop dance club, restaurant, cantina, karaoke, and souvenirs all under one roof. Strippers and whores were too much trouble for the money they generated. He was tired of scraping the barrel.

His men destroyed my cane, but Stephan gave me a gold and ivory over mahogany walking stick. It had his family crest. "Anyone fucks with you, show them this and watch them bow."

He would keep enough crime to afford the police and military on the payroll, enough guns to keep rival cartels from attempting to roll on him. He hadn't seen the error of his ways, just a new way to make more cash. If petty crime paid better, Donald Trump would be running whores. Real green was in legit, big business crime. Stephan was on his way. Me, he promised to forget.

I trusted him only because killing me was harder than leaving me alone.

CHAPTER 40

The sun and hot sand felt good on my hip and leg. My limp was pronounced; two months later I still needed a cane. My head was in Serenity's lap. She was idly stroking my hair and watching Freedom, Angel and Adolpho's kids splashing and laughing, playing a variation of tag that involved a long clump of seaweed being worn as a wig.

Adolpho was out on a charter. The boat, a gift from Señor Sanchez Jr., had allowed Adolpho to quit his job at the whorehouse.

Serenity gave the business to Kenny and Gregor, with the understanding they would get out of guns and armaments and into information only. I tried to get Gregor to retire, but he reminded me he was a young man with a life to build. He did promise to bring the family down for spring break.

It was strangely hot the night I said good-bye to Mikayla. When I buried Moses I let a lot of his shit go. It was time I let her go.

Pussy, Mikayla said.

I was looking out to sea, Angel leaning against my good leg.

Pussy. Walking away.

"You could be right. Maybe the fight's just gone from me. Maybe I'm a pussy."

You are.

"You have to leave me alone now."

I know. Will you miss me?

"Always."

When I looked back from the sea, she was gone.

Peter was short-listed for a Pulitzer. Maybe he'll win. Maybe he won't let success drive him mad.

They did finally make the Moses McGuire movie. After his tragic death it was a done deal. In the end they didn't go with The Rock to play me. They went with a shorter younger hunk, and Gregor became East Indian. Hollywood. Peter set it up so that payments due to the dead Mr. McGuire would go into a trust fund for Freedom MacGowan's college. She would need all the edge I could give her.

In the spring we would enroll her in a private Catholic school run by nuns who had escaped the death squads in Nicaragua. They had been to war. I hoped it would be a good match. If not, we would find her another, and another. Raising Freedom was a long-haul proposition. Tough as she was, she slept in a sleeping bag at the foot of our bed, curled up with Angel. She never took off her Saint Jude medal. She often woke screaming. When I asked her what it was she would go silent, as if giving it a name would make it real.

I was not one to give her advice. I still chewed pain pills like Chiclets and drank too much. They say time heals all wounds. Bullshit. Time just gives you enough scar tissue to make it bearable.

I hope I'm full of shit.

I hope one day Freedom wakes free of what was done to her, free of the guilt she carries for the lives she took. I hope one day I will wake with the uncomplicated joy of simply living. But if I don't, an Angel, Serenity and Freedom are enough to keep the gun barrel from ever going back into my mouth.

CPSIA information can be obtained at www.ICGtesting.com
Printed in the USA
BVOW04s1906071213

338477BV00003B/160/P